D1339555

2063766

THE SEA AND THE SAND

THE SEA AND THE SAND

Frederick Harsant

Book Guild Publishing
Sussex, England

First published in Great Britain in 2006 by
The Book Guild Ltd
25 High Street
Lewes, East Sussex
BN7 2LU

Copyright © Frederick Harsant 2006

The right of Frederick Harsant to be identified as the author of
this work has been asserted by him in accordance with the
Copyright, Designs and Patents Act 1988.

All rights reserved. No part of this publication may be reproduced,
transmitted, or stored in a retrieval system, in any form or by any
means, without permission in writing from the publisher, nor be
otherwise circulated in any form of binding or cover other than
that in which it is published and without a similar condition being
imposed on the subsequent purchaser.

All characters in this publication are fictitious and any
resemblance to real people, alive or dead, is purely coincidental.

Typesetting in Baskerville by
IML Typographers, Birkenhead, Merseyside

Printed in Great Britain by
Antony Rowe Ltd, Chippenham, Wiltshire

A catalogue record for this book is available from
The British Library.

ISBN 1 84624 036 0

To my wife, Joan, who gave me so much encouragement and who meticulously read and corrected the several versions of the novel as I developed it on the computer.

Contents

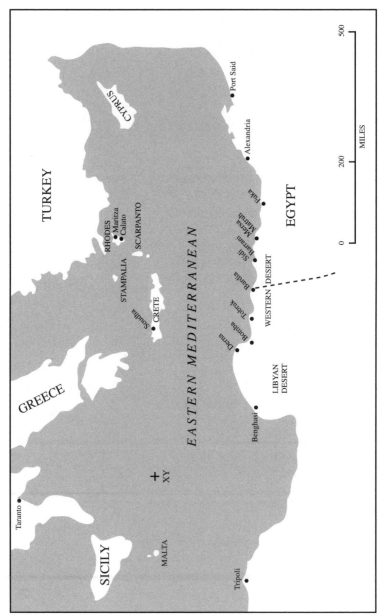

The Eastern Mediterranean and Western Desert

viii

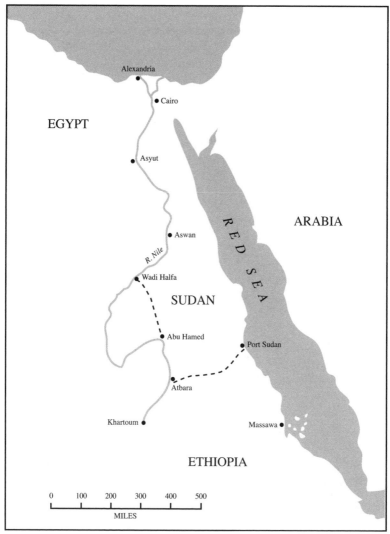

The Nile and the Red Sea

Author's Note

In *The Sea and the Sand* I have endeavoured to capture the life and the spirit aboard an aircraft carrier in the early part of the Second World War.

The events recorded in this novel loosely follow events in the Mediterranean, Red Sea and South Atlantic in 1940/ 1941. Almost all the incidents are based on what happened either to myself or to my friends. The characters and the romantic stories are fictitious.

Chapter 1

Tobruk

The voice of the Deck Control Officer could be clearly heard over the low rumble of the carrier's engines. Then the comparative silence of the night was shattered by the noise of Pegasus engines as first one, then another coughed into life.

Lieutenant (A) Bolo Hawkins RNVR looked across at the Swordfish aircraft on either side of him. Bolo was sub-flight leader in K – King; 'Biddy' Bidwell, pilot of L – Love, newly promoted to Lieutenant RN, was on his right and Sub Lieutenant 'Bing' Crosby, nicknamed after his famous namesake, was on his left.

Three more Swordfish, in a vic formation, were lined up ahead, led by Lieutenant Commander Savage, the Commanding Officer of 999 Torpedo-Spotter, Reconnaissance Squadron.

The six aircraft had been detailed for a dive-bombing attack on ships known to be in Tobruk Harbour. The year was 1940. The aircraft carrier was *HMS Peregrine*, an old carrier, converted from a First World War battleship.

Bolo thought of *Peregrine*'s history as he revved up his engine before take-off. *Peregrine* had served for years in the Far East. Almost all the pilots and observers were either long-serving RN officers or Air branch RN officers with short service commissions. Bolo was a 'hostilities only' RNVR officer. *Peregrine*'s squadrons had already tasted action. They

1

had searched the Indian Ocean for the German raider, *Atlantis*, without success, and had sunk an Italian destroyer and a submarine on their way through the Red Sea.

At first, the squadron officers had looked askance at the Wavy Navy rings on Bolo's reefer jacket. But they were used to the unusual, for whilst the ship had been in the Far East in 1939 the Royal Navy had finally taken over responsibility for the Fleet Air Arm from the Royal Air Force. Some of the naval pilots had formerly worn RAF tunics, and several of the maintenance crews were still in the RAF, awaiting replacement by Navy personnel. Bolo's log-book, however, showed many hours of flying, more than most of the *Peregrine*'s pilots could claim, and his undoubted skill was soon acknowledged when he became a sub-flight leader.

Now Bolo was about to undertake his first operational sortie. An RAF reconnaissance had revealed the presence of several merchant ships in Tobruk Harbour. Mussolini had a desperate need to prove himself to his associate, Hitler, and for this he had chosen to invade Egypt. His intention was to build up stores in ports like Tobruk, ready for the invasion, and the ships in harbour were part of his supply fleet.

The *Peregrine* was now turning into wind. Again a green light flashed briefly from the bridge and the Deck Control Officer waved his torch in a circle. The CO in A – Abel rolled forward to the take-off position and took off, followed by his two wingmen. Bolo gestured with an arm towards Biddy and Bing and received a thumbs-up sign. He waved his chocks away, taxied to the take-off position and opened his throttle, holding the plane back with his brakes. The biplane shuddered and shook with the surge of power, and, with full boost, Bolo released the brakes. Slowly the plane trundled forwards, slowed by the weight of six 250-pound bombs slung under the wings, a crew of three and a full tank of fuel.

The tail came up, but Bolo held his wheels to the deck until nearing the bows. Then he eased the stick back gently, feeling the weight of the bombs. The speed had reached sixty-five knots, but still the aircraft sagged to below deck level after it had left the carrier. Slowly, as his speed built up, Bolo gained height and began a turn to port, climbing steadily. As he passed down the port side of *Peregrine* he saw that L – Love was airborne and M – Mike was just leaving the flight deck.

In the faint light of the deck illuminations, he could see the shadowy figures of the deck party clearing away chocks, and on the bridge Commander Flying, known as 'Wings', peering over the port side at the departing aircraft.

Flying as slowly as being airborne allowed, Bolo waited for his sub-flight to catch up with him. Biddy, in L – Love, he had come to respect. He had taken part in the attack on the destroyer and had faced the fire of the enemy. Like himself, Bing, in M – Mike, had yet to prove himself.

'Pilot, course two-one-zero degrees. Climb to seven thousand feet. Let me know your climbing speed.'

This was the voice of Lieutenant 'Sandy' Sandiford, Bolo's observer, coming through the gosport tubes, speaking-tubes forming the intercommunication system between the three aircrew.

'Right, Sandy. My climbing speed is seventy-five knots. How long to the target?'

Sandy, after a brief calculation on his course and speed calculator, replied, 'Approximately one hour twenty minutes.'

'Okay. Can you see any sign of "Love" and "Mike"?'

'They're just coming up on either side of us.'

Bolo had been flashing the letter K on his navigation lights so that his wingmen could join up with him. He would keep these lights on until they were fifty miles from the target, when all lights would be switched off and the difficult part of the flight would begin. He could see the flashing light of his leader, 'Abel', ahead of him, and he closed on this steadily.

'Permission to test guns, sir?'

3

This was the voice of PO Mercer, his telegraphist-air-gunner, or TAG, as he was known.

The wing aircraft were now closed up on either side and it was clear for Mercer to fire. A short burst was sufficient.

Flying was now instinctive for Bolo. An occasional glance at his speed, his height and his turn-and-bank indicator was enough to keep him on course. He had fixed a bearing of a distant star against his bombsight and by keeping this steady he was on a steady course. This saved constant corrections, which would have made life difficult for the pilots formating on him. They had closed to just behind his wing tips and the sub-flight now formed a compact unit.

'My altitude is now seven thousand feet and I'm levelling off. Speed eighty-five knots,' said Bolo into his intercom.

'Very good, Bolo,' his observer replied. 'We shall be switching off lights in about five minutes.'

'Right, Sandy. I'll wait for the CO and switch off when he does.'

Bolo was now closed up below and astern of the leading sub-flight. When the CO's lights were extinguished he could just see the faint, blue light of his CO's exhaust and the shadowy silhouettes of the three aircraft ahead of him. The half moon helped. He was aware of his own sub-flight aircraft rising and falling gently on either side as they strove to maintain station. By 0500 hours there was a suffused light towards the east, heralding the dawn.

At this stage of the war the Fleet Air Arm had no radio-telephony. Simple messages could be conveyed from one aircraft to another by hand signals, which were used mainly to confirm the instructions already given at briefing. The Fleet Air Arm had made little progress in its aircraft and its communication systems since the First World War. It was thus by waggling his wings that the CO indicated he was going into line astern. Bolo dropped back and indicated to his wing men to follow suit.

The squadron was now approaching the coast to the west of Tobruk. Savage's plan was to cross the coast a mile or two to the west of Tobruk and come out of the dark side. The Italians were not yet using radar, so he hoped for complete surprise.

In K – King, Sandy Sandiford studied the scene below him. He could see the glint of water and the line of foam marking the coast, and towards the east the shadowy jumble of buildings and sheds marking the town and port.

Now the squadron was turning in for the attack. At last the anti-aircraft fire had started, wildly and indiscriminately. Shell-bursts pockmarked the sky over the harbour, but none came near the approaching aircraft. Already the close-range weapons had opened up, firing their tracers in graceful arcs of flaming onions at nothing in particular.

Sandy could see the ships in the harbour, two medium-size merchant ships and a tanker at anchor, and along the mole a depot ship with a destroyer alongside. The Italian naval vessels had now joined in the anti-aircraft barrage.

He watched the black puffs, now visible in the lightening sky. They seemed harmless enough and impersonal, as though they had little to do with the approaching aircraft. As they drew closer, lines of tracer bullets rose vertically from the destroyer.

'The CO's going down now,' Sandy informed his pilot.

'Yes. I've got him. I think he's going for the merchant ships. We'll take the depot ship and destroyer.'

Already Sandy could see bombs bursting across the tanker, which was enveloped in flame. Now they were almost over the depot ship.

'Going down,' said Bolo.

Sandy felt the familiar lift of his stomach as Bolo raised the nose of his plane and rolled over into a near vertical dive.

Down, down, down.

Over his pilot's head, Sandy could see the flaming onions

rising towards them, slowly at first and then with incredible speed as they rushed past on either side. The ships below seemed to rotate as Bolo turned and lined up on his target.

Sandy glanced at his altimeter. Five thousand feet, four thousand, three thousand.

And still going down.

Sandy was aware of running figures on the decks below as gunners began to leave their weapons for shelter. Then at one thousand feet Sandy felt the bombs go, and Bolo was pulling out of his dive at water level. Now Sandy's stomach was pressed down towards his boots and he almost blacked out. He looked astern and saw the stick of bombs had fallen across the depot ship and the destroyer with great flashes of flame.

'Well done, Bolo!' he shouted. 'You've hit both of them.'

Bolo was throwing his aircraft around, now corkscrewing, now jinking up and down as he avoided the enemy flak and made eastwards out of the bay.

Both of the merchant ships had been hit and one was sinking. The tanker, depot ship and destroyer were on fire and their flames cast a faint glow in the shadowy dawn light.

Petty Officer Mercer was firing at ships, docks and any targets that presented themselves. A quick sidestep to avoid another fleeing aircraft and they were out past the entrance, with the wide sea ahead of them.

All six aircraft had come through, but not without some damage. As 'Mike' closed up on 'King', Sandy could see the damage on the bottom starboard wing. A line of holes was punched through the fabric of the wings and a wing strut was hanging brokenly.

'Keep an eye on him, Sandy,' said Bolo, as Bing brought his aircraft alongside.

Sub Lieutenant 'Harold' Lloyd, the observer of 'Mike' waved to Sandy. A method of communicating sometimes used between observers was zogging, making short or long strokes with the forearm to denote dots and dashes in the Morse code. Sandy used this now.

'Are you okay?' he zogged.

'Yes. All okay. Engine okay.'

Sandy reported this message to his pilot and then concentrated on his navigation. He took a back bearing of the still-visible smoke of the burning harbour, and laid this off on his Bigsworth chartboard until it met the projected track of the fleet. Bolo was, in fact, following his Commanding Officer, but Sandy liked to check his own navigation and keep his own plot.

'You should sight the Fleet on your starboard bow, about twenty miles away steering west,' he told his pilot.

They had been flying for an hour since the attack and Bolo was feeling cramped and hungry. He peered ahead and to starboard.

'I've got them,' he exclaimed, 'ten degrees off the starboard bow.'

Bolo felt a warm glow of satisfaction. His first operation was nearly over. He had been blooded. And he had been so busy flying his aircraft, dropping his bombs, taking evasive action, and keeping an eye on the leader that not once had he thought about the danger of the operation. Not once had he been afraid. What a lovely sight the Fleet was! At first, a faint smoking blur in the middle distance, that became toy warships and finally the Fleet in all its iron strength. The battleship *Ramrod* was followed by the *Peregrine* and the cruiser *Nottingham*. Ahead of the three large ships, in a broad vic formation, were five destroyers, with a destroyer on either side of the battlefleet.

A recognition flare went up from the CO's aircraft and the Fleet began to turn into wind.

'Send a signal on your Aldis, Sandy,' said Bolo, 'about the damage to "Mike". We shall stay with him until he has landed.'

7

Sandy picked up his Aldis lamp and flashed a signal to the carrier. The reply came back that the other four aircraft were to land first, then 'Mike', then 'King'.

As they approached the carrier the squadron broke into line ahead with a quarter of a mile between each aircraft, circling the carrier in an anti-clockwise direction. Bolo formed up on 'Mike's' starboard quarter.

The CO was the first to land-on, his hook catching an arrester wire and bringing him to a halt. The deck-handling party rushed forward and released him and pushed him backwards to the after lift, where he was lowered to the hangar. This operation took several minutes. In the meantime the next aircraft lined up on the carrier and approached until waved round by the batsman. Eventually the lift started ascending and Bats began to control the next aircraft's approach, guiding him in and controlling his speed until he gave the signal to cut engine, leaving the aircraft to glide in and hook on to the arrester wire.

At the beginning of the war, in the older carriers this was a fairly slow operation and it was twenty minutes before 'Mike' was signalled in. Bolo watched Bing approaching carefully. 'Mike's' damaged mainplane was juddering and shaking and Bolo wondered whether it would survive the landing. Bing, however, was a good pilot. He brought his machine down with hardly a bump and then was brought to a halt by the arrester wire and bundled aft down the lift.

Now it was Bolo's turn. He straightened out a hundred yards astern of the carrier, arrester hook down, then saw the Deck Control Officer's bats pointing above horizontal. Too high. Ease the engine and allow the plane to sink a little, he told himself.

Bats horizontal: just right. Keep going.

Bats pointing downwards: you are too low. Give it a touch of throttle and gain height.

You are almost over the round-down.

Cut. Cut your engine and pray.

You jerk forward as the hook catches and the plane comes to a quick stop. Squadron maintenance crews rush forward, unhook you, wheel you back to the aft lift and, when it descends into the hangar, manoeuvre you into your stowage position and make you fast. Then you relax, thank your crew, and with your observer make your way up to the operations room.

As Bolo and Sandy opened the door into the operations room a burst of chatter greeted them. Most of the pilots and observers were talking in post-operational, over-loud and rather excited voices.

'Did you see the tanker go up?' Sub Lieutenant Temple was saying. 'I nearly got caught in the explosion as I followed the CO down.'

Sub Lieutenant (A) Temple, nicknamed 'Holy', pilot of B – Baker, was normally a quiet, mild-mannered young officer. He had joined the squadron a year before. This was his first operation.

'I didn't care much for those flaming onions coming from the destroyer. You don't think they're linked together with wire or something?' said Sub Lieutenant (A) 'Wes' Weston.

'Not likely!' exclaimed his pilot, Biddy Bidwell, a regular RN Lieutenant who had volunteered for the Fleet Air Arm two years before. 'I think they must be tracers fired from some sort of multiple pompom. Probably one in four shells is a tracer, giving that spaced-out effect.

'You were lucky, Bing,' he went on, turning to his young sub-flight colleague. 'Your plane was peppered with bullet holes.'

'Yes. I don't know how they missed me,' said Bing Crosby, pilot of M – Mike. 'When Chiefy saw the broken strut, he was amazed the wing had held.'

9

'Well, that leaves you with eight lives,' said Bolo Hawkins, with a smile.

'I shall be more careful next time,' said Bing.

Bolo glanced across to the end of the room where the CO was talking to Wings, the Ship's Commander (Flying). Wings was responsible to the Captain for all flying operations. Compared to Wings, Lieutenant Commander Savage, the CO, Bolo thought, was rather a severe-looking man, with a reserved manner. He was well respected for his flying and his courage, but he tended to keep his feelings to himself and not reveal too much to the squadron officers.

Wings, in comparison, beneath his undoubted air of authority, was friendly and forthcoming with the young officers. A man of about thirty-five years, Dartmouth trained, he had been flying for several years. His latest joy was to take up one of the two Gladiators, fighter biplanes, and practise aerial combat. Always on the lookout for a fellow creature, he had noted Bolo's experience with a variety of aircraft and, whilst the squadron was ashore at Dekheila, the Fleet Air Arm station close to Alexandria, he had given him some training in the Gladiator and in aerial combat. At present, the *Peregrine* had no trained fighter pilots aboard.

Wings now turned to the assembled crowd of flying-crews.

'Well, gentlemen,' he said, with a glint of humour in his eyes. 'Now for the hard part. We have to determine just what happened at Tobruk. I'll ask Lieutenant Commander Savage to begin and you'll each have a turn to say your piece.'

Gradually the picture emerged.

'Abel', 'Baker' and 'Charlie' had attacked the moored merchant ships, scoring hits on all three. The tanker had blown up and one of the merchant ships had started to sink.

'King', 'Love' and 'Mike' had gone for the depot ship and destroyer. At least five hits had been observed, two on the destroyer and three on the depot ship. Other bombs had hit the sheds alongside, which had gone up in flames.

'In other words, you left a complete shambles,' said Wings, and a chorus of assent greeted his summary.

The Air Staff Officer, an observer lieutenant commander who was standing quietly beside Commander Flying, now came in with a question.

'How good was the enemy defence?'

The CO turned to Bolo.

'Lieutenant Hawkins can answer that better than I,' he said. 'I was too involved to see clearly.'

Bolo pondered for a moment. The temptation to overrate the opposition was there, but what was wanted was an honest opinion.

'When the first sub-flight went in,' he said, 'the enemy flak was wild and erratic. The ships in the harbour and the shore defences were firing anywhere and everywhere. I thought we caught them by surprise. When my flight went in, the destroyer and depot ship were more under control and putting up a moderate defence, particularly with close-range weapons.'

'I see,' said the ASO. 'Anyone like to add anything to that?'

'Yes, sir,' said Sandy, Bolo's observer. 'As we dived to within firing-range, when we were most vulnerable, I saw one or two of the gunners leave their guns and run for shelter.'

This was confirmed by Biddy Bidwell.

'That's interesting to know,' said Wings. 'It gives us a moral ascendancy and will encourage us to press home our attacks.'

Wings made to leave the room.

'Before you go, gentlemen,' said the ASO, 'I want each of you to leave written statements of what you remember of the action. I shall remain here to give help if you need it and the ship's schoolmaster will assist, too.'

The atmosphere quietened as the flying-crews settled to their task, using the forms provided by Schooley.

Chapter 2

HMS Peregrine

'Bing, on the way down let's go and see what they're doing to "Mike",' said Bolo.

The two officers made their way from the operations room, down through the island, the superstructure on the starboard side of the carrier that housed the bridge and operations room, and past watertight doors into the hangar. This was an enormous metal hall that ran the length and breadth of the ship. It was filled with aircraft, eighteen Swordfish and two Gladiators, tethered to ringbolts in the deck. Overhead and along the side spares were stored: mainplanes, tailplanes, rudders, ailerons, and a host of such articles as landing-wheels, tyres, spare hooks and engine cowlings. Fitters and riggers were working on the aircraft, and those recently returned were being refuelled and rearmed. The hangar was alive with activity and there was little room between the closely packed aircraft.

Bolo and Bing made their way to where 'Mike' was stowed.

Already the damaged strut had gone and the lower mainplane was being removed. This operation, carried out by air-riggers, was supervised by Chiefy himself. Chief Air Artificer Tom Stillson, the senior non-commissioned officer of the squadron, oversaw everything to do with maintenance. He now approached Bolo and Bing.

'Well, Chiefy, what's the verdict?' said Bolo. He studied the face of the man in front of him as he gravely looked at the damaged aircraft and pursed his lips in concentration. Tom Stillson was now approaching forty. He was a small man, with a fiery energy and a no-nonsense approach where men and machines were concerned.

'We can repair this aboard ship, sir,' he said, 'but it won't be ready today.'

'Well, keep at it. You never know. The Eyeties might be out in force and we could need it this evening.'

'Very good, sir. We'll see what we can do.'

'What was it like, sir? I mean when you were attacking the ships.'

Bolo regarded the keen, eager face of the young fitter who asked the question. Naval Airman Bailey was the fitter of M – Mike. A small group of ratings gathered round to hear the answer.

'Not too bad,' said Bolo. 'There was some flak, as you can see, but the old stringbag is a wizard aircraft for this sort of caper. I threw "King" all over the place and she stood up to it like a Trojan – thanks to you chaps.'

A muttered appreciation greeted this remark.

'Did we do any damage, sir?'

'Yes, plenty. Two ships sunk, one on fire and a destroyer and depot ship damaged.'

They had heard the rumour, but this information, coming from Bolo, was food and drink to the men. They worked hard and seriously in the hangar, and success in action was their reward as much as that of the pilots. Their enthusiasm was obvious.

'That was well said, Mr Hawkins,' said Chiefy quietly as they walked away from the crowd. 'They'll work all the harder for it.'

When Bolo and Bing reached the wardroom, they found their friends well tucked into breakfast.

'Come on, Bolo. You'll miss breakfast if you don't hurry,' called Sandy.

'I will if you greedy lot have anything to do with it,' said Bolo, finding a vacant seat next to his observer. 'There's no doubt about it,' he continued. 'There's nothing like action to work up an appetite.'

Everyone agreed.

'What's the programme today, Bolo?' Sandy asked.

'I don't know yet. The CO wants us to meet in the guest room after breakfast and he's going to brief us before we get our heads down. The Captain's going to speak to us first.'

At 0900 the whole squadron was grouped in the wardroom round the loudspeaker, cigarettes glowing comfortably.

'D'you hear there? This is the Captain speaking.'

They bent forward, listening attentively.

'First, my congratulations to 999 Squadron for this morning's effort. We've just received a wireless report from an RAF aircraft. All three ships at anchor in the harbour are sunk and the two ships alongside the mole are badly damaged and down by the stern.'

A small cheer greeted this news.

'We believe,' he continued, 'that the Italians intend to mount an attack from Libya across the border into Egypt, threatening our naval base at Alexandria. The ships at Tobruk are part of the build-up for that attack. A convoy of merchant ships has also been located at Benghazi, and it is almost certain that a task force of Italian battleships and cruisers is at sea covering that convoy.

'At the same time, we have a convoy coming through from Gibraltar and Malta bringing more men and stores to Alexandria. This convoy is being covered by the C-in-C in *Warspite* with *Malaya* and five destroyers, but we think that this force is far smaller than that of the Italians.

'Our task is to search out the Italian Fleet and attempt to bring them to battle or drive them back to port. For that purpose, we shall carry out aircraft searches ahead of our Fleet. The first, by 998 Squadron, will take off in half an hour; 999 Squadron will stand by as a strike-force. At 1500, 999 will mount a search with 998 standing by as strike-force.

'That is all.'

A stunned silence greeted the Captain's final statement. It was broken by Lieutenant Price, the Senior Pilot.

In a quiet voice, he said, 'Well, chaps. Now you know. The war is really on and there's an Italian Navy out there waiting for us.'

'Into the guest room, everybody,' he continued. 'The CO is waiting to speak to us.'

Lieutenant Commander Savage studied the officers as they settled themselves into and on the arms of the comfortable armchairs in the small room, adjacent to the wardroom, generally used for guests.

'Gentlemen,' he said, 'I've been talking to Wings and the ASO and they want me to put you fully in the picture. If 998 Squadron sight the enemy, we will send off a strike of eight aircraft.

'I'm afraid your plane won't be ready,' he said, turning to Bing Crosby.

'We shall approach the enemy in vic formation and try to get ahead of them before attacking. We shall be armed with torpedoes, so the attack formation will be line abreast. I shall waggle my wings when I want you to go into that formation.

'If 998 Squadron don't sight the enemy, we shall be required for a search at 1500. I shall put up a list on the squadron notice-board. Briefing in the operations room at 1400.

'Seven aircraft of 998 Squadron are on the present search. The remaining two are doing the anti-submarine patrols. When we are searching, 998 Squadron will arm with torpedoes for the strike and our remaining aircraft will be on A/S patrol. M – Mike will have to do the last patrol of the day. I hope she'll be ready, Steve.'

15

The CO turned to his Senior Pilot, Lieutenant Steve Price RN, who was responsible for the availability of squadron aircraft.

'I'll keep an eye on it, sir,' Steve replied.

'I've been talking to the Ship's Navigating Officer,' the CO continued. 'He tells me that we shall hold this course westwards all day. If the Italian Fleet is at sea it is likely to be north west of Benghazi, covering their convoy to Benghazi and threatening our convoy coming through from Malta. Now, we are not trained for night deck-landings. I think they will have to come eventually, but at present we've got to get back before dark. So if we sight the enemy this afternoon, the aircraft sighting will stay with the enemy until he is relieved, and all aircraft, strike-force and shadowers, must be back on board by 2200.

'We do not expect the present search to sight the enemy, so get your heads down until lunchtime. After lunch check your aircraft before going up for briefing.

'Anything you want to add, Gordon?'

Lieutenant (A) Gordon Power, the Senior Observer, addressed the observers in the squadron.

'If we are called upon as a strike-force we shall be wanted in a rush,' he said. 'While pilots are checking their engines, observers must go to the ops room and get the latest ship's position and course and the wind direction and speed. Although you are following my navigation, you must be ready to navigate yourselves back to the carrier. Understood?'

When the observers murmured their acknowledgement the meeting broke up and the officers made their way to their cabins or the wardroom ante-room to rest or relax as they thought best.

Sub Lieutenants Bing Crosby and Harold Lloyd should have been feeling happy. They had been lucky to escape with their lives when their aircraft was hit by enemy bullets. In fact, they felt depressed, unwanted, not part of the team as their aircraft, 'Mike', was unserviceable.

'Come on Harold; let's go and see how they are getting on with "Mike",' said Bing.

Quickly, the two officers made their way up to the hangar. There they found that a team of air-riggers had already removed the damaged lower wing and were manhandling its replacement into place. A petty-officer artificer was supervising this work. In the cockpit an electrical artificer was checking the electrics, and engine fitters were checking over the engine. A dozen men were working on the aircraft and Chiefy was keeping an eagle eye on the whole.

'What do you think now, Chiefy? Can she be ready any sooner?'

'The job is going well,' Chiefy replied. 'Barring accidents I think we'll be ready late this afternoon, after all. We'll need a test run, say, at about 1800 hours.'

The faces of Bing and Harold lit up.

'That means we do the last A/S patrol today and can be in the morning strike tomorrow, if there is one.'

Bing and Harold felt that they were back in the squadron again, and they retired in good heart to the cabin they shared.

Chapter 3

Enemy Fleet in Sight

It was nearly lunchtime and Bolo had been half asleep in a wardroom armchair, recovering from his recent activities and reflecting on the events of the past year that had seen an incredible turnabout in his life ...

A year before, he had lived for cricket. Throughout the early summer of 1939 he had played regularly for Sussex. Then had come the trial for his country and a place in the England 'A' team. He was a fast bowler and this was reflected in his attitude to life. Honest and direct, he was without the guile of the spinner or the deceit of the googly bowler. He lived in the spirit of cricket. Play the game. Use your initiative but follow your captain's lead and do your best for the team. In many ways a Fleet Air Arm squadron was like a cricket team. You followed your commanding officer and did your best for the squadron.

He was twenty-three years old when war broke out and he had immediately contacted the Admiralty. With a pilot's licence and more than two hundred hours' flying, he was welcomed by the Navy into the Fleet Air Arm. After an induction period he was sent to Lee-on-Solent to train observers. This was not quite what he had wanted, but he was aware how little he knew of the Navy and his experience at

Lee gave him an opportunity to study its ways and to make himself a naval officer in fact as well as in uniform. Six months after joining he was promoted to lieutenant, a rank appropriate to his age, experience and role as an instructor.

His duties were simple. The observers under training at Lee were the last of the short-service commission officers and the first of the hostilities only officers under training. Either sub lieutenants or midshipmen, according to their age, or leading airmen if they were hostilities only, they spent four and a half months at Lee training as observers. Bolo flew mornings and afternoons, taking up observers for practice in navigation, wind finding and wireless telegraphy. He flew them in Sharks, Walruses and Proctors, with an occasional trip in a Swordfish or Skua.

When not on duty it had been his great pleasure to visit his old cricket club, where he had first met Joyce. Joyce was the daughter of a great friend of Bolo's, an old cricketer of the club, who had given Bolo much valuable advice and encouragement. Joyce had attended most of the games in which Bolo played and gradually they had become close friends.

On 10th June 1940 Italy had declared hostilities against England and the war had entered a new phase. The Mediterranean had become all-important and the aircraft carrier *Peregrine* had been recalled from the China Station to strengthen the Eastern Mediterranean Fleet. A few days later Bolo received his new appointment from the Admiralty. He was to fly to Alexandria and join *HMS Peregrine* as a pilot in 999 Squadron.

He was replacing a senior lieutenant who had been appointed Commanding Officer of another squadron. A new sub-flight leader was required. Bolo was the most senior officer available, and after watching him go through his paces Lieutenant Commander Savage had had no hesitation in selecting him for the role.

19

At first this was regarded with some suspicion by the pilots but, without his being aware of it, Bolo's quiet manner and undoubted ability had won him friendship and support from his colleagues ...

'D'you hear there? Nine-nine-eight Squadron stand by to receive aircraft.'

Bolo awoke with a start and saw that his friend, 'Biddy' Bidwell, in the chair next to him, was also waking and stretching.

'Come on, Biddy. That's the search party returning. Let's go and watch them land-on.'

The two friends quickly made their way to the goofers' platform, a deckspace at the after end of the island where flying-crews foregathered to watch take-offs and landings. There they met Bing Crosby and Harold Lloyd, Sandy Sandiford and other members of the squadron.

A Swordfish from 998 Squadron was ranged on deck, waiting to take off for the anti-submarine patrol. They could see the aircraft of 998 Squadron circling the carrier, which was beginning its turn into wind. It settled on a course with the smoke indicator blowing straight down the carrier deck. The affirmative flag was hoisted on a port boom and a green was flashed from the bridge.

Away chocks.

The Swordfish rolled forwards with its two depth charges to take up a patrol position fifteen miles ahead of the fleet.

Already the first of 998's aircraft was approaching, circling towards the round-down like a predatory falcon. Bats was in position bringing the aircraft in. A destroyer was stationed on the port quarter of the carrier to pick up survivors if an aircraft crashed into the sea. It was a scene witnessed by the officers many times, but they never tired of it. Last to land was the relieved A/S patrol aircraft. Then the carrier swung back on to its course and returned to its habitual state of vigilant rest.

Bolo and Biddy made their way to the ops room, where the flying programme for the afternoon was posted on the squadron notice-board.

999 Squadron

Flying Programme

Take-off 1500

Aircraft	Pilot	Observer	TAG
		A/S PATROL	
H	S/Lt Andrews	S/Lt White	L/A Naylor
		SEARCH	
A	Lt Com Savage	Lt Power	CPO Goodrick
B	S/Lt Temple	Lt Burd	PO Black
C	S/Lt Wickers	S/Lt Reddington	L/A Denton
F	Lt Price	Lt Williams	PO Bower
G	S/Lt Martin	S/Lt Dowling	PO Adams
K	Lt Hawkins	Lt Sandiford	PO Mercer
L	Lt Bidwell	S/Lt Wilson	PO Jarman
		Take-off 1800	
		A/S PATROL	
M	S/Lt Crosby	S/Lt Lloyd	L/A Gibbons

'You're at the extreme left of the search, and I'm next to you,' said Bolo. 'Let's hope we sight the Italians.'

After lunch the aircrews made their way to the hangar where fitters and riggers and artificers were making last-minute checks. A good relationship existed between the flying personnel and the maintenance crews. It was centred on the aircraft, each of which had its own pilot, observer and

21

F/2063766

WEXFORD
COUNTY
LIBRARY

airgunner as well as fitter and rigger, all of whom took a pride in their own aircraft. Sub-flights shared air-artificers and the squadron shared the specialists such as the armourers and radio mechanics.

Esprit de corps was built up first round the individual aircraft, then the sub-flight and finally the squadron. Officers and men played together in the squadron football team and against each other in the deck-hockey teams.

In addition to flying, officers in the squadron had their individual squadron responsibilities. Lieutenant Price, the Senior Pilot, was responsible for the availability and maintenance of all aircraft. Gordon Power, the Senior Observer, was responsible for squadron navigation and the continued training of all observers and TAGs. Lieutenant Burd was the Squadron Adjutant, Lieutenant Bidwell the Stores Officer and Lieutenant Hawkins the Sports and Recreation Officer. Other officers assisted in these responsibilities or had minor duties. In this way they developed their powers of leadership and responsibility.

A strong sense of comradeship was evident in the hangar that afternoon as aircrews talked to maintenance crews before making their way to the operations room for briefing. The Air Staff Officer was the first to address the meeting.

'I shall first give you an overall picture of the situation,' he said. 'The Commander in Chief, with Force B, including the battleships *Warspite* and *Malaya* and five destroyers, is to the west of us, covering a convoy from Malta to Alexandria. Force A, consisting of five cruisers and a number of destroyers, is making a sweep to the north.

'Our task is to find an Italian battlefleet believed to be covering an Italian convoy to Benghazi. As the Captain said, this fleet is a threat to our convoy and we must bring it to battle or drive it back to port.

'Strict wireless silence is to be maintained unless you sight the enemy. In that case, get off a first sighting report as quickly as possible and an amplifying report as soon as you have ascertained the numbers and disposition of the enemy and its position, course and speed.

'The reference position, XY, for all reports is 36 degrees north, 18 degrees east. The Fleet's position at 1500 will be 116 degrees bearing from XY, distance 175 miles. We shall maintain a course of 285 degrees and a speed of 20 knots.

'You must keep an eye open for enemy fighters. There is an aerodrome at Benghazi which might be within range.'

He was followed by the Squadron Senior Observer, Gordon Power, who gave details of the parallel search. Aircraft would take departure from a smoke-float dropped by the CO and fly on diverging courses, at an angle of sixty-five degrees, on either side of the Fleet's course, breaking off one by one until all seven aircraft were flying on the same westerly course ahead of and away from the Fleet, at a distance of fifteen miles from each other.

Gordon then gave each observer his precise tracks. All aircraft would return to the carrier two and a half hours after departure. Recognition signals, wireless frequencies and call signs could be obtained from the list on the notice-board.

Schooley came next with weather information. Aboard *Peregrine* the ship's schoolmaster had a mixed bag of responsibilities. As well as his role in education, he helped with the ship's navigation and was the ship's meteorological officer.

At two thousand feet, the height the squadron would be flying, winds would be light, force three, from the west, with some patchy cloud above that height.

'Right, gentlemen,' the CO concluded. 'Keep a good lookout. Pilots, remember that accurate flying is essential to keep an even space between the parallel lines of the search. We shall take off in half an hour.'

Lieutenant Bidwell and Sub Lieutenant Weston followed Bolo and Sandy down to the flight deck where, at the after end, a familiar sight greeted them. The CO's aircraft already had its wings locked into flying position. Behind it seven other aircraft, with wings folded, were packed like pilchards in a tin. A TAG was in each, tuning his wireless set, whilst in the cockpits mechanics sat waiting for the pilots. Crewmen waited with each aircraft, ready to remove chocks, push the aircraft forward and lock the wings into flying position.

Wes Weston climbed into his observer's cockpit and began to lay off the ship's and his own projected tracks on his Bigsworth chartboard. From his open cockpit he could see all the other aircraft, silent, still, waiting expectantly. Biddy, his pilot, had climbed into his cockpit and was beginning his pre-flight drill, what he could manage with folded wings.

Then came the signal, 'Start up. Start up.' And the silence was shattered by the developing roar of the nine-cylinder Pegasus engines.

Wes watched as the carrier turned into wind.

First the CO took off, then 'Baker', followed by 'Charlie' and the others, until it was 'Love's' turn. Biddy revved his engine a little and taxied to the starting position. There his wings were locked into place. Wes clipped the safety line from the floor on to his harness and sat on his stool waiting. He heard the roar as Biddy revved up his engine. He felt the shudder as the machine began to vibrate. He saw the mechanics remove the chocks. And then they were off, with the usual slow start and the building up of speed as the power of the engine took over. He saw the staring faces of the Captain, Commander Flying and the Air Staff Officer watching from the side of the bridge as they sped past. There was a final bump and they were airborne, sagging downwards below deck level at first and then rising and turning as the speed built up.

Looking aft, he could see the carrier's deck stretching away from him with the solitary A/S Swordfish waiting to take off for its patrol.

'There's the smoke-float,' he exclaimed as they circled past the stern of the carrier and out to starboard. 'Make for that and then fly a course of 220.'

He had allowed a few degrees for the wind and the small variation. L – Love was already at two thousand feet and Biddy had settled on a cruising speed of ninety knots.

'Permission to reel out the wireless aerial, sir?'

This was PO Jarman's voice and Wes heard Biddy give an affirmative. He looked over the side of the cockpit and watched the wire aerial with its weighted end unwind in a long curving arc below the Swordfish. Now Jarman was able to fine-tune his wireless set.

'How long on this course, Wes?' asked Biddy.

'We've got forty-five miles to go before we turn and that will take half an hour. I'd like to take a wind before then and that will cost us three minutes. We took departure at 1515, so you can expect to turn on to a course of 285 degrees at about 1548.'

'Okay, Wes. Let me know when you want to take a wind.'

Before he was ready for that, Wes took a backbearing on the carrier and checked his course. He was a careful and methodical young man, very tidy in his appearance and confident in his manner. Of medium height and stature, he was a stalwart of the squadron deck-hockey team, where his physical fitness and agility made him a successful centre-forward. His squadron job was to assist the Adjutant, 'Dicky' Burd, with the administration.

He took an aluminium dust marker out of its tin, picked up his voicepipe and said, 'I'm ready now for that wind. Stand by. Now!'

On that word he threw the dust marker over the side of the aircraft and started his stopwatch. At the same time Biddy began a carefully controlled rate two turn to port until he was on a reciprocal course. At one and a half minutes precisely Wes told his pilot to complete another rate two turn to port and fly along the original course. With a series of bearings of the dust marker Wes was able to estimate the distance and direction of the drift in three minutes and from this work out the direction and speed of the wind at the height at which he was flying. Wes would take at least one more wind before the flight was concluded and more if he suspected a change of wind direction.

At 1548 Biddy turned on to his new westerly course, whilst Wes searched all round with his binoculars. Later in the war, Fleet Air Arm aircraft would be equipped with ASV, a primitive form of radar, but at this stage they had to rely on the human eye.

At 1630 Wes was carefully circling the horizon with his binoculars when a faint suggestion of movement caught his eye, just above the horizon. He steadied the glasses on the bearing.

'Biddy, I think there is something about twenty miles away fine on the port bow, about red one-oh. Continue on this course until I'm sure.'

Biddy searched the horizon in the direction indicated, but could see nothing with the naked eye.

Then Wes spoke again.

'Yes. There are several large ships there. I can see them clearly in the glasses. It must be the enemy fleet.'

'Right!' said Biddy. 'Get a sighting report off. I'll continue on this course.'

Enemy Fleet in sight bearing 270 degrees distance 15 miles. My position is 157 degrees XY 137 miles. Time of origin 1634.

Wes put the message into simple code and passed it to his petty officer telegraphist-air-gunner.

'Send that off, Jarman, and let me know as soon as it's acknowledged.'

'Steer across their stern, Biddy,' Wes told his pilot. 'Keep the range at about seven miles. They may not see us then.'

Wes plotted the enemy fleet's position on his chartboard and began to write out his amplifying report.

Three battleships, six cruisers and seven destroyers in position 165 degrees XY 133 miles. Steering (they crossed the track of the enemy at that moment and Wes took a bearing which gave him the enemy course) *285 degrees. Estimated speed 20 knots. Time of origin 1645.*

'Message acknowledged, sir,' said PO Jarman.

'Very good. Now send this new report.' Wes passed the coded message to his TAG.

This was an electric moment for Wes, the first time in the war that an enemy battlefleet had been reported. He could visualise the scene aboard *Peregrine*. On his first report the torpedoes, already prepared and available, would be loaded on to the Swordfish. Maintenance crews would be making last-minute checks, and the order would go out, '998 Squadron range aircraft.' Telegraphist-air-gunners would be checking the guns and wireless sets, and pilots and observers would be hastening to the ops room for briefing. By about 1700 the strike would be launched and would reach the Italian Fleet by 1830, roughly.

He reached for his speaking-tube.

'Biddy, we've got a problem. The strike-force will arrive at about 1830. We shall have been flying for over three and a half hours by then. If we stay till then we may not have enough fuel to get back to the carrier.'

'We've got to stay and shadow until 998 arrives, Wes, even if it means ditching. I'll fly as economically as I can and try to stretch out our fuel.'

Biddy turned his aircraft a hundred and eighty degrees to cross back astern of the enemy fleet. Wes was now plotting the enemy's track and he would use this for his own navigation. It freed him from the need to plot the many changing courses that Biddy might make over the next hour or so.

It was on the third crossing that the inevitable happened. Black puffs appeared ahead of 'Love'.

'They've seen us,' Biddy shouted. 'That's four-inch they're firing. I'll close the range a bit and you can get a more accurate assessment of their speed.'

Wes fixed his binoculars on the line of battleships. He saw the kick in the wake of the first ship.

'They're turning to starboard,' he called. 'This will bring more guns to bear.'

'I'll open the range,' said Biddy, 'and stay on their starboard side.'

Both officers knew how important it was to inform the carrier and the strike-force of the change of course. The strike was almost certainly on its way, aiming to intercept the Italians on their old course. They would miss their target completely unless they were given fresh information.

The Italian Fleet had steadied on their new course to the north at an increased speed. Wes made some rapid calculations and gave a new signal to his TAG to transmit.

Enemy has altered course to 350 degrees. Speed 26 knots. Position 163 degrees XY 130 miles. Time of origin 1710.

It looked as if the Italians were turning for home at Messina or Taranto. This was good for 'Love' as it cut down the distance for the strike-force and for 'Love's' return. Maybe now they would manage to get back and land on the carrier.

Wes made some more calculations on his chartboard.

'Biddy,' he said, 'the ETA of the strike-force is now 1800. If we shadow from the starboard beam of the Eyties we shall be nearer the carrier for our return. We might just make it.'

'Good thinking, Wes,' said Biddy. 'Keep your eyes open for the strike-force.'

The Italians had almost ceased firing, reserving their guns for when Biddy took his aircraft to have a closer look. Wes sent a further report on the enemy's movements at 1745 and ten minutes later he spotted the approaching squadron at about six thousand feet.

It was in three vics of three aircraft. Wes could see the CO was aiming to get ahead of the Italian Fleet. Still in tight formation, the attacking squadron began its shallow dive to build up speed for the approach. Now the Italians had opened up and shell bursts speckled the sky ahead of the torpedo bombers.

No guns were now firing at L – Love and they were able to follow the squadron and watch the attack.

Laboriously, the slow Swordfish had managed to get ahead of the enemy fleet and now, deployed in line abreast, they levelled off at a hundred feet above the waves. The Italians were firing every gun that would bear, including their big guns, in a barrage that seemed impossible to penetrate.

'They're bunched together too closely,' Biddy exclaimed. 'They make too good a target.'

At that moment one of the aircraft was enveloped in a shell-burst, and plunged into the sea. The aircraft next to it, damaged by the same shell, pulled up and away, its starboard wing dropping.

'They'll never make it,' cried Wes.

As if to prove the point the fleet turned 180 degrees, away from the oncoming torpedo bombers. The squadron was still two miles from the enemy, in a hopeless position to attack the battlefleet. The cruisers, which had been ahead of the battle-ships, were now astern of them, and in the way of the attacking aircraft.

'Look! They're dropping their fish,' Biddy cried.

The aircraft were turning away, their torpedoes launched, astern of the cruisers. There was no chance of their hitting a battleship. But there was one explosion, a hit on the after-most cruiser.

'We can't wait any longer,' said Biddy. 'We must make for the carrier.'

'Message from a 998 plane to the *Peregrine*, sir,' said PO Jarman. 'He has taken over shadowing and is sending out an enemy report.'

'Okay. Give us a course back to the carrier, Wes,' said Biddy.

'Right – 082 degrees,' said Wes promptly. 'ETA 1900. The Italian alteration of course has helped. We are now only forty-two miles from the carrier.'

'Good!' his pilot replied. 'We're low on fuel, but I think we'll make it.'

The last Wes saw of the Italian Fleet, it was its turning 180 degrees, back on to its northerly course.

Twenty minutes later, the British Fleet hove in sight. As soon as Wes flashed a recognition signal, the Fleet turned into wind, and, without wasting any time, Biddy brought his aircraft down to make a safe landing. The fuel gauge was reading zero. But they were safe.

The CO was waiting for Biddy and Wes and accompanied them to the bridge to report directly to the Captain.

'Pilot, check the positions with Sub Lieutenant Weston,' said the Captain, 'while Lieutenant Bidwell gives us a rundown on what happened.'

The ASO accompanied Wes and the Ship's Navigation Officer to the chartroom, but Wings joined the Captain and the CO of 999 Squadron to hear Biddy's account.

First Biddy gave a brief account of the sighting of the enemy fleet and their turning away northwards. Then he came to 998's attack.

'They followed our usual pattern,' he said 'and attacked in close formation from ahead, going into line abreast for the launch. I don't think this is a successful method.'

'Why is that?' Wings asked.

'For two reasons, sir. When they were bunched together they presented too good a target. One shellburst destroyed one plane and damaged another. Then the enemy fleet did a hundred and eighty degrees turn and put the squadron in a hopeless position. The Italians are too fast and too manoeuvrable for these tactics. Our Swordfish are too slow to respond.'

'What is the answer, then?' said the Captain. 'This is the first attack of this kind on an enemy fleet.'

'Well, sir,' said Biddy. 'The real answer is faster aircraft, but I don't suppose we'll get any.'

'The Barracuda and Firefly are in the pipeline,' said Wings, 'but I'm afraid it will be three years or more before they are available.'

'There is possibly one other answer,' said Biddy, who had been thinking about the attack on his way back to the carrier. 'If we could put more aircraft up and attack simultaneously from different directions, then whichever way the enemy turned, some aircraft would be in a good attacking position. This would also have the merit of spreading our aircraft out and making them less vulnerable to enemy gunfire.'

'This is very interesting. What do you think, Wings?'

'I'd like to work on it, sir,' Wings replied. 'I'd like to talk it over with Lieutenant Commander Savage and the ASO. Are we putting up another attack tonight?'

'No. We're not ready for a night attack or night deck-landings. I expect the Admiral will turn north as soon as 998 Squadron has landed on. We shall try to cover the Italians and launch another torpedo attack at first light – our aircraft can take off in the dark.'

Lieutenant Commander Savage had been listening intently to the discussion. He had been particularly impressed with Lieutenant Bidwell's account of the attack and his suggestions for improving it. He now added his own suggestion.

'I wonder,' he said, 'if we can put up a combined attack, with some aircraft dive-bombing and others launching torpedoes. It would help if both squadrons were involved.'

'Wings?' The Captain turned to Commander Flying.

'I'll look into it, sir, and make a recommendation when 998 has returned.'

Wes had now joined Biddy and with a last word of commendation from the Captain, the squadron officers made their way down to the wardroom and a lively reception from the remainder of the squadron, who had landed earlier from their search.

Chapter 4

Torpedo Attack

'Wake up, sir. Wake up.'

Bolo clutched for a moment or two at his fast receding sleep and then became fully awake. A torpedo attack on the Italian Fleet! That was what he was being called for.

'What time is it?' he asked the marine steward who was waking him.

'Three o'clock, sir.'

It all came back: the search, the sighting, the other squadron landing-on after their attack and, just before darkness fell, the landing-on of the shadowing aircraft and the anti-submarine patrol. The last report of the Italian Fleet was that it was continuing northwards at twenty-six knots.

Bolo sensed the change of direction as *Peregrine* turned into wind. That would be for the two aircraft of 998 Squadron, flying off to establish the whereabouts of the enemy fleet. If the Italians had continued on their course of 350 degrees at 26 knots, they would be about forty miles ahead of the British Fleet. If either of the search aircraft sighted the Italians, he was to stay and shadow and report their position, course and speed, whilst the second aircraft returned for A/S patrol.

Bolo joined the other airmen for a quick coffee or tea in the wardroom before they all assembled in the briefing-room.

Wings addressed the crews.

'As soon as we get a sighting of the enemy fleet,' he said, 'the squadrons will take off. Aircraft are presently being ranged on deck. First to take off will be five aircraft of 998 Squadron. They will each be armed with two two-fifty-pound bombs and two five-hundred-pound armour-piercing bombs. They will climb to eight thousand feet and carry out a dive-bombing attack.

'999 Squadron will be ranged on deck immediately behind 998 Squadron. They will be armed with torpedoes and will fly at six thousand feet. The Commanding Officers will brief you on the plan of attack.'

He was followed by Schooley, who provided the latest meteorological information, and the ASO who gave details of the position, course and speed of the British Fleet. Because of the threat of an Italian air attack, the Fleet would turn on to a course of 130 degrees, away from the Italian mainland, immediately after the two squadrons were launched. The attack on the Italian Fleet, therefore, would be the last chance of doing some damage.

Then 998 Squadron retired to the rest room for briefing by their CO, whilst Lieutenant Commander Savage addressed his squadron.

'One aircraft of 998 Squadron was lost and one was damaged in their torpedo attack,' he said. 'Two of their aircraft are out on a search and that leaves them only five aircraft to coordinate a dive-bombing attack with our torpedo attack.

'We learned some lessons from their torpedo attack and from some suggestions made by Lieutenant Bidwell, who witnessed it. The dive-bombing attack by 998 is intended to create a diversion and commit the Italians to avoiding action. We'll endeavour to come out of the dark side, from the west, immediately following their attack. We must not provide them with a good target by being too bunched up.

34

'I'll drop a flame-float five miles north-west of the carrier and circle it whilst you form up on me. We'll fly in close squadron formation, climbing to six thousand feet. I hope to pass to the west of the enemy fleet until we are on his port beam. I'll waggle my wings as a signal for the second and third sub-flights to break off and act independently. My sub-flight will attack from the west; the second sub-flight will attack from the north, whilst the third sub-flight attacks from the south. In this way, at least one sub-flight should be in a good position for launching torpedoes, whatever evasive action the enemy takes.

'I want you to start your dive towards the enemy battlefleet five minutes after I signal you away. That'll give you time to get into your correct positions and coordinate our attacks. When you start your run-in, each sub-flight leader will waggle his wings as a signal to his sub-flight to open out into line abreast, at a distance of about two hundred yards. In this way we hope to disperse the enemy gunfire and give ourselves more of a chance.

'Maintain maximum speed in a shallow dive and try to drop your torpedoes at about half-a-mile range. Aim at any of the battleships if you can. Otherwise go for a cruiser. Any questions?'

'Yes, sir,' said Holy Temple. 'Will we be doing a night attack?'

'No, the intention is to attack at first light, that is about 0530, providing we get a sighting from one of the search aircraft.'

He was interrupted at that point, by a messenger from the bridge, who handed a note to him. He glanced at it and read it out to the squadron.

'"Enemy fleet sighted in position 353 degrees from XY, distance 154 miles. Course 346 degrees. Speed 26 knots. Time of origin 0415."'

He looked at his watch.

35

'It is now 0430. Out to your aircraft. Take off at 0445.'

In an orderly confusion, the pilots and observers hurried down to the flight deck, where mechanics had already started and were running the engines. By 0445 the CO of 998 Squadron was taking off, followed quickly by the aircraft of his squadron and then 999 Squadron.

Bolo soon spotted the flame-float dropped by the CO, and above it he could see the letter 'A' being flashed on 'Abel's' navigation lights. 'Abel' was making a slow circle round the flame-float and as Bolo formed up astern and to starboard of his CO, he noticed his own sub-flight closing up on his wing tips. Very quickly the squadron aircraft were in close formation, and as soon as they set out on their north-westerly course the CO began climbing and switched off his lights.

Bolo kept his eyes on the aircraft on his port bow, 'Charlie', the starboard aircraft in the leading sub-flight. At first, the shadowy, barely seen aircraft required all his attention. As the squadron climbed, the light grew a little brighter and he could see the leading sub-flight more clearly. The sun was just below the horizon and a faint tinge of red was appearing.

He had had little time to brood on the impending action and it was not in his nature to worry about what might happen. He had a job to do and he would do it to the best of his ability. He hoped they would not be shot down. Even more, he hoped they would score a hit.

Bing Crosby in M – Mike was not so sure of himself. He was very conscious of the damage done to them on the previous attack and he glanced nervously at his starboard wing, seeing, in his mind's eye, the line of bullet holes and the damaged strut. He would have liked to be anywhere but in his aircraft about to torpedo an enemy fleet. But then the sense of unity with the squadron took over. He was part of a team and his aircraft was slotted into its position in the formation. Whatever he felt, he would follow the pre-determined plan and play his part in the attack.

In L – Love, Biddy was thinking quite differently. He was a Royal Navy career officer, and this was what he was trained for. He was interested in the CO's tactics, of which he approved, and was thinking how he would develop his part whichever way the Italians turned. He looked forward to testing out the CO's theory. Clearly pre-war training had not really prepared the naval squadrons for their role in a modern war. The Navy still regarded the battleship as the bulwark and main offensive weapon of the fleet. Aircraft carriers were subsidiary, of use in detecting the enemy and slowing him down, not for defeating him. The war in the Mediterranean was bound to test these beliefs and Biddy was glad he was in the right theatre of war at the right time.

'I think I can just see the enemy fleet to starboard, about green six-oh.' Wes Weston's voice cut into his thoughts.

He risked a quick glance and thought he, too, had caught a faint glimpse. And then Bolo was signalling, waggling his wings to indicate he was breaking off.

Sandy had kept Bolo informed of the whereabouts of the Italian Fleet and when he saw the CO's signal, Bolo was ready. He made a slow turn to starboard, noting the time on his cockpit clock. This took his sub-flight back to the port quarter of the Italian Fleet and when Sandy had checked his bearing he began the turn in.

The guns of the enemy had now opened up and the sky above them was pitted with gun bursts. The flashes of the guns could be clearly seen and as Bolo drew closer the fleet was revealed. Three battleships in line ahead formed the centre, flanked by three cruisers on either side. The destroyer screen formed a broad 'v' ahead of the battlefleet.

'Five minutes since we broke off, Bolo,' said Sandy in his calm, unhurried voice.

'Right. I'm starting the attack.'

Bolo waggled his wings and waved his sub-flight away to a position two hundred yards on either beam. He put his nose down and let the speed build up. He was aiming to come out of the shallow dive astern of the enemy and turn in to intercept them no matter which way they turned. The air now was black with shell-bursts. Streams of tracers rose vertically from the large ships as their close-range weapons opened up on the dive- bombers.

Bolo's speed had now built up to a hundred and thirty knots. He could see 'Love' and 'Mike' two hundred yards away, one on either side of him. Still they were not fired at. They had not been seen. Then the destroyers opened up. That would be the second sub-flight, approaching from the north.

Bolo's aircraft juddered. He saw the flash of shell-burst a hundred yards ahead, and soon the air around him and ahead was full of bursts. The torpedo attack had been spotted. The enemy was putting up a barrage ahead of them.

Events moved rapidly in a dream-like sequence. The enemy ships now turning to port, taking evasive action from the dive-bombers. Huge splashes alongside the battleships, the battleships now committed and making a good target for Bolo's attack. *Pull out of the dive. Trim the aircraft. Arm the torpedo. Jink away from the shell-bursts, round the nearest cruiser. The sea fifty feet below. A bow-shot on the nearest battleship. Fifteen hundred yards. One thousand. Steady. Press the tit. Hold it for a second. Then up and away, jinking, side-stepping, avoiding the flak.*

Sandy watched the mad scramble with bated breath. He was more aware of Bolo's skill now than ever before. He saw the aircraft on either side of him launch their torpedoes just as he felt his own go, and saw the torpedoes running towards the enemy.

The battleships were turning again. They were attempting to comb the tracks of the torpedoes of the CO's flight. But this opened them up to the torpedoes of Bolo's flight. Surely, they hadn't missed?

An explosion amidships on one battleship! Another on a cruiser! Two torpedo hits. Smoke coming from a second battleship. That would be a hit by the dive-bombers.

As Bolo circled astern of the enemy fleet, Sandy watched the stricken vessels falter and recover. The enemy was able to continue northwards, their speed scarcely reduced.

Now Sandy could see 'Love' and 'Mike' joining their sub-flight leader. And there was the CO, flashing the letter 'A'. Soon the squadron, all nine of the planes, had formed up and were flying southwards to join the carrier. Ahead of them were the five aircraft of 998 Squadron. Incredible. Not one aircraft lost!

'How long before we sight the carrier?' Bolo's voice broke into Sandy's thoughts.

'It's now 0545. We should see them about fifteen miles ahead in an hour's time.'

As they circled the carrier, Bolo could see the single Gladiator ranged on deck. That would be Wings, taking off to defend the Fleet against the expected aircraft counter attack. Bolo came to a quick decision. As soon as he landed he would seek permission to take off in the second Gladiator to assist Wings.

The Fleet was turning into wind. The Gladiator was taking off, a solitary, ancient biplane, to defend the Fleet against the might of the Italian Air Force. The squadron was breaking off in sub-flights to circle the carrier and wait their turn for landing-on.

Cut!

Bolo was down and taxiing to the lift where he left a fitter in the cockpit whilst he hastened to the bridge.

'Yes,' the Captain agreed. The remaining Gladiator would

be ranged and flown off as soon as all the Swordfish had landed.

Half-an-hour later, Bolo was in the cockpit of the Gladiator, climbing as fast as he could to join Wings. Wings was circling at fifteen thousand feet above the carrier and Bolo could see him as he climbed. Unlike the Swordfish, the two Gladiators were fitted with R/T, and Bolo called his leader.

'Hello Red One, this is Red Two. How d'you hear me? Over.'

'Red Two, this is Red One. Loud and clear. Over.'

'Red One, this is Red Two. I will join you as soon as I can. Over.'

'Red Two, this is Red One. Glad to have you. Out.'

The carrier and the Fleet looked tiny, peaceful and vulnerable as Bolo climbed to fifteen thousand feet. He tucked in behind Red One's starboard wing tip to await events, keeping an all-round lookout for enemy aircraft.

The first warning of attack came from the carrier: 'Fifteen bandits, distance ten miles, approaching from the north at angels ten.'

The language of the RAF seemed strange to Bolo. The ship had no radar and the R/T was primitive. Fighter control hardly existed in this early stage of Fleet Air Arm operations.

'Roger. Am turning north to intercept. Stay with me, Bolo, and watch for enemy fighters.'

Bolo maintained his station on Wings' starboard quarter and soon he could see the cluster of dots ahead and below. They were SM 79s, Italian high-level bombers, and they were already opening out into attack formation.

'Stand by,' came the voice of Wings. 'We'll attack from up sun and try to break up their formation.'

On the deck of the carrier, Action Alarm had been sounded and guns were manned and waiting. Some of the squadron officers had talked themselves into manning Lewis guns, borrowed from the squadron stores and set up by the armourers as extra defence.

Biddy and Wes had control of one such gun, Biddy as the gunner and Wes standing by with a fresh drum of ammunition. They could see the Savoias approaching from astern, deadly and menacing. The big guns had opened up and gun-bursts enveloped the approaching bombers. They seemed to bear a charmed life, for they came on steadily, ignoring the gunfire. A mile from the Fleet, the British fighters struck. Biddy saw the two Gladiators tear into the enemy pack, apparently unseen, and, in a moment, the orderly approach of the Italians was changed to one of confusion. One big bomber was plunging into the sea astern of the carrier. The others were weaving and turning, now within range of the close flak.

'Break off and leave it to the ships,' called Wings.

Bolo had felt an exhilaration unlike anything experienced in Swordfish. The Gladiator had responded to his lightest touch and was very manoeuvrable. He had followed Wings into the centre of the pack, selected his target and made a stern attack, coming in from above. The enemy squadron was caught completely unawares and had broken up in confusion. Bolo let his machine go past the Italians and then pulled away to starboard and back, making a beam attack from below on his next target. Again a quick and accurate burst, and then out past the enemy formation, another turn and another attack, this time from the quarter.

Bolo had lost sight of his leader, but there was no doubt of the effect the two fighters were having. The enemy formation was scattered across the sky and aircraft were dropping their bombs indiscriminately and without much hope of hitting.

Then came the order to break off, and the madness was over. The Italians were retreating. The Fleet was steaming on, still in good formation, and Wings was doing a victory roll over the carrier. One enemy shot down and the attack driven off.

Chapter 5

Alexandria Harbour

Ras-el-tin, the site of Pharos, the ancient lighthouse on the promontory, stood like a sentinel, guarding Alexandria. As the earthy, ancient smell of Egypt came out to greet them, Bolo stood to attention, lining the flight deck with the rest of his squadron for the entry into harbour. It was a ceremonial that Bolo enjoyed, with the Marine Band playing 'Wings over the Navy', and *Peregrine* dipping her flag to salute the Admiral as they passed *Warspite*. Slowly, the great ship approached its mooring-buoy and made fast. The Marine Band played its final tune, 'Hearts of Oak', and officers and men were dismissed. Bolo hurried, with his borrowed telescope, his symbol of office, to the quarterdeck, where he was Officer of the Day.

The scene was a lively one. Signals were being flashed to *Peregrine* from the Flagship. The ship's number one cutter was being manned and lowered. Bumboats were already approaching with their wares, fruit or leather wallets and handbags. Feluccas with their single lateen sails were plying busily between the ships, joined by many ships' boats going about their business. Voices in broken, excited English offered Egypt to the men lining the *Peregrine*'s side-decks.

A motor-boat was approaching *Peregrine*'s starboard gangway. On being hailed, it gave a time-honoured response, *Ramrod*. This meant that the Captain of *Ramrod* was aboard, and coming to visit *Peregrine*'s Captain.

'Man the side,' Bolo ordered.

Joined by the Petty Officer of the Watch and the ratings who formed the guard, he stood to attention as Captain Hendy of *Ramrod* climbed the companionway. As the Captain stepped on to the quarterdeck the bosun's pipe sounded, the men came to attention and Bolo raised his hand in salute. Commander Christie, *Peregrine*'s Commander, whom Bolo had hastily sent for, stepped forward and presented himself, and accompanied Captain Hendy down below to the Captain's day cabin.

Bolo enjoyed this ritual as he enjoyed most things in the Navy. It spoke of centuries of tradition, of a history that began when King Alfred first contemplated a Navy. The Officer of the Day no longer wore a sword, but the telescope was part of the ritual. So was the uniform. During the daytime, most officers wore white shorts and open neck shirt. Bolo was dressed in the more formal number tens, long white trousers and white tunic with black epaulettes revealing his rank.

Bolo was glad of the overhang of the flight deck, for the day was very hot, with temperatures in the nineties. By lunchtime, he was ready to finish his spell of duty and retire to the wardroom ante-room, where his squadron friends were gathering for pre-lunch drinks. A sense of excitement was building up. Flying personnel rarely drank at sea, but the tradition was developing of holding an officer's party in the wardroom ante-room after dinner on the first night back from operations.

Most of Bolo's friends were going ashore after lunch to explore the mysteries of Alexandria, but Bolo had spent several days in the port waiting for the *Peregrine* and now preferred to spend the afternoon resting in his cabin. He looked thoughtfully at the photograph on his bookcase. It revealed a slim twenty-year-old girl, with hair curling to her shoulders. Her most striking feature was her grave, wide-set eyes, grey-green in colour, that gazed steadily from the picture. Bolo's mind went back to the day when he had first met Joyce. The year was 1938 …

'John, we're going to try you out as a regular bowler in the First Eleven this year. We need to fill Corny Wilde's place, now that he's retiring.'

John Hawkins flushed with pleasure as he listened to Mark Fender, Captain of Sussex County Cricket Team. Throughout 1937 he had played regularly for the Second Eleven, developing his skills as a fast bowler. Under the guidance of Corny he had learned to use the seam, swinging the ball either way, and to vary his pace. Towards the end of the year he was rewarded with more and more wickets and an occasional place in the first team.

John was in whites, about to make his way to the nets for some early practice. It was late April and already the sun was warming the field, drying out the turf and making it possible to use the outdoor nets. He saw the familiar figure of Corny ahead of him, accompanied by a girl. He hurried forward to greet his old friend.

'Hello, John,' said Corny. 'Let me introduce my daughter, Joyce. She's just finishing her Easter holiday.'

John took the hand offered to him and found himself confronting a slim girl of medium height with dark brown hair and a twinkle in her eyes.

'Daddy has told me about you,' she said, 'and how your bowling has come on. I've been wanting to meet you.'

'I'm glad to meet you, too, Joyce. Your father hasn't told me anything about you. He's been keeping you a secret! Are you at school or college?'

I'm in the sixth form at Hinchinbury School. I hope to go to university if I do well enough in my highers.'

John realised that Joyce must be about eighteen years old.

44

There was a mixture of youthful freshness and serenity in her demeanour that he found attractive. He wondered why he had not met her before. He knew that Corny had lost his wife the previous year and he thought it possible that Joyce had been tied up with school and housekeeping. That might explain the gravity that underlay the twinkle.

Joyce and her father accompanied John to the nets, where he limbered up, ready to bowl under the critical eye of Corny. Soon his rhythm was going and the balls flowed smoothly. On his fifth ball he tried an in-swinger and was rewarded by the crack of the ball against stumps and a small handclap from Joyce.

Joyce stayed at the nets until John had finished his practice and then accompanied him to the pavilion for a refreshing drink.

John saw nothing of Joyce that summer until the end of July. The team was at home in Hove and Joyce and her father were near the pavilion as the cricketers left the field. John was strangely moved by this meeting. He had thought little about her since he had last seen her – after all, she was a schoolgirl. Now, in a pretty, free-flowing, floral dress, she was attractive and disturbing. She greeted him warmly.

'Well bowled,' she said, referring to the four wickets he had taken.

'Hello, Joyce. How's school?'

'I'm finished with all that. Now I'm looking forward to university.'

'Did the exams go well?'

'Well enough, I think. And now I've got two months of this gorgeous summer to enjoy without a care in the world.'

And Joyce had enjoyed that summer. Long summer afternoons in a deckchair, watching the cricket, were followed by walks with John in the quiet country lanes or along the promenade, or curled up in an armchair talking to her father and John.

John particularly remembered one walk, after Joyce and he had driven to the New Forest and had lunch at a pub. As they came to a particularly rocky climb John had lent a helping hand and Joyce had not released it when they reached the summit. Hand in hand they wandered along the path beneath the tall, shady beeches. Joyce was particularly good at botany and named the flowers and plants as they passed. Then, as they approached a glade by a small pond, a movement caught their attention and a small herd of deer emerged from the woods and approached the pond. John and Joyce stood entranced, watching the deer and revelling in the attractive power of nature.

Just for a moment John put his arm around Joyce's shoulders and she leaned against him. Then a low-flying aeroplane flew past and the mood was broken. They looked up and watched the plane, an early Hurricane, circling in the sky, and their talk turned to the atrocities in Germany and the danger of a world war as they wandered slowly back to John's car.

At the beginning of October Joyce left for university and, with cricket over, John found a new interest. He joined the local flying-club and was putting in as much time as possible into his flying before the weather broke. By the middle of October he was ready for his first solo.

'Right then! It's all yours,' said his instructor, Peter Gale. 'Just a few circuits and bumps and, when you are ready, come in to land. I'll meet you in the bar.'

With that Peter walked away, as was his custom, deliberately not looking back at John, leaving him to come to terms with his first solo flight.

John felt the quiver in his stomach as he began to taxi towards the downwind end of the grass field. The quiver was not one of fear, however, but rather one of anticipation. John had made several successful landings and take-offs that morning with Peter in the second cockpit and he felt quite capable of doing the same thing without his instructor.

46

The Tiger Moth handled so easily. Opening the throttle, John felt the power surge as the aircraft gathered speed. It virtually took off on its own and John scarcely needed to touch the controls. Pulling the aircraft into a climbing turn, he soon found himself circling at two thousand feet above the aerodrome.

Then a new feeling took over. Until now he had been concerned with the technique of flying, following his instructor's suggestions, listening to criticisms, practising his use of controls, perfecting his technical knowledge. Now he felt free of that, free of the land, free as a bird. To one side of him were the South Downs, rolling away east and west. Chanctonbury Ring stood out clearly and Devil's Dyke passed beneath him. Suddenly a picture of Joyce came to mind, Joyce laughing breathlessly as they reached the top of the steep slope above the Dyke and stood looking at the Devil's handiwork.

Joyce. Was he in love with her? She was still so young, little more than a girl. Was it a brotherly concern? One thing he felt for sure. He would like to have Joyce with him in the second cockpit to share his emotional upsurge and enjoy with him the freedom of the skies.

He looked out seawards. Sunshine and blue sky and sparkling water added to his mood of jubilation and uplift. And then further out he saw an aircraft carrier, escorted by two destroyers, steaming westwards towards a distant, threatening cloud. It was time to go back.

John approached his first touchdown in his usual forthright manner. He had practised this many times with Peter, and with relaxed concentration he eased his throttle and allowed the Tiger Moth to glide down until the wheels barely touched the earth. Then pushing the throttle gently forward, he allowed the plane to fly itself off. Already his handling of the controls was becoming gentle and instinctive, allowing the machine to have its way yet exerting

47

a firm control when required. On his fifth approach, he landed and taxied to the hangar.

Bolo smiled to himself as he tidied up his memories and stowed them away. It was time to go to the hangar and see how work was progressing on K – King. He had reported a slight oil leak to Leading Air-Mechanic Sid Hapwell, his engine fitter, who had promised to deal with it immediately.

He found the fitter wiping away the grease from his hands as he surveyed the engine.

'I found the leak, sir,' said Hapwell. 'One of the scraper rings was slightly worn. Just as well you reported it. It might have led to more serious trouble.'

'Thank you, Hapwell. It's good to know all is well with the old chap. By the way, who's responsible for the picture?'

Bolo indicated the painting on the fuselage just forward of the pilot's cockpit.

'That was Tiny Rawlings' idea, sir,' said Hapwell, nodding towards the huge air-rigger who was inspecting the ailerons.

'What's this, Rawlings? It looks like Old King Cole to me.'

'That's right, sir. It is Old King Cole.' A broad grin spread across the air rigger's face. 'As he is K – King, we thought we would give him a name, and Old King Cole seemed a good choice. Hope you like it.' A flicker of doubt crossed the rugged features.

Bolo appeared to pause for a moment of contemplation while both rigger and fitter waited anxiously.

'A splendid idea,' he said, smiling, 'and very well done. I think Old King Cole and I are going to get on well together. I must introduce him to the rest of the crew when they return from shore-leave.

'By the way,' he went on, 'wasn't it a make-and-mend this afternoon?'

48

'Yes, sir,' said Hapwell. 'But I wanted to make sure Old King Cole was on top line. And he is now.'

'What about you, Rawlings?'

'Well, sir, Sid is my oppo, my mate, like. I thought I'd keep him company, so I dealt with Old King Cole while he was tinkering with the engine.'

'Well, thank you both. I very much appreciate it,' said Bolo. 'Now you can get your heads down, or whatever else you do on a make-and-mend.'

'We're catching the 1600 liberty boat for a run ashore, sir. We're meeting some of the lads for a bit of a celebration.'

'Good show. Enjoy yourselves. You deserve it.'

'Thank you, sir. We will.'

At 2100 hours, the wardroom ante-room was full. The shore-party had returned for the evening. Dinner was finished. The bar was busy. Pink gins, horse's necks and John Collins were being served as fast as they could be prepared. Spirits were more popular than beer. Beer was sixpence a glass, gin twopence, whisky or brandy threepence. On a wine bill limited to two pounds a month for sub lieutenants, you could go further on spirits than on beer.

Sub Lieutenant Pincher Martin was already at the piano, playing a medley of popular songs. Now, as the officers of the two squadrons gathered around him, he began playing the songs they were waiting for, songs they could sing, nautical songs, sentimental songs, comic songs and bawdy songs. Soon everyone was singing lustily.

'Soon we'll be Sailing', 'Red Sails in the Sunset', the new Fleet Air Arm song, 'Wings over the Navy', 'A Muvver was Barfin 'er Baby One Night', 'While the Train was in the Station, You Must Practise Constipation'.

Bolo was amused and interested in the developing party. He realised that everyone was letting go the tension of the past few days. Flying personnel abstained from liquor whilst engaged in operational flying, but they more than made up for it now.

49

> I don't want to join the Navy,
> I don't want to go to sea.
> I'd rather hang around
> Piccadilly Underground,
> Living on the earnings of a high born lady ...

'Lydia Pink' was toasted next, 'the saviour of the human race', followed by 'My Rhubarb Refuses to Rise'.

Finally, they came to 'The Sampan Man', a song developed in the Far East.

> Have you seen the Sampan Man, the Sampan Man,
>   the Sampan Man?
> Have you seen the Sampan Man who lives in Wei
>   Hai Harbour?

Each officer in turn sang the refrain to a neighbour, beating him about the head and shoulders as he did so. The answer was sung in return, accompanied by further blows.

> Yes, I've seen the Sampan Man, the Sampan Man,
>   the Sampan Man.
> Yes, I've seen the Sampan Man who lives in Wei Hai
>   Harbour.'

As the familiar song echoed round the ante-room, so it became more riotous and more vigorous.

Pincher now began playing a conga and the party soon sorted itself out into a long conga line that threaded its way out of the ante-room, into the wardroom and back again.

The two squadrons were now ready for the next phase of the party. A pause to empty glasses, then at the command, 'At them, 999' and 'Go to it, 998' the two squadrons met head on in a gigantic rugby scrum in the middle of the ante-room.

50

Heaving, pushing, laughing, falling, heads down, arms locked, the squadrons struggled with each other. First one way the battle moved, then as ship's officers joined in to support the weaker side, back it went the other way.

Men grunted. Bodies sweated. Collars and ties were ripped off.

Suddenly a sharp command rang out above the hubbub.

'Dogs o' war – Wings.'

Commander Flying, who had been watching the antics of the young men with some approval, suddenly looked horrified and made for the door. He did not stand a chance. The rugby scrum broke up and made for the Commander. Wings disappeared in the middle of the melee and in short time a pair of trousers was held triumphantly aloft.

With great dignity Wings accepted his trousers back from the satisfied and victorious young officers, bowed to them and, with a twinkle in his eye, walked solemnly from the room, carrying his trousers over his arm.

Chapter 6

Rhodes

For the fifth time Bolo turned to cross the track of the Fleet. K – King was carrying out an anti-submarine patrol fifteen miles ahead of the destroyers forming the screen to the battlefleet. He could see the ships, stretched out in the hazy, early autumn sunshine, *Warspite*, with the C-in-C aboard, leading the battlefleet, followed by *Peregrine* and then *Malaya*. On the starboard side of the battlefleet was a line of three merchant ships. To starboard of these were two cruisers in line astern, thus giving the merchant ships the all-round protection of the Fleet's guns. Ahead of the convoy was the destroyer screen, in a broad vic formation, and Bolo could just make out the safety destroyer astern of the battlefleet.

He recalled yesterday's address by the Captain to the ship's company.

'Following the success of 998 Squadron's attack on Bomba, we are proceeding westwards to link up with Force H from Gibraltar, consisting of *Ark Royal* and the battlecruiser, *Hood*, with a destroyer escort. They are escorting a convoy from England with much-needed supplies for our forces in the Western Desert. We shall meet up south of Malta and exchange convoys. Force H will take over the merchant ships we are escorting and escort them via Gibraltar to England, whilst we take over their merchant ships for onward passage to Alexandria.

'With Force H are the new aircraft carrier, *Illustrious*, and the *Valiant*, a battleship of the same class as *Warspite*, that has undergone a complete re-fit, together with the anti-aircraft cruisers' *Calcutta* and *Coventry*. These ships are just what we need to boost our own forces in the Eastern Mediterranean. After we link up with *Illustrious*, the two carriers will mount a combined attack on the airfields of Rhodes.

'We expect to sight Force H tomorrow evening at about 1800 hours. That is all.'

Bolo hoped that he had drawn the lucky straw. He was on A/S patrol from 1600 to 1830 and he hoped to make a first sighting of Force H before he had to land.

Whilst 999 Squadron was covering the A/S patrols, 998 Squadron was standing by as strike-force. Yesterday, three aircraft from that squadron had made a dawn attack on Bomba, a supply port for Mussolini's Western Desert Army. One submarine had been attacked and sunk as it approached Bomba Harbour; a destroyer at anchor had been sunk; and a supply ship with a submarine alongside had been damaged and left in a sinking condition. *Peregrine*'s record since Italy entered the war had been superb and the score was rising every month. How would she fare with another carrier in the area? *Illustrious* was very much more modern than the elderly *Peregrine*, and was equipped with Fairey Fulmars, the Navy's latest fighters. What price the old Gladiators?

'I think I can just see Malta to the north-west.'

Sandy Sandiford's voice cut in on Bolo's thoughts and brought him back to matters in hand. He could see the faint smudge of cloud on the horizon that must be Malta, about twenty-five miles away. It was too far away in the slight haze to see clearly with the naked eye.

'Yes,' said Sandy. 'It is Malta. I can see it clearly now through the glasses.'

The time was 1700.

'Surely we must be getting fairly close to Force H,' said Bolo.

'Yes,' his observer replied. 'According to my calculations Force H is about thirty miles away. We could sight them within the next half-hour.'

'Aircraft approaching from the south-west,' suddenly shouted PO Mercer, the air gunner, who had been keeping an all-round observation for enemy aircraft.

'Got them!' cried Bolo and Sandy together.

'They could be enemy fighters from Tunis,' said Bolo. 'Keep an eye on them.'

Sandy watched the formation of three single-engined monoplanes approaching. He trained his binoculars on them, following them as they turned in towards the Swordfish.

Suddenly, he shouted, 'It's okay. They're Fulmars. They must be from *Illustrious*.'

The three Fulmars had indeed been sent off from *Illustrious* to investigate a suspicious contact picked up by the carrier's radar. Already the new equipment in the new carrier was proving itself. *Peregrine* had to wait for enemy aircraft to be sighted before being able to attack them; *Illustrious* could detect an aircraft up to thirty miles away, and send its aircraft to investigate and attack if it were an enemy.

The Fulmars circled the Swordfish, their leader waving a greeting as they passed, before heading off towards *Warspite* and *Peregrine*.

'Let's go and have a look,' said Bolo. 'Force H must be ahead just out of sight.'

He turned his aircraft on to a westerly course and three minutes later saw the Fleet ahead. It was really two fleets. *Illustrious*, *Valiant*, two cruisers and a convoy of four merchant ships, screened by several destroyers, was a mile ahead of the second fleet, dominated by *Hood* and *Ark Royal*, with its own cruisers and destroyers.

Bolo was particularly impressed with *Illustrious*. *Peregrine*, his own carrier, was a converted battleship, built during the First World War. *Illustrious*, the first of its class, had only recently been completed and had yet to take part in offensive operations, but her Fulmars had already shot down Italian shadowing aircraft and provided a defensive umbrella of fighters for the convoy. She was long and sleek and powerful. Even at a distance she looked purposeful and full of menace.

'We'd better get back and let *Peregrine* know we've met up,' said Sandy.

'Right! Give me a course,' said his pilot, and Bolo quickly settled on the course of 080 degrees. As they approached the *Peregrine* Sandy flashed his message: *Force H bearing 260 degrees distance 25 miles. Time of origin 1725.*

As soon as the message was acknowledged Bolo resumed his A/S patrol. Almost immediately he was joined by a Swordfish from *Illustrious*, presumably the A/S patrol of Force H. Bolo waggled his wings in greeting and received a friendly wave from the other pilot before they each resumed their patrols.

The crew of M – Mike had a grandstand view of the joining up of the two fleets. As they approached each other, signals were passed by lamp and flags. *Warspite*, *Peregrine* and *Malaya* with their cruisers and destroyers completed a hundred and eighty degree turn. They were joined by *Valiant* and *Illustrious* on their port side and the four merchant ships from the Force H convoy on their starboard side. The two anti-aircraft cruisers accompanying *Illustrious* stationed themselves outside the merchant ships, whilst the destroyers from *Illustrious*' screen joined the defensive circle round the capital ships and convoy.

Meanwhile, the merchant ships from Alexandria continued westwards to join Force H, which had completed a hundred and eighty degree turn to head back towards Gibraltar.

Never had Bolo seen such a gathering of ships. When the two fleets met he watched three aircraft carriers, four battleships, six cruisers, some twenty destroyers and seven merchant ships, all manoeuvring to gain their new positions. A great feeling of pride and confidence in the British Navy swept through him, and he felt almost sorry for the Italian Navy.

It was now 1830 and time to return to the carrier. The huge Fleet was already turning into wind. *Illustrious* was flying off the next A/S patrol and landing-on its Fulmars and Swordfish. In a very short space of time it was Bolo's turn. He had been impressed by the efficiency of *Illustrious*. He must not let *Peregrine* down.

A close circuit round the stern of the carrier. Hook down. Batsman's flags steady. Over the round-down now. Cut. A smooth landing, efficient and no fuss. As the Fleet swung back on its easterly course, K – King was already being lowered in the after lift.

The next day, whilst *Peregrine*'s aircraft took care of the A/S patrols, *Illustrious* mounted a twelve-aircraft search to scour the seas ahead and on either side of the Fleet for enemy surface ships. The search party was due to return at noon and, shortly before that time, a number of *Peregrine*'s pilots and observers gathered to watch.

Lieutenant Biddy Bidwell was particularly interested in the new aircraft carrier. He was speaking to a group of 999 officers.

'What a graceful ship she is!' he said. 'And she carries many more aircraft than we can, forty against our twenty-one. At present she has two squadrons of twelve Swordfish and one squadron of fifteen Fulmars.'

'She's fast, too,' said Sandy Sandiford. 'I believe she can reach a speed of thirty-two knots.'

'Very useful in a light wind,' said Bolo, 'particularly when landing-on her Fulmars.'

'She has a useful deck armour,' said Biddy. 'We have bulges for protection against torpedoes but very little deck armour. We would be vulnerable against a bombing attack. *Illustrious* has three-inch deck armour, which should give her some protection against all but the heaviest bombs.'

'Are there many ships in her class?' Holy Temple asked.

Biddy was the acknowledged authority on the Navy. He was a career officer and deeply interested in ships and tactics.

'Five more carriers of the *Illustrious* class are on the stocks,' he replied. 'I can see the time coming when they operate as a carrier squadron, with two hundred planes available. Just think of that. Two hundred planes. We've been operating with twenty.'

'And doing a lot of damage,' said Sandy.

'Here they come now,' said Bolo.

The officers watched keenly as the Fleet turned into wind to fly off a new fighter patrol and a relief anti-submarine Swordfish patrol. Circling the *Illustrious* were the three returning Fulmars and twelve Swordfish from the search. First the Fulmars landed.

'Look,' cried Bolo. 'They're not waiting for the lift to go down and up as we do.'

As soon as the first Fulmar landed, the crash barrier was lowered and the Fulmar taxied past it. Immediately the aircraft was past, the barrier was raised while the next aircraft landed-on. Whilst this was happening, the lift was taking the first fighter down to the hangar. *Peregrine*'s officers were astonished at the speed of the operation. They were even more astonished when the Swordfish landed-on.

'Like a lot of Red Indians,' said Bing Crosby.

The Swordfish were circling their carrier one behind the other at a distance of little more than two hundred yards. As one Swordfish landed, the next approached until waved away by Bats. As soon as the crash barrier was raised behind the previous Swordfish, the aircraft approaching was flagged in.

57

A Swordfish landed approximately every thirty seconds. In six minutes all twelve Swordfish had landed and the Fleet was turning back on its easterly course.

'It would take us about half an hour to land twelve aircraft,' said Bolo.

As *Peregrine* was providing only A/S patrols, which meant an aircraft flying off and on every two and a half hours, the squadron officers had an opportunity to catch up with squadron work or private letter-writing. Steve Price, the Senior Pilot, spent his afternoon in the hangar checking that all aircraft would be ready for the following morning's operation. Gordon Power, the Senior Observer, gathered all the air-gunners together to brief them for the following morning. Bolo, the squadron Sports Officer, had a word with the squadron deck-hockey team and decided to challenge the *Illustrious* squadrons to matches. Dicky Burd, the squadron Adjutant, spent the afternoon in the squadron office, catching up with Admiralty bumph.

Sandy Sandiford had a special meeting with the squadron Armourer. He had an idea, which he wanted to explain to Bolo, and to support this he asked the Armourer to fit him up with twenty extra smoke-puffs for his Verey pistol. A smoke puff does just what its name indicates. It is a cartridge which produces a puff of smoke about fifty feet from where it is fired. Generally, it is used to attract attention.

Whilst he was supervising the stowage of the extra smoke-puffs, Bolo came along to have a word with Leading-Air-Mechanic Hapwell, his fitter, about K's engine. He was intrigued with the smoke-puffs and asked Sandy what they were for.

'You know how rumours fly about Winston Churchill's secret weapons. Well, these smoke-puffs are one of them.'

'What do you mean?' chuckled Bolo.

'Tomorrow morning we're attacking an aerodrome. Aerodromes mean fighters. The smoke-puffs are our secret weapon. If an Italian is coming at us from astern and he sees a series of smoke-puffs,what is he going to think? They have to be shell-bursts from our special cannon, and he is flying right into them. His first reaction is going to be to sheer off and avoid us. It may give us just the chance we need.'

Bolo was impressed with Sandy's argument and agreed, if it came to it, to give it a try.

'I have some ideas of my own,' he said. 'We have almost no defence against fighters – other than smoke-puffs and one Lewis gun. What we have got is manoeuvrability. Get hold of PO Mercer and I'll explain what I have in mind.'

Mercer was talking to another air-gunner in the hangar and Sandy soon fetched him, explaining his ideas about smoke-puffs as they came back to 'K'.

'With all due respect, Mercer, I'm sure you'll agree that one Lewis gun doesn't stand much chance against four, or even eight, machine-guns. What we have got, however, is manoeuvrability. If I close the throttle and pull the stick back and to one side, the plane will go into a tight corkscrew turn. It won't stall. Before it does that I'll open the throttle, shove the nose down and then pull out – preferably at sea level.'

Bolo described the movement with body-actions and his crew were impressed.

'I want you, Sandy, to give me a running commentary on the approach of any fighter, telling me which direction he's coming from and giving an estimate of his distance. When he's between two and three hundred yards away, I propose to turn into him with a corkscrew turn. He shouldn't be able to keep within our turn and his bullets or shells will pass outside us. As he passes, Mercer, give him a long squirt. If you can keep your feet and overcome your blackout quickly enough,you should have a good target.'

'I'm with you, sir,' said Mercer. 'I'll fan through him from astern to ahead. That should get him. Do you want me to fire at him on his approach?'

59

'No. Leave that to Lieutenant Sandiford's smoke-puffs. Remember, in this situation surprise is the keynote. And he has three surprises coming, the smoke-puffs, the corkscrew turn and your sudden burst of machine-gun fire.'

Bolo shivered in the chill air as he made his way up to the briefing-room. The time was 0330. *Illustrious* and her attendant ships had detached themselves at dusk the day before. They would be ten miles ahead now and far enough away from *Peregrine* to avoid a mix-up in the darkness between the squadrons. Already bombed up, 999's Swordfish were being assembled on the flight deck. Bolo joined Sandy and PO Mercer in the briefing-room, to be addressed by the Air Staff Officer.

'Fifteen aircraft from *Illustrious*,' he said, 'are going to attack the airfield at Calato. Your target is the airfield at Maritza. These two airfields have been a thorn in our flesh since Italy entered the war. Rhodes is close to Haifa and not far from Port Said, so that bombers from the two airfields have been a constant threat to our ships using Haifa or entering the Suez Canal.

'The purpose of this operation is to destroy enemy aircraft on the ground and damage or destroy hangars and aircraft workshops. To achieve this you have each been armed with six two-hundred-and-fifty-pound bombs and eight incendiary bombs.

'The attacks from the two carriers are timed to arrive at 0530, in the first light of dawn. We believe that the Italians have not yet installed radar, so, coming out of the dark, the attacks should be a complete surprise.

'We know the Italians have squadrons of Fiat CR 42 fighters at both bases, so don't hang around. Go in. Drop your bombs. And get out quickly.

'Take off will be at 0415 and departure at 0430. At

departure, the ship will be in position 197 degrees from Cape Prasonisi on the southern tip of Rhodes, distance 38 miles. We shall maintain a course of 045 degrees and a speed of 20 knots. The distance to the target is 75 miles.'

He then gave them call signs and recognition signals.

The ASO was followed by Schooley, who gave a met report. There was little or no wind, so for take-off the carrier would work up to its maximum speed of twenty-four knots. Dawn was at 0530.

Lieutenant Commander Savage completed the briefing. He would drop a flame-float five miles ahead of the Fleet and would circle it at one thousand feet whilst the squadron formed up on him. He would flash the letter 'A' on his navigation lights and all aircraft would keep their navigation lights on until formed up. As soon as the squadron had formed up he would switch off his navigation lights and set course for the target. All lights must be switched off at the same time. He would start climbing at a speed of eighty knots and level off at eight thousand feet.

No specific targets would be given but lines of parked aircraft would have priority. Where possible the squadron should drop its two-hundred-and-fifty-pound fragmentation bombs on aircraft and the incendiaries on the hangars.

Wings, who had been listening to the briefings, wished them all good luck as they rose and made their way quickly down to their aircraft. There was a subdued air about the squadron. This was the first time they had attacked an aerodrome and they were conscious of their vulnerability to fighters.

The take-off was difficult, but not impossible. With their heavy weight of bombs, Bolo would have liked more wind speed over the deck. The very light wind did not help. Following his usual routine, he opened his throttle and held the aircraft on his brakes. Then, releasing the brakes, he moved forwards, building up speed. As they cleared the flight deck he put the nose down slightly to gain the extra speed he needed to remain airborne, levelling out just above the sea until he had enough speed to start climbing. He soon spotted the CO's flame-float and within minutes began to close up on his leader. At the same time Sandy reported that his wingmen were closing up on him. The squadron had now become very efficient at these night manoeuvres and was soon heading north-eastwards to its destiny.

At first the flight was smooth, the air calm, but increasingly Bolo became aware of turbulence. It became more difficult to maintain formation and by the time they passed six miles to seaward of Lindos, which Sandy was able to identify, they knew the worst. A wind had got up and was heading them. They were already ten minutes late and would be later still by the time they arrived over Maritza.

At 0530, dawn was breaking and they were still twenty miles from their target. To his dismay Sandy suddenly saw a series of flashes and explosions on his port quarter. That would be *Illustrious* squadrons attacking on time. He reported this to his pilot.

'That's going to alert the fighters,' said Bolo. 'We can expect trouble.'

As if in agreement, the CO waved his arm, indicating he was going into a shallow dive to increase speed. Time was important now. Could they reach the target and get out before the enemy fighters were airborne? By 0545 they were approaching land. The squadron was in a tight formation.

Bolo could see Rhodes Town on his starboard side and the rocky crags and scrub of Mount Kompali and the spinal mountain range of Rhodes Island to port. He thought what a terrible area it would be to force-land in. Twenty miles to the south, he could see huge columns of smoke. The *Illustrious* raid would be over now and the attacking squadrons would be on their way out. Black shellbursts appeared in the sky ahead of them as the Italian guns opened up.

'Enemy fighters approaching, sir, from below on the starboard bow.' Mercer's voice cut with razor-edge sharpness into his thoughts.

He could see the squadron of nine Fiat CR 42 fighters to the right and about two thousand feet below, climbing rapidly.

'Keep your eye on them, Sandy, and let me know what they're doing.'

Bolo could see Maritza airfield now five miles ahead. The white buildings showed up sharply in the early morning sunshine. The squadron's height was now seven thousand feet and their speed in the shallow dive was up to 130 knots.

'Enemy fighters have broken formation and are attacking from the starboard beam in line ahead.' Sandy's voice was calm as he reported the enemy movements.

Bolo, watching his CO intently, saw the hand signal to break away, and, giving his sub-flight a signal to break first, he turned to starboard into the enemy fighters, weaving and ducking to spoil their aim.

'The enemy is going for the CO, and the other flights,' Sandy's voice informed him.

Bolo turned back towards the airfield buildings.

'God! The CO's bought it.'

Sandy watched in dismay as A – Abel, attacked by three fighters, began to spin earthwards, pouring out flames and smoke. Yet another Fiat bore into it, guns flaring. Abel did not stand a chance. No one baled out.

Sandy could see another Swordfish falling out of the sky and yet another, twisting and turning, being chased by a Fiat. This is a shambles, he thought. We'll never get out of this.

'There's a line of six bombers on the tarmac. I'm going to dive-bomb them.' Bolo's voice was calm and reassuring.

'Enemy fighter approaching,' shouted PO Mercer.

The Fiat was five hundred yards astern. Sandy began firing his smoke-puffs as fast as he could load the Verey pistol. At the same time he kept up a running commentary for Bolo's benefit.

'Fighter four hundred yards astern and to port ... Three hundred yards.'

Several smoke-puffs could now be seen between 'Mike' and the enemy.

'He's breaking off. He's breaking off.' Sandy's voice was excited and jubilant.

Without waiting, PO Mercer trained his gun on the fighter as it broke away and gave him a short burst.

Bolo had not deviated from his course and was now in a good position to bomb.

'Going down now. Hang on, chaps.'

Sandy felt his stomach rise as Bolo put the nose down and soon they were screaming towards the target. Standing up, with his G-string holding him in, he peered over his forward bulkhead and over Bolo's shoulder. He could see the line of six Savoia Marchettis, Italian bomber-torpedo planes, on the tarmac. At either end was a bunker with machine-gunners firing at them as they dived. Suddenly the hangar at the edge of the tarmac erupted in flames and he could see a Swordfish pulling out of its dive.

The line of Savoias seemed to be turning clockwise as Bolo lined up on his target. At a thousand feet Sandy felt the bombs go. Bolo was pulling out towards the hangars, whilst Mercer sprayed everything within reach with his machine-gun.

The Swordfish shook violently as the bombs burst. Sandy saw the line of Savoias disintegrate as the two-fifty fragmentation bombs exploded along it. Now Sandy could feel the heat from the blazing hangar as Bolo flew past it to the next one. The incendiaries fell through the roof of the hangar, which was soon a furnace.

Sandy had a fleeting impression of another Swordfish pulling up from its dive with its bombs exploding amongst the workshops and then they were clear, at five hundred feet, working their way across the northern plain of Rhodes to escape out to sea and safety.

'Enemy fighter approaching,' shouted Mercer, urgently.

Sandy saw the Fiat wheeling in for a stern attack. Quickly he prepared his smoke-puffs.

'Enemy fighter astern at five hundred yards…' he told Bolo. Four hundred yards … Three hundred yards.'

He was now firing the smoke-puffs, but the fighter ignored them.

'Brace yourselves,' came Bolo's terse warning.

Immediately earth and sky chased each other over Sandy's head as Bolo threw the aircraft into a corkscrew turn to port. The fighter's burst of machine-gun fire passed harmlessly to starboard as he tried desperately to follow Bolo round and down. As he passed, Mercer, who had recovered quickly from the turn, fired a long burst. The Fiat did not come out of his diving turn and hit the ground with an explosion that again shook the Swordfish.

By now they were crossing the coast. The Swordfish, what was left of them, were racing out just above sea level. The CO had gone. Bolo looked for Steve Price in F – Fox. He was Senior Pilot and next in command. There was no sign of him. Bolo waggled his wings for the remaining aircraft to form up on him.

Sadly, Sandy counted the score. In formation were Holy Temple in B – Baker, Andy Andrews in H – Howe and Bolo's own wingmen, Biddy Bidwell in L – Love and Bing Crosby in M – Mike. 'Abel', 'Charlie', 'Fox' and 'George' had all gone. The squadron would never be the same again.

Chapter 7

New Arrivals

The mood in *Peregrine*, and especially in 999 Squadron, was sombre as the aircraft carrier steamed into Alexandria Harbour. At the last debriefing after the attack on Rhodes the sad story had emerged. The lack of coordination between *Illustrious* and *Peregrine* and the chance effect of the adverse wind were the prime causes of the disaster. The Italian Fiat CR 42s had been alerted by the *Illustrious* strike and were already airborne when *Peregrine*'s aircraft crossed the coast. Secondly, 999 Squadron had no pre-planned defensive tactics and were picked off one by one by the Italians. Thirdly, the Swordfish in general were quite unprepared for the fighter attack. Where aircraft had thought out a defensive plan, as with Bolo's corkscrew evasion and Sandy's dummy cannon, they had escaped the enemy.

Bolo found himself the senior officer left in the squadron. They were stood down from harbour duties and, after lunch, Bolo took the opportunity of calling the flying crews together.

'Look, chaps,' he said to them. 'We've been brought up all standing by this last action. But we can't let the boat founder. We've got to look more carefully now at what we are doing. We can't bring our friends back, but we can learn from our mistakes. Our aircraft are slow and vulnerable, but highly manoeuvrable and we must make the most of that. Have any of you got ideas?'

'We were attacked,' mused Biddy Bidwell. 'The Fiat was coming up fast, so I closed my throttle, slowed up and turned away. He went past without getting his sights on us.'

'I got in a burst as he passed,' exclaimed PO Jarman, his air-gunner. 'I think I may have hit him.'

'We tried something,' said Dicky Burd, diffidently. 'I think it possibly worked. I'd torn up some toilet rolls into small pieces and as the Fiat came up behind us I let a cloud of bumph go. The Fiat immediately turned away.'

The flying crews all laughed at this account.

'Both of these are good ideas,' said Bolo.

He had achieved what he wanted. The squadron had stopped feeling sorry for itself and was thinking positively.

'What about our efforts, Sandy?' he continued, turning towards his observer.

Sandy described the smoke-puff cannon and Bolo's corkscrew turns.

'I think we could develop this,' he went on. 'If the observer gives a running commentary on the approach of the fighter, and judges the best time for the corkscrew turn, he can give the order and control the action. The order could be something like this, "Corkscrew starboard. Go, go," with the pilot doing a violent corkscrew turn to starboard on the word go.'

'That sounds like a good idea, Sandy,' said Bolo, 'and if we add in the braking effect of closing the throttle that Biddy suggested, so much the better. I'll have a word with Wings to see if he can arrange a training session with his Gladiator. I also think we can do more as a squadron. We need to remain in formation, so only the aircraft that are attacked do the corkscrew turns. The air-gunners in the remaining aircraft can put up a defensive fire with their Lewis guns.'

The TAGs nodded in agreement.

'I like that, sir,' said PO Mercer, speaking for the air-gunners. 'We should get an attacking aircraft in our crossfire, though we'll have to be careful we don't hit each other.'

The discussion became general and ideas were batted to and fro. Bolo relaxed and allowed the arguments to develop until an interruption came on the Tannoy.

'Will Lieutenant Hawkins please report to the Captain.'

Good Lord! What have I done? thought Bolo as he hurried to the Captain's day-cabin.

The Captain was at his desk when Bolo knocked, and it was Wings who indicated an armchair to him. Bolo had never been received by the senior officers like this before. He guessed it was because he was the senior officer left in the squadron. The Captain turned towards Bolo.

'I'm very sad at what happened to your squadron,' he said. 'How are they bearing up?'

'They were deeply depressed at first,' replied Bolo, 'but now they're beginning to bear up and think of the future.'

'It's the future I want to talk about,' said the Captain. 'I've received some signals from the Admiralty and from the C-in-C. A new Commanding Officer has been appointed to your squadron. Lieutenant Commander Simpson DSC, RN was Senior Pilot of a Swordfish squadron in a fleet carrier. He is being flown to Alexandria by the RAF and will arrive the day after tomorrow.'

Bolo breathed a sigh of relief. Coming from a fleet carrier, he was bound to have good operational experience, and this was confirmed by his DSC.

The Captain had paused and was regarding Bolo intently.

'On my recommendation,' he continued, 'you will become Senior Pilot of the squadron and Lieutenant Sandiford will be Senior Observer. Congratulations.'

In somewhat of a daze, Bolo accepted the handshakes of the Captain and Wings. He could not believe promotion could come so rapidly, not in the Navy, with its RN officers and its traditions. After all, he was merely RNVR hostilities only.

The Captain continued to speak. What more was to come?

'*Illustrious* has brought out a number of young officers, from England, pilots and observers, as well as some air-gunners, to form a pool of available aircrew at Dekheila. They're all newly qualified RNVR hostilities only personnel, and it was intended that they continued operational training, but they've now been posted to your squadron. There are two sub lieutenants, five midshipmen and three leading airmen telegraphist-air-gunners. Chief Petty Officer Cutter, also from a fleet carrier, is appointed as Senior Telegraphist-Air-Gunner.'

Bolo's first reaction was one of horror. From having a balance of senior, experienced RN officers, the squadron would change to one where younger officers predominated. How would these young RNVR officers blend with the RN? Fortunately, he was RNVR himself and he must exert every bit of influence and leadership he could muster to help the newcomers to fit in and adapt. The RN officers would also have to adapt to change, and they might find this more difficult.

The Captain had been studying Bolo's reactions and now said with a smile, 'I can see you are aware of the problems. Your new CO will want all the help you can give him.'

'You can prepare the ground,' said Wings. 'Lieutenant Commander Simpson won't know the squadron personnel. I think he'll want to mix the old and the new, so that new observers will have experienced pilots, and new pilots experienced observers. Talk it over with Lieutenant Sandiford and prepare some suggestions.'

'Aye, aye, sir. I'll get on to that as soon as I see the new officers.'

Bolo breathed deeply as he left the cabin and made his way thoughtfully to the wardroom. Life was changing rapidly, for him, for the squadron and for the carrier. He found his observer waiting for him and quickly told him the news. Sandy was clearly delighted at his own promotion and congratulated Bolo on his.

'The newcomers from *Illustrious* are due shortly,' Bolo said. 'Let's go and greet them.'

The two officers made their way to the quarterdeck, where they were joined by Wings, to watch the approach of the pinnace bringing the new aircrew.

'My God!' murmured Wings. 'They're still children.'

Some of the young men in the boat certainly looked very young, with pink cheeks and the purple patches of the RNVR midshipman. Yet they would be just as qualified as the sub lieutenants, though only nineteen years old. The Navy made a break-off point at twenty years. If you were twenty years or more, you became a sub lieutenant on qualifying. If you were nineteen you became a midshipman.

Peregrine had spent the last four years away from home, mainly in the Far East, and was unused to the new look of the RNVR. To the older officers, midshipmen were officers under training. In fact, following tradition, the Commander had allotted the midshipman's flat, a large cabin, to house the five midshipmen, whilst the sub lieutenants had been given cabins. The four airgunners stepped aboard first and were escorted to their messes by PO Mercer. The oldest of the incoming officers was a man of about twenty-two years with a shock of fair hair, fair almost to the point of whiteness.

He saluted the quarterdeck as he stepped aboard and was greeted by Wings.

'My name is Kennedy, sir,' he said. 'I'm the senior officer of this party.'

'This is Lieutenant Hawkins, Senior Pilot of 999 Squadron, and this is Lieutenant Sandiford, Senior Observer.'

'Don't I know you?' said Bolo.

'Yes, sir. I was at Lee-on-Solent for my observer's training and you were often my pilot.'

'Yes, I remember. We did some NAVEXes together. By the way, the chaps call me Bolo.'

'Right, Bolo,' said Kennedy. 'I'm usually called Snowball, for obvious reasons.'

He turned to introduce his companions and Bolo studied each one as he was presented.

'Midshipman Dorrington, observer. We call him Dorrie.' Tall and willowy.

'Midshipman "Hatters" Dunn – pilot.' Lean with sharp features.

'Sub Lieutenant "Hank" Phipps – pilot. He's an American but can't help it.' Broad shoulders, piercing eyes.

'Midshipman John Hampden, observer. We call him "Hampers".' Medium height, pink and podgy.

'Midshipman "Killer" Compton, pilot.' A puckish face with elfin ears, rather like a frog, but a twinkle in his eye.

'Midshipman Hewitt, observer. I believe you also knew him at Lee.' Hewitt was very young-looking, with keen, intelligent features.

'And what is Hewitt called?' Wings asked with a smile.

'I haven't got a nickname yet, sir,' said Hewitt. 'People call me Bill.'

As each officer was introduced, he was greeted by Wings, Bolo and Sandy with a handshake and a smile.

'Well, gentlemen. Welcome aboard *Peregrine*,' said Wings. 'Lieutenant Hawkins and Lieutenant Sandiford will look after you. I'll see you later, when I introduce you to the Captain.'

'Come on fellows,' said Bolo, 'I'll take you down to the wardroom and introduce you to the squadron. Leave your luggage. The working-party will look after it.'

There was a general air of breeziness and confidence in these young officers that Bolo found appealing. They would help to dispel the despondency in the squadron following the loss of their colleagues. In the wardroom, over the first drinks of the evening, a lively discussion soon developed over the merits of *Illustrious* and *Peregrine*. *Illustrious* was newer and technically more efficient. *Peregrine* was older and vastly more experienced.

Later that evening, after dinner, Sandy Sandiford joined Bolo in his cabin to discuss the new aircrew list.

'You will have to be the CO's observer, Sandy,' said Bolo. 'You'll be responsible for navigating the squadron. I think it best that Dicky Burd flies with me as back-up leader.'

'Agreed,' said Sandy. 'What about the third sub-flight?'

'I shall keep my flight as the third sub-flight, and Biddy Bidwell will lead the second sub-flight in F – Fox. We must give him the next most experienced observer. Wes Weston should rise to the occasion.

'Young Bing Crosby and Harold Lloyd are just beginning to gain confidence. I think I'd like to leave them together in M – Mike for the time being. As I know Snowball Kennedy, I'll have him in my flight with young Compton – Killer Compton – as his pilot in L – Love.'

The two officers worked on the squadron organisation, pairing experience with newness and sub lieutenants with midshipmen so that it would be clear in each aircraft who was senior officer. They finally produced the organisation they would offer to the new CO:

999 Squadron

A/C	Pilot	Observer	TAG
A	Lt Com Simpson RN (CO)	Lt 'Sandy' Sandiford RN (Sr Observer)	CPO Cutter Chief TAG
B	S/Lt 'Holy' Temple RN (A)	Mid. Bill Hewitt RNVR (A)	PO Black

C	Mid. 'Hatters' Dunn RNVR (A)	S/Lt 'Knocker' White RN (A)	L/A Naylor
F	Lt 'Biddy' Bidwell RN	S/Lt 'Wes' Weston RN (A)	PO Jarman
G	S/Lt 'Hank' Phipps RNVR (A)	Mid. 'Dorrie' Dorrington RNVR (A)	L/A Kirk
H	S/Lt 'Andy' Andrews RN (A)	Mid. 'Hampers' Hampden RNVR (A)	L/A Roberts
K	Lt 'Bolo' Hawkins RNVR (A) (Senior Pilot)	Lt 'Dickie' Burd RN	PO Mercer
L	Mid. 'Killer' Compton RNVR (A)	S/Lt 'Snowball' Kennedy RNVR (A)	L/A Gibbons
M	S/Lt 'Bing' Crosby RN (A)	S/Lt 'Harold' Lloyd RN (A)	L/A Davey

'There. I think that's it. The new CO may want to change it, but it will do for starters. Let's go to the wardroom and see what the lads are doing.'

The wardroom was in full song. A replacement at the piano had been found for Pincher Martin. 'Dorrie' Dorrington's tall figure was drooped over the keys as he banged away lustily at the *Peregrine* song.

> We are the carrier *Peregrine*,
> The best ship you have ever seen.
> We search the sea for an enemy fleet
> In winter cold or summer heat
> And never return till the search is complete
> And never have sight of an enemy fleet
> And still you will find we are keen.
>
> We fly our Swordfish aeroplanes
> Whether it snows or whether it rains
> Except when the engine will not start

73

And body and mainplane fall apart
And the Looker cannot find his chart
And the Sparker cannot raise a spark
And we start all over again.

The new boys had soon picked up the words and on the third attempt were joining in heartily, supported by the bulk of 998 Squadron. Bolo noticed two figures on the fringe of the crowd – unhappy and not joining in. Putting an arm over the shoulders of Bing Crosby and Harold Lloyd, he gently propelled them into the throng, singing as he went. First one, then the other, started singing the familiar words until, with Bolo's encouragement, they were fully involved and singing as loudly as the rest.

The next morning Bolo summoned the squadron to a meeting in the guest room. He told them that the new CO, Lieutenant Commander Peter Simpson, would arrive on the following day. On the day after that *Peregrine* would put to sea to fly off the remaining aircraft of 999 Squadron for training at Dekheila. There, the four replacement Swordfish would be waiting. Half the squadron maintenance personnel would disembark to Dekheila immediately to service the new aircraft and receive the old ones when they arrived. The remainder would stay with *Peregrine* and see the squadron Swordfish off the aircraft carrier. On *Peregrine*'s return to Alexandria all squadron personnel would disembark to Dekheila.

'What about the new pilots and observers?' said Killer Compton. 'Shall we disembark before *Peregrine* leaves harbour?'

'No, Killer. At the suggestion of Wings I have reorganised the squadron so that as far as possible, experienced pilots are flying with new observers and experienced observers with new pilots. These are only suggestions at present and they'll have to be agreed by Lieutenant Commander Simpson. I'm afraid it will mean a fairly radical reorganisation of the squadron, but I think it's better for us to accept it first and not leave it to the new CO to persuade us. So, here's the new list, which I'll post on the squadron notice-board.'

As he read out the list, some faces fell as pilots lost their familiar observers, but the crews accepted the reasoning behind the reorganisation and almost immediately the new teams of pilot and observer were getting together and getting to know each other.

'How would you like to see the flesh-pots this afternoon?' Holy Temple addressed the small group enjoying a pre-lunch drink in a corner of the wardroom.

'Good idea!' exclaimed his observer, Bill Hewitt.

'Count me in,' said Killer Compton.

'And me,' added Dorrie Dorrington.

'I'm always good for a flesh-pot,' Hank Phipps drawled.

'Good! That makes five of us,' said Holy. 'The motor-launch is leaving at 1430, so we'll catch that.'

The five young officers landed at the steps in the old inner harbour at Ras el Tin, and soon found themselves in the ancient streets of El Khudar. Almost immediately they were besieged by a horde of young beggars.

'You want feelthy pictures, mister?' said one youngster of about twelve years, brandishing a handful of picture post-cards.

Bill Hewitt could see the photographs of nude women in unlikely postures.

'Good Lord!' he exclaimed. 'Is this typical?'

'I'm afraid it is,' said Holy. 'And it will get worse – much worse.'

The next moment Bill felt his arm grabbed by a young boy of about ten.

'You like my sister?' he was saying. 'Very good! Very clean! Very cheap!'

When Bill drew away from the embrace, the boy went on, 'You like my mother?' And then, desperately, 'You like me?'

The young men, newly arrived from England, were shocked. Even Killer, who was usually good for a laugh, was subdued.

'Some of these families are very poor and will go to any lengths to earn money,' said Holy. 'This is the East. The morality is not quite the same as in England. The worst exhibition you'll be offered is a woman mating with a donkey.'

The young officers hurried through the squalid streets. On one corner a one-legged child begged for alms.

'As I understand it,' said Holy, 'this is a professional beggar. The child is deliberately maimed by his parents to enhance his appeal.'

The others stared in disbelief.

'Come on, let's take these two gharries and go on to the Cecil.'

He called to the two Arabs who were driving their horse-drawn open cabs, and piled into one with Bill Hewitt and Killer Compton, whilst Hank and Dorrie took the other.

The young officers soon recovered from the initial shock they had received on landing in Egypt, and the sights fascinated them. The Arab men in their jellabahs and the Arab ladies almost hidden by their yashmaks intrigued them. On a corner they saw two elderly men sitting quietly smoking hookahs. A colourful water carrier offered them drinks as they paused at a crossing.

And then they were in the wealthy quarter of the Zaad Zagoul, with spacious well-laid-out gardens that must have cost a fortune to maintain in this hot climate. Many of the pedestrians were dressed in western style, though some of the men wore a tarbouche above their western suits.

'The lingua franca of Alexandria is French,' said Holy, 'a result of the French occupation of Egypt. Many of the streets have French names, like the Rue des Soeurs we've just passed. And the Café aux Jardins we're passing now is very good for its cakes. But we're going on to the Cecil Hotel for a cup of tea. It's particularly favoured by the British and it's our general meeting place.'

When the gharries arrived at the Cecil, Bill Hewitt was impressed with the quiet opulence of the building. The door was opened by a splendid Arab in spotless white. The carpets had a thick pile, and white-clad waiters showed them to leather armchairs with solid oak tables for their tea.

'What a change from the poverty in the dock area!' exclaimed Bill.

The extremes of poverty and wealth here are probably a bit like Victorian England,' said Holy.

The young RNVR officers were too young to have experienced much of the wealthy background suggested by the Cecil. Bill Hewitt, particularly, was out of his depth. He came from a poor, hardworking family. He had obtained a scholarship to a grammar school where, both academically and in sports, he had done very well. At the outbreak of war he had applied for a commission in the Fleet Air Arm and to his surprise he had been called up immediately for training as an observer officer. For the first nine months he had been classed as a leading naval airman. The white band on his hat denoted that he was an officer under training.

It was not until he qualified and became a midshipman and went to Greenwich Naval College for a conversion course that he became aware of the social status of a naval officer. He must not leave the college in uniform without a black cane and leather gloves. The only case he could carry was a black leather briefcase. Meals, at Greenwich, consisted of several courses, and the several knives and forks were arranged accordingly. He learned to distinguish which knife and fork to use without waiting to see what the others did. Hence the course was popularly called the 'knife and fork course'. He also learned that the port was passed round the table in an anticlockwise direction and that naval officers remained seated for the loyal toast.

He had now become accustomed to having his uniform cleaned and pressed and laid out for him and his shoes cleaned and polished, but he was still not used to the opulence of a top hotel. However, he was learning fast. Now, he fitted into the background, absorbing the atmosphere and enjoying his tea and cakes.

In the evening, Holy took his friends to La Belle Etoile, a nightclub in the Rue des Soeurs. Again, this was a new experience for Bill. He and his companions were shown to a table where they had a good view of the dance floor. A beautiful young Greek girl in a glittering sheath of a dress was singing a haunting melody in French. By the bar, several girls were standing, gazing at the singer. When the song ended, a quickstep was played and men and women from the tables around began to dance. Bill noticed that three young officers in army uniform from the next table crossed to the girls at the bar and invited three of them to dance.

'What's the form here?' Hank asked. 'Are those dancers available?'

'Yes, they are,' said Holy. 'They'll expect you to buy them a drink. They'll probably ask for champagne, which will be very expensive, and is almost certainly coloured lemonade.'

'Well, what are we waiting for?' cried Hank. 'Who's coming?'

There were two girls left at the bar, aged about twenty, slim and elegant.

'I'm with you,' said Killer, getting up.

Bill watched Hank and Killer approach the girls, and, after a short chat, the two couples were dancing. Bill laughed. Hank had a breezy style that had nothing to do with the quickstep being played. He was talking amiably with his partner, whom he held in a crushing grip. Killer was deadly serious, trying out his steps in a painstaking way, but it was only the nimbleness of his partner that prevented his tripping her up.

At the end of the dance, the three young officers at the table stood up as Hank and Killer brought their partners to the table and introduced them.

'This is Simone,' said Hank. 'She's French but she speaks some English.'

'This is Kara,' said Killer. 'She's Greek and also speaks English.'

The waiter was called and the 'champagne' duly ordered.

'Tell me, Simone,' said Hank, 'are you part of the establishment?'

'What does that mean – establishment?'

Hank laughed. 'Do you work here?'

'No, I do not work. I dance. During the dancing I dance with the customers. During the cabaret I dance with the corps de ballet.'

Simone's simple English was enhanced by her French accent. She was an outgoing girl and was soon popular with the group.

Her friend, Kara, was quieter, more remote. She was content to let Simone do most of the talking.

A new dance had started – a slow foxtrot. Bill braced himself.

'Would you care to dance this?' he said, turning to Kara.

Kara rose to her feet, non-committally, no doubt fearing another difficult dance.

Bill felt the music sink into him. He was an excellent dancer, and his long, slow hesitant steps exactly matched the mood of the music. At first surprised, Kara responded to the subtle leadership of her partner, her steps matching his. Their bodies just touching, they moved as one. Bill half-closed his eyes and gave himself up to the dance. Kara was so light on her feet and so responsive that he hardly knew she was there, and yet he was aware of her body so close to his. He had the sensation of floating.

The experiences of the last twenty-four hours passed through his mind: joining the *Peregrine*; the wardroom party; the poverty of Egypt and the beggars; the wealth of Egypt and the Cecil. And now this. How on earth had he, Bill Hewitt, come to find himself dancing in a night club in Egypt with this exotic Greek girl?

The music had stopped. The dance had finished. The applause was dying. And still Bill stood with his eyes half-closed, with Kara resting in his arms, a half-smile on her face.

'Come on, Bill. Break it up.'

That was Killer's voice. They were right next to their table. And with a laugh, Bill led Kara, hand in hand, back to the table.

Whilst never quite reaching that emotional pitch again for Bill, the rest of the evening went very well. The girls stayed with the boys, except for the half-hour when they joined the other girls for a dance sequence. The table was lively and the girls danced with all the boys in turn.

It was a very happy and contented group that returned to the *Peregrine* at midnight, four of them most impressed with their first experience of the Middle East.

Chapter 8

Dekheila

At first light, the next morning, *HMS Peregrine* left her mooring accompanied by four destroyers. Once outside the harbour, the destroyers took up formation, three ahead as anti-submarine screen and one on the port quarter as safety vessel. All the officers of 999 Squadron were on the goofers' platform, awaiting the arrival of their new CO, Lieutenant Commander Simpson. He was due to arrive in the new A – Abel at 0800 and had asked for a squadron meeting at 0900 before take-off at 1000.

At eight o'clock, a solitary Swordfish was seen approaching as *Peregrine* turned into wind. With the tightest turn possible round the stern of the carrier, the Swordfish made a perfect landing.

'He knows how to fly!' said Bolo to the approving officers. 'Come on, Sandy, let's go and greet the CO.'

At nine o'clock all flying-crews, pilots, observers and TAGs were mustered in the briefing-room. Talk ceased and everyone rose to his feet as the slight figure of the lieutenant commander, accompanied by Bolo Hawkins, made his way to the front.

'Gentlemen,' said Bolo, 'your new Commanding Officer, Lieutenant Commander Simpson.'

'Thank you, Bolo,' said the CO and, turning to the squadron, 'will you please be seated?

81

'Well, I hope we shan't be as formal as that again,' he said as the squadron settled into their seats. 'It's a bit like the first day of term when the headmaster is new and so are half the boys.

'I've had a chat with Bolo and Sandy and I understand how those of you that were left felt after your last op. Bolo tells me that you are already recovering from the loss. He has also given me suggestions for the 999 Squadron's new organisation. I accept this and trust the new crews will settle in together.

'The squadron's nucleus is now one of the most experienced in the Fleet Air Arm. At the same time, 999 Squadron probably has the largest number of young and completely inexperienced flying-crews. It is up to us to develop our skills as rapidly as possible. The Captain has given me a fortnight for operational training – and then it is back to war. I shall draw up a programme of intensive training at Dekheila, to give us a chance of getting together as crews, practising our skills and operating as a squadron.

'The crews for flying off will be as in the list drawn up by Bolo. That means that Midshipman Dunn, Lieutenant Bidwell and Sub Lieutenant Phipps and their crews will join the shore party. Your replacement aircraft are waiting for you at Dekheila. Lieutenant Bidwell will be in charge of the shore party. You will disembark with the remainder of the maintenance crews as soon as the ship returns to its mooring.'

After dealing with a few questions, mainly from the new boys, the CO dismissed the squadron. By now the six aeroplanes were ranged on deck, their wings spread ready for take-off.

'Wish me luck,' said Killer to Bing Crosby as they made their way to their aircraft.

'What! For flying off? A piece of cake!' exclaimed Bing.

Bing had taken his CO's words seriously. He and Harold

Lloyd were no longer new boys. They were the experienced nucleus of the squadron. It was up to them to set an example.

Killer was not really worried about the take-off. He had already achieved several take-offs on a training carrier and twice on the *Illustrious* during the passage from England. He was looking forward to the Dekheila fortnight and even further ahead to operational flying. He enjoyed flying, particularly when taking part in a dummy bombing or torpedo attack. He loved the sensation of the steep dive, the pull out at sea level, the aircraft racing in just feet above the waves towards the target, the release of the dummy torpedo, and the feeling of exhilaration when he achieved a hit.

And yet Killer had not always been like that. At school he had taken Highers as a qualification for entering medicine. His father was a doctor and he had always expected to go to Bart's and follow in his father's footsteps. Here he was, controlling a lethal machine, preparing to kill and maim. Ah, well! He must put his ambitions into storage and concentrate on the present.

The coastline was just ahead and Killer could see a hangar, with a few aircraft parked outside it, some adjacent huts, a large one-storey building with more huts, and a number of tents in rows. Was this Dekheila? Where were the runways? Where were the living quarters?

Bolo was waving to him and he obeyed the signal to close up. Bolo was leading his own sub-flight, following the CO leading the other two aircraft as a sub-flight. In tight formation they followed the CO in a shallow dive towards the windsock when the CO waved them to break away for landing.

Puzzled, Killer followed Bolo round until he saw the marks of many tyres on the hard sand. A desert landing-strip. This was Dekheila aerodrome. He landed and taxied towards the hangar. When he stopped, the heat hit him and soon the sweat was pouring off, underneath his khaki bush shirt.

Squadron mechanics, disembarked before *Peregrine* had left harbour, were already dealing with his machine and he was glad to make his way to the mess – or wardroom, as it was still called.

The mess was relatively cool, with fans revolving overhead and plaited straw walls. A lieutenant was circulating round the walls with a fly swatter, solemnly swatting any fly he could see. On one wall Killer could see the fly swatter's assistant, a lizard with a long tongue waiting for an unwary fly to settle within range. Even as he watched, a fly settled, the tongue darted out with incredible speed, and the fly was caught.

The squadron quickly settled into the routine at Dekheila. Killer discovered that the tents were their sleeping quarters, two officers to a tent. He shared tent number fifteen with Snowball Kennedy, his observer. He soon found that the bed boards were too hard and, like most of the officers, purchased a lightweight camp-bed with its own palliasse.

Flying started at 0800 and consisted of dummy parallel searches, dummy dive-bombing attacks on a rock five miles out to sea from the aerodrome, dummy torpedo attacks on an obliging destroyer and fighter evasion tactics.

Each afternoon was a make-and-mend when you could get your head down if you wished. With the other younger officers, Killer found the nearby beach too attractive. The sea was warm and they soon discovered a use for the bed boards. There was a good surf breaking on the golden sand and the bed boards made good, if somewhat clumsy, surf-boards. Surfing became the popular pastime and occupied most afternoons.

From 1700 the flying crews spent two hours at the squadron office, discussing tactics and brushing up ship and aircraft recognition.

Killer found the long three-hour NAVEXes rather dull. They were in the form of parallel searches out to sea. Whilst Snowball practised his navigation, taking winds each half-hour, Killer's role was to maintain, as nearly as possible, the exact course and speed given by Snowball. If at the end of the exercise they were some distance away from where they should be, Snowball's navigation would be checked by Sandy Sandiford, the Senior Observer. If the navigation were correct then the error was down to Killer's flying. With several practices, pilots and observers came to respect, and rely on, each other. Meanwhile the telegraphist-air-gunners practised their W/T, ciphering and sending signals to base.

On the day following their first NAVEX, the squadron gathered in the squadron office to be briefed by the CO on their first dive-bombing exercise. He explained how he wanted them to form up on him in echelon formation and follow each other down, one at a time, for the bombing run.

Half an hour later the squadron was in formation, circling the aerodrome and climbing until they were at five thousand feet with the target; a rock, five miles ahead. Each aircraft as it came to the target was to dive and drop one of its practice bombs at about a thousand feet.

After dropping his own bomb, the CO circled a little way past the target to watch the practice. B – Baker and C – Charlie both missed. Biddy Bidwell in F – Fox was quite good, a near miss. Hank Phipps in G – George undershot and Andy Andrews in H – Howe overshot. Bolo's was an excellent run, hitting the target. Killer Compton in L – Love was too low. He hit the target but would have been blown out of the sky if the bomb were real. Bing Crosby in M – Mike missed to one side. Possibly three hits, including his own, and one aircraft blown up by its own bombs. And this on a stationary target without defensive fire. Not good enough.

He dropped a smoke-float and began to circle it, flashing the letter 'A' on his navigation lights. This was another good practice. Learning to form up quickly was important. Bolo Hawkins and Biddy Bidwell were soon in position, followed by the others, except for Hatters Dunn in C – Charlie. He was following round in a circle and taking much too long. He would have to explain to the new pilots how they must cut across the circle to form up quickly rather than follow round.

Again they climbed to five thousand feet and bombed. This time there were three hits and two near misses; still not good enough, as the CO told his squadron at the debriefing.

'After all, we are bombing a stationary target as big as a fat destroyer. How would we do if the target were moving?'

The squadron had four more practice bombing runs on the rock, and on the last the CO declared himself satisfied. All of the bombs had either hit the target or were near misses.

At the end of the first week, *HMS Heron,* one of *Peregrine's* screening destroyers, was seen steaming ten miles off the coast from Dekheila. She was the target for a dummy torpedo attack.

Lieutenant Commander Simpson had discussed this with Bolo and Biddy. They had had experience of a real torpedo attack on a real enemy target, particularly Biddy, who had witnessed one as well as taking part in one. The CO had followed their suggestions and at briefing he outlined his plan of attack.

He would approach from up-sun and aim to get five miles ahead of the target. On the order to attack, Biddy would lead the second sub-flight to port of the target and Bolo would take his sub-flight to starboard. They would make a coordinated attack from three sides, so that whichever way the target turned, one sub-flight would be in a good dropping position. On the dive down, aircraft were to open up to two hundred yards apart to disperse 'enemy' gunfire.

'Try to drop your fish from fifty feet at a range of about a thousand yards. And watch out for each other when you break away,' he concluded. 'We don't want any accidents.'

It was now nine o'clock and Killer was concentrating on

his sub-flight leader, Bolo Hawkins. Snowball was giving him a running commentary on the intercom.

'Target about seven miles on the port bow, steaming east at twenty knots.'

Killer risked a quick glance and saw they were aiming for a spot about five miles ahead of the target. A minute later the CO waggled his wings, the order to attack.

Immediately, Bolo put his aircraft into a shallow dive to build up the speed. At the same time he broke away to port, making for the starboard beam of the target, waving his sub-flight to open up the formation.

Snowball Kennedy watched the aircraft take up their allotted positions. Then he saw Bolo waggle his wings.

'"King" turning in now,' he told his pilot.

The sub-flight was three miles to starboard of the target, in line abreast. The angle of dive became steeper as Bolo sought to get into a good dropping position.

'They're turning towards us,' exclaimed Snowball. 'That will shorten the range.'

Killer responded immediately by increasing the dive to near vertical. Snowball could now see the target immediately over Killer's head, looking very close. He could see a group on the bridge and men manning guns that were being ranged on them. If this were real they would be facing a fearsome hail of exploding shells.

They were almost at sea level. Would Killer never pull out?

And then Snowball's stomach went down to his feet and his knees sagged as the extra gravity hit him. Killer had pulled out and was skimming the wave tops, with the target half a mile ahead. They were on the starboard bow of the target and Killer was aiming just ahead of it.

'Torpedo gone,' Killer shouted, and again Snowball sank to his knees as Killer pulled the aircraft around and away, jinking and weaving to avoid imaginary gunfire.

Suddenly there was a Swordfish crossing directly ahead

of them. Snowball's heart was in his mouth, but Killer was cool and very professional. Almost casually he flipped his aircraft below and behind the other. And then they were clear.

'The CO has dropped a smoke-float,' said Snowball. 'We have to form up again for another try.'

'I enjoyed that,' said Killer. 'Do you think we got a hit?'

'I think it's possible,' replied Snowball. 'We were in a good position when you dropped. The film will show.'

And, indeed, when the film taken by the camera to simulate the dropping of the torpedoes was shown, the squadron was deemed to have scored three hits, one of them Killer's. Snowball was beginning to have confidence in his young pilot, as Killer now had confidence in Snowball. Perhaps he had a tendency to overplay his hand, as with the first bombing run, but Killer was showing superb control of his aircraft and plenty of grit and determination.

In the second week a Fulmar squadron from *HMS Illustrious* arrived. Bolo talked to the Senior Pilot of the Fulmars and then to his Commanding Officer and arranged for some practice at fighter evasion. As a demonstration, the Senior Pilot of the Fulmars would attack Bolo's Swordfish over the aerodrome. For this demonstration, Bolo was joined by his old observer, Sandy Sandiford, and his aircraft had been equipped with the R/T used by the fighters, so that the Swordfish crews and Fulmar pilots crowded on the dispersal area could listen in as well as watch the combat.

They watched intently as K – King approached at about two thousand feet. Suddenly the Fulmar appeared, diving down from five thousand feet on the starboard quarter of the Swordfish.

'Fighter approaching, starboard quarter from above. Range four thousand yards.'

Sandy's voice was steady as he controlled the action.

'Fighter, three thousand yards, starboard quarter.'

PO Mercer braced himself at his Lewis gun. Bolo, tense at first, now relaxed and awaited developments.

'Two thousand yards.

'One thousand yards. Stand by to corkscrew starboard.

'Five hundred.

'Three hundred.

'Corkscrew, go, go.'

Sandy braced himself on his stool and watched events. He felt the drag as the throttle was closed, and suddenly the sky and earth went crazy as Bolo brought the Swordfish in the tightest possible turn to starboard and downwards. The Fulmar, although expecting it, was completely out-manoeuvred and went hurtling past to port. As it passed, Mercer followed it with the Lewis gun, shooting a cine film instead of bullets.

The Fulmar had turned hard to starboard to follow the Swordfish down, but at five hundred feet, following Sandy's running commentary, Bolo opened his throttle and did a climbing turn to port, again catching the Fulmar pilot out of position and unable to bring his guns to bear. Three times the two aircraft carried out these manoeuvres, with Sandy trying different ranges, two hundred yards and four hundred yards, before giving the corkscrew order.

Then Bolo approached the aerodrome at five hundred feet and the onlookers on the ground held their breath. They saw the Fulmar screaming down from astern of the Swordfish. At three hundred yards, just when its fire would be effective, the Swordfish corkscrewed violently to port and pulled out almost at ground level. The Fulmar flashed past with the pilot, unable to get the Swordfish in his sights, using all his concentration to avoid crashing into the sand. The Fulmar pilots as well as the Swordfish crews cheered as the machines swept past. It had been an exhibition of superb flying.

'Time for coffee. Then everyone into the cinema to see the results,' announced the CO.

An hour later the small cinema was crowded with both squadrons. The photographers had done a good job and were ready with the cine films on the projector. There were two films, one taken by the Fulmar pilot when he pressed his firing button, and one by the Swordfish air-gunner when he pressed his. The films would show if hits had been scored.

The first film to be shown was the Fulmar's. The cinema lights went out and the film started. A view of earth and sky was seen, revolving round each other. There was no sign of the Swordfish.

'I fired my guns just too late,' came the voice of the Fulmar pilot. 'I simply couldn't turn tightly enough to get him in my sights.'

The next sequence caught a glimpse of the Swordfish dead centre and moving out to port.

'I started firing just before he turned and I think I would have hit him,' commented the Fulmar pilot.

'Yes,' said Sandy. 'I waited till you were two hundred yards away before giving the corkscrew order. I think that's too late.'

In the third sequence the Swordfish was further away when the camera started, and swam right into the centre of the picture, before going off screen to starboard.

'I'd have got him on that one,' said the Fulmar pilot.

'That was the time we tried the corkscrew at four hundred yards,' observed Sandy.

'I think that's too early for us to turn,' commented Bolo. 'It gives the fighter a chance to get inside our turn.'

'I agree,' said the Fulmar pilot. 'Between two and three hundred yards was most difficult for me.'

The last sequence was the most dramatic. The Swordfish flashed across the screen away to starboard and the ground came up, revolving and frighteningly close.

'I nearly bought it on that one,' was the Fulmar pilot's comment. 'I followed you round and down and then realised

I would hit the deck if I didn't do something. So I had to yank the stick back hard. I forgot to release the firing button, so you see what I saw.'

'Right!' said Bolo. 'It will be interesting to see if we did any damage.'

The first sequence of the Lewis gun film from the Swordfish showed the Fulmar away to the left of the camera and disappearing off to the left.

'I had a go, but I didn't think I got him on that one,' said Mercer. In the second sequence, the Fulmar did not appear.

'I could have got him in my sights dead astern before we corkscrewed,' stated Mercer, 'but I obeyed instructions and waited till the corkscrew. He was then too near me and too fast to get my sights on him.'

The third sequence showed what was clearly a hit but the general agreement was that the Swordfish would have been shot out of the sky before the Lewis gun fired.

In the fourth and final sequence the Fulmar came fairly and squarely into the Lewis gun's sight. It could only have meant a number of bullets striking home, and the Swordfish crews gave a cheer.

'Lights on!' shouted Lieutenant Commander Simpson. He and the Fulmar Commanding Officer took the stage and spent the next half-hour discussing the merits of the evasive tactics with both squadrons.

It was generally agreed that corkscrewing at between two and three hundred yards' range and taking the aircraft down to sea level presented the most difficult target to the attacking fighters, and all the Swordfish crews were to be given an opportunity to practise the next day.

Three Fulmars were to assist 999 Squadron, one for each sub-flight. Fighter evasion practice was to take place in allotted positions over the sea. It was the turn of L – Love, and Killer was looking forward to the exercise. The first two practice runs, at a thousand feet, went according to plan, although Snowball felt that on the first exercise the Fulmar might well have got in a burst. The third run was at five hundred feet.

'Fighter approaching. Three thousand yards from astern, slightly to port.'

'Two thousand yards.'

'One thousand. Stand by to corkscrew port.

'Five hundred.

'Four hundred.

'Three hundred. Corkscrew. Go, go!'

Killer threw his aircraft into a violent turn to port and downwards to sea level.

'You're too low. Pull out,' shouted Snowball.

He was too late. As Killer pulled on the stick, the tip of the port lower wing touched the sea and Snowball gazed in horror as the wing dragged through the water. He watched the wing tear away, three or four feet of it, almost up to the first strut. And then Killer pulled the plane clear.

Leaning over the bulkhead, Snowball watched Killer fighting his machine, using all his skill on the controls to prevent it from spinning in. The drag of the broken wing made the aircraft yaw and roll, but Killer was able to keep it flying and gain height as he made for the coast.

Snowball saw that Bolo, who had been watching the exercise from a safe distance, had closed and was flying alongside to port. Killer needed all his attention for the aircraft, so Snowball kept silent and waited. He held his breath as Killer approached the touchdown, and both he and L/A Gibbons, the TAG, braced themselves for the crash.

Killer held the Swordfish steady, just above the ground, and with the gentlest caress, feathered down on to the sand.

Fire engine and ambulance came tearing up to them, but all was well. A shaken observer clambered down and was greeted by his pilot.

'Sorry about that, Snowball. I miscalculated. Hope it hasn't put you off.'

Snowball thought for a moment. This was the kind of flying that had given Killer his nickname. But Snowball wasn't going to be killed off. Killer would not make that mistake again. And he had flown superbly after the accident.

'I'm all right, Killer,' he said, 'as long as you don't do it again.'

Chapter 9

Stampalia

Bolo greeted Sandy as he entered Lieutenant Commander Simpson's cabin. The CO had invited them, after dinner, to join him for a discussion on the squadron's progress. They had landed on *Peregrine* in the early afternoon, and the Captain had told them the Fleet was to make a sweep westwards into the Mediterranean.

Lieutenant Commander Simpson had proved to be a very different character from his predecessor, Lieutenant Commander Savage. Whereas Savage was formal, reserved, even withdrawn, Simpson was easy in his manner, outgoing and informal. He was now known to everyone as 'the Boss', a nickname given to him in his absence by Killer Compton, and now used generally.

Under the leadership of the Boss, camaraderie and loyalty in the re-formed squadron had developed rapidly. At Dekheila, the Boss had taken to sitting with his pint in a cane chair on a veranda after dinner in the cool of the evening. Bolo and Sandy initially, then most, if not all, of the squadron, had joined him. At first the talk had been technical, mostly about the day's events and future practices. Then the CO had started to reminisce about the pre-war Navy, the early days of the Fleet Air Arm, the brief marriage with the RAF when squadrons were manned partly by RAF personnel, the parties when the hangar had been trans-

94

formed into an underwater grotto, with everyone in suitable fancy dress. Gradually the talk turned to the war, the causes of the war, and the hopes for the future.

In the quiet evenings, against the vast backdrop of the desert, the squadron had drawn together. Bolo realised that this was the effect the CO was having on them. In talking about social problems, it did not matter whether you were RN or RNVR, a lieutenant or a midshipman. You were an individual with a view to express and you were encouraged to express it. So the CO drew his young colleagues out and drew the squadron together.

'Well, Bolo, what do you think?' the CO asked, as Bolo settled himself into an armchair.

'I think the last fortnight has been good for us, Boss,' Bolo replied. 'The new boys have shaken down well, and the squadron is just about ready to go to war again.'

'Are you happy, Sandy?' said the CO, turning to Sandy Sandiford.

'I'm happy with the way the chaps have come on, particularly with navigation and fighter evasion.'

'Good! Now, I've had a word with Wings and the Air Staff Officer. At present we're doing a routine sweep to the west. The Eyeties have occupied Sidi Barrani and are heading towards Alexandria and Cairo. Their biggest problem is supplies, so we're going to attack their supply line at Benghazi. The objective will be to hit the docks and sink or damage any ships in harbour. We shall have to carry out searches and A/S patrols and probably a dive-bombing attack on Benghazi. Are we up to it?'

'I think we could carry out a reasonable search,' said Sandy. 'Midshipman Hewitt is a little bit nervous and unsure, but he's a quick learner and he's done well in the NAVEXes. Holy Temple, his pilot, will have a steadying effect.'

'Yes, I like Holy,' replied the CO. 'He's very steady.

Midshipman Dunn in C – Charlie is a bit unsure of himself though.'

'He's got Knocker White as his observer,' said Sandy. 'I feel sure Knocker will add to his confidence.'

'What about your sub-flight, Bolo?' said the CO.

'Bing Crosby and Harold Lloyd in M – Mike have had plenty of experience. They seem to have matured considerably since the new boys joined us.'

'Well, they're old hands now,' replied the CO. 'I expect they're living up to that.'

'I'm not yet sure about Killer Compton in L – Love. He's impulsive and inclined to be rather overconfident, but he's an excellent pilot. I think he'll finish up dead or winning a VC. Snowball Kennedy, his observer, is first-rate material. He's mature, steady and confident and a very good navigator. He'll be good for Killer.'

'The second sub-flight seems to be coming together well,' said the CO.

'Yes,' said Bolo. 'Biddy Bidwell, Wes Weston and PO Jarman in F – Fox are a good team. They're all experienced and have proved themselves in action. Hank Phipps, in G – George, is an extraordinary chap – quite a character, almost unreal. Sometimes I think he's playing the part of an American he's so American, if you know what I mean.'

'You mean the Yankee drawl and the breezy gestures. He's a very confident young man.'

'He's also a sound pilot,' said Bolo.

'And Dorrie Dorrington, for all his air of sleepiness, is sound enough,' said Sandy. 'He's also an unusual character. Did you hear the classical music he played at Dekheila? At one time I heard a whole movement from a Mozart concerto that he played without a note of music in front of him. The next moment he was playing the Navy songs for the boys. I think the two of them, with Leading Airman Kirk, will make a good team.'

'The crew of H – Howe; what about them?' said the CO.

'Andy Andrews has always been a quiet chap,' said Bolo. 'He's done his job, so far. Nothing spectacular but plenty of experience.'

'Midshipman Hampden is rather similar,' said Sandy. 'Hampers is also quiet and unobtrusive. I think we'll have to keep an eye on them.'

'That's it then,' said the CO. 'We're on A/S patrol tomorrow. I've put the list up on the squadron notice-board. I'm taking the first patrol and then it's in alphabetical order.'

'We'll say goodnight, Boss, and let you get your head down,' said Bolo.

Bolo, after a walk round the quarterdeck with Sandy, retired to his cabin. Here he took out the letter from Joyce that had awaited him in the ship on his return from Dekheila.

The summer vacation was ending and Joyce was going up to Cambridge to start her third year. Her Part One examinations had been successful and she had obtained an Upper Second in English. The beaches of Brighton and Hove were now inaccessible with barbed wire along the front and the piers had been disconnected at the shore end. Petrol was in short supply and food rationing was in full swing.

As he read the details of Joyce's everyday life, Bolo thought of the girl herself. She was now twenty years old and had developed into a graceful, attractive young woman. Walking along the beach at Dekheila, with the sea on one side and the desert sand, stretching away to the horizon, on the other, Bolo's thoughts often returned to England, and inevitably to Joyce. In his cabin now, as at Dekheila, he could almost feel the softness of her arm tucked into his as they walked along the beach at Hove or beneath the cliffs from Black Rock to Rottingdean. Much of their time together had been spent walking, and the moonlit stroll to Rottingdean had been one of their favourites.

And how they had talked and revealed themselves to each other! Joyce was fond of music. She had introduced Bolo to Mozart, Brahms and Beethoven and he had sat with her for hours listening to, and gradually learning to enjoy, the great symphonies. She had recited poetry to him and he had been touched by the power of Shakespeare, by the lyrical poetry of Wordsworth and by the emotional appeal of Keats.

Bolo had found his world enlarging. After leaving school, cricket had been all-consuming. Then he had learned to fly and this had broadened his horizons. But Joyce had added a new dimension to his life. Through her he had discovered an emotional response to music and literature and thence an interest in society and his fellow men. These interests at present were undeveloped and ill-defined, but they had affected Bolo's relationship with his colleagues. He had begun to think about them as individual people who needed to work closely together for their common good and common safety. Unconsciously he became aware of their strengths and weaknesses, of the difference of their characters from his own. Without realising it he was beginning to develop the skills of leadership. What he did realise was that this new awareness, this awakening to a wider world, was the result of Joyce's influence.

Joyce had ended her letter, 'with love, yours, Joyce.' 'With love' – did that mean what it said? Did Joyce love him, or was it a conventional, friendly ending? This was now important. Surely those magic moments when Joyce had first held his hand, had leaned against him, had walked arm-in-arm with him, had sat with her head against his shoulder listening to music, had kissed him goodbye: surely those moments were significant? Bolo realised now how much they had meant to him. Surely they had a significance for Joyce?

Bolo had been reserved in his friendship because he thought of Joyce as a young girl. Now he felt that in some ways Joyce was far older than himself. Emotionally she was

98

more mature and it was this maturity that had brought him out. With Joyce he felt more complete.

Other subtle changes were occurring in his relationship. More and more he found himself thinking in physical terms, of the soft contours of Joyce's body, the delicate touch of her lips, the fragrant scent of her hair. He now knew that his desire for her was physical and sexual as well as intellectual and emotional, and that his future, if he had one, was bound up with Joyce.

'D'ye hear there? This is the Captain speaking.'

All activity in the wardroom ceased and everyone crowded round the Tannoy.

'A signal has been received that Italy has invaded Greece. We have been instructed from London to give whatever assistance we can. As a result of this the Admiral has decided to strike at Stampalia, where the naval headquarters of Mussolini's Eastern Mediterranean Fleet is based. Both squadrons will carry out this strike at dawn tomorrow. That is all.'

The buzz of conversation was immediately interrupted again by the Tannoy.

'D'ye hear there? This is the Air Staff Officer speaking. There will be a general briefing for all aircrews in the briefing-room this afternoon at 1500. That is all.'

How do you think this Italian invasion of Greece will affect us, Boss?' said Bolo.

A group of pilots and observers had gathered round the CO to discuss the latest news.

'I think Mussolini is making a mistake,' said Lieutenant Commander Simpson. 'He has enough on his plate with the invasion of Egypt. His army is stretched to the limit in North Africa and he'll need all his ships and naval strength to keep his African armies supplied.

'The Greeks have an excellent naval base at Soudha Bay on the north coast of Crete. If we can use that, it gives us a base halfway between Malta and Alexandria, which we badly need.'

'Do you think this attack on Stampalia is just a diversion for us, to show the flag, so to speak, to the Greeks?' said Sandy.

The CO pursed his lips and paused for a moment.

'I suppose in a way it is. At the same time it gives us a chance to hit Musso's naval bases. I believe he keeps some light naval forces and submarines in Stampalia. Anyway, we shall no doubt learn more at three o'clock this afternoon.'

At three o'clock the briefing-room was packed. Commander Flying and the Air Staff Officer, together with the Commanding Officers of the two squadrons, occupied the stage. The Air Staff Officer was speaking.

'Stampalia is one of the Italian Dodecanese Islands. It has two or three good natural harbours. One of these is at Skala, the chief town of the island, one is at Maltezana, now used as a seaplane base, and one is at Agrilithi Bay, where light forces, MTBs and gunboats are moored. Above Agrilithi are naval barracks and offices, forming the headquarters of the Italian Eastern Mediterranean Fleet.

'The seaplane base at Maltezana will be attacked by 998 Squadron, and 999 Squadron will attack the offices and barracks at Agrilithi. Now that Italy has invaded Greece in the north, the Greek islands in the Aegean as well as Crete will be vulnerable, particularly to ships based on Stampalia. Our attack is a pre-emptive one, to deter the Italians from using Stampalia as a base for their shipping and seaplanes. It is also intended to be a morale booster for the Greeks.

'The Fleet, which is now south of Crete, will alter course and pass through the Kaso Strait during the night. As you know, there is an Italian aerodrome on Scarpanto on the eastern side of the strait, where both bombers and fighters are based, and we must be well clear of them by daylight.

'Both squadrons will take off at 0430 when *Peregrine* will be sixty miles south of Stampalia. The Fleet will proceed due west along the north coast of Crete at a speed of twenty knots to Soudha Bay, where we will anchor and refuel. Your attack is timed to take place at about 0530 just as dawn is breaking. You should rejoin the *Peregrine* at 0630, eleven miles north of Heraklion. At 0630 the Fleet will be at that point steering west at twenty knots.'

Charts of the area had been handed to observers before the meeting and crews had been following the details on these charts. Now they were given photographic enlargements of the bombing areas. With these, 999 proceeded to the operations room for further briefing, leaving 998 Squadron in the briefing room.

In the operations room, the Boss took up the tale.

'After take-off I shall fly on a course of 015 degrees for ten minutes, when Sandy will drop a flame-float from a height of 1,000 feet. I want you to form up on me at that height. As soon as we are in formation, I shall proceed to Stampalia, climbing to six thousand feet; 998 Squadron will fly from the carrier on a course of 345 degrees, so the two squadrons should be well separated.

Our target is in the hills above Agrilithi Bay, next to a village called Kastellano. The village is on one side of a narrow road, the barracks and naval headquarters on the other. Our task is to destroy the barracks and naval headquarters. As far as we know, there are no civilians in the area, so all the buildings can be considered targets. Remember, the site is approximately 1,000 feet above sea level, so don't try to pull out at 500 feet.

'You will note on your charts that Stampalia is like two islands joined by a narrow isthmus. Maltezana, 998 Squadron's target, is on the isthmus; our target is on the

101

eastern hump. I shall fly over the isthmus and turn east, approaching Kastellano from the west, the dark side. This will set the target up against the dawn light. I shall give the order to form line astern just before we turn east.

'We don't know what the defences are like as this target has never been attacked before. So I want you to dive-bomb immediately you are over the target, one run only, and make your escape southwards down Agrilithi Bay and out to a small uninhabited island called Kunupia, five miles south. We form up there and fly back to the *Peregrine*.'

The CO had illustrated his plan on a large-scale blow-up of the area. Now he asked if there were any questions.

'Can we expect any fighters, Boss?' Bolo asked.

'No, we don't expect fighters. The nearest fighter base is Scarpanto, about seventy miles away. We should be well away before they can possibly arrive.'

'What bombs are we carrying, sir?' asked Holy Temple.

'The usual for this type of mission – six two-fifty-pound fragmentation bombs and six incendiary bombs.'

'How do we know which target to select?' asked Killer.

'You don't. As you come over the target area, select one of the buildings that hasn't already been hit.

'Remember to pull out about a thousand feet above the ground, that is two thousand feet above sea level.

'No more questions? Right! I'll see you up here for a final briefing at 0330 tomorrow morning. After dinner tonight I advise you to get your heads down. It's going to be an early start.'

Bolo Hawkins and Sandy Sandiford joined the CO as he made his way down to the wardroom.

'I've made this attack as simple as possible,' he said to them. 'What we didn't tell the boys was that this is a soft target to blood the new chaps. That is why I have made it an in-out attack and given instructions to form up over Kunupia Island for the return flight to the carrier. There's bound to be some anti-aircraft fire, but I'm not expecting too much.'

Midshipman Bill Hewitt shivered slightly as he made his way across the darkened flight deck to B – Baker. He had been awakened at 0300 and, after the ritual coffee or tea in the wardroom, had assembled in the ops room for the final briefing. It was not the cold that made Bill shiver. It was a kind of nervous anticipation, a fear of the unknown; not a fear of action so much as how he would react in action. Even the thought of it made him tremble.

'All right, Bill?'

Bill felt the hand on his shoulder and turned to find Sandy Sandiford smiling at him. Sandy walked with Bill to the waiting aircraft.

'I think I'm OK,' said Bill. 'I have a few jitters in my tummy, but I expect I'll be all right.'

'The first time is the worst,' Sandy replied, 'although I always feel a bit tensed up at this stage. I find the tension eases once I'm in the cockpit.'

Bill was grateful for those words. If others felt as he did and got over it, then so would he.

The two squadrons were packed tightly, with wings folded, on the after end of the flight deck. On the order to start up, the silence was shattered as sixteen Pegasus engines burst into life. 999 Squadron was putting up nine aircraft and 998 seven. Two of 998's aircraft would be left behind to cover the early A/S patrols. The carrier turned into wind and quickly, one after the other, the Swordfish aircraft were rolled forward to the starting position, where their wings were unfolded and locked for them to take off.

A few minutes after take-off B – Baker was circling the flame-float and forming up on the right of the CO. Holy Temple was very sure of his movements and this and the routine of forming up had had a reassuring effect on Bill. His stomach soon settled down as his attention became absorbed in the task of plotting the navigation.

A cloud had passed from beneath the moon and the seascape lay revealed. They had left the shores of Crete and Scarpanto, dark and mysterious, astern on either quarter. Ahead were the small clusters of Nisia and Sophrana Islands. Bill was enchanted by the sight of Sophrana beneath him, surrounded by breaking waves like a necklace of pearls, gleaming in the moonlight.

What a waste of human effort, he thought. Here am I crossing the wine-dark sea of Homer's *Odyssey* on a mission to bomb and destroy part of one of these Greek Islands. One day, please God, I'll return here in my own boat and visit Stampalia and explore the islands as they should be explored, as Ulysses explored them, by boat.

Sirina lay to starboard, surrounded by its cluster of tiny islets, and then Holy called through the intercom.

'I can see Stampalia, about fifteen miles ahead. Our height is five thousand feet and we're still climbing.'

'Thank you, Holy. What's our speed?'

'Still seventy-five knots.'

'Right!'

Applying himself to his chartboard, Bill quickly put some times on the pre-plotted tracks. Now he was able to give all his attention to the developing action.

The CO waggled his wings and the squadron formed line astern. The coast was passing beneath them. To port, Bill could easily see the small *chora*, or principal town, of the island, called Skala, with its ancient castle guarding the harbour.

The CO was now turning to starboard and the desolate scrubland of Agrilithi lay beneath them. Bill could clearly see the barracks, a parade ground with rows of stone houses on one side and a large building on the other. Scattered shell-bursts pockmarked the sky and several lines of tracers fanned skywards. It was all so remote – so impersonal. Bill could not feel that they were attacking human beings down there who were firing back to blast them out of the sky.

A ball of flame and smoke belched from the houses. That was the CO's attack. B – Baker was already hurtling downwards and the cry came from Holy, 'Bombs gone.'

Now they were streaking down a valley and towards a long narrow bay that led seawards. Behind them Bill could see smoke and flames obliterating the target. He saw they were passing over a small destroyer anchored in the bay and then they were out at sea, making for Kunupia Island to reform with the squadron.

Behind them, Killer Compton was fifth in line to attack.

'I can't see a damn thing over the target,' he shouted to his observer, Snowball Kennedy. 'But I can see a destroyer in the bay. I'm going to have a go at that.'

'Okay,' said Snowball, 'but drop your incendiaries first.'

Killer released the incendiaries into the smoke beneath him, and, easing out of his first dive at four thousand feet, he continued for a mile or so to the south and then threw the plane into the steepest dive Snowball had ever experienced. Guns on the destroyer were blazing away at them, but at one thousand feet Killer released his bombs and continued towards the entrance to the bay, pulling out at sea level. Looking astern, Snowball saw the bombs straddle the bows of the destroyer, with possibly two hits.

'Well done, Killer,' he called into his intercom. 'You've got at least two hits.'

As Holy Temple flew B – Baker southwards, away from the target area, Bill could see the pall of smoke behind them. Away on his starboard side he observed some heavy flak coming from Skala. That would be enemy warships concentrating their fire on the aircraft of 998 Squadron attacking Maltezana. Even as he watched he saw the splash of

105

bomb-bursts, with the occasional one ringed in red flame, signifying a hit.

He had been surprised by the speed of the operation. It was all over before he had had time to feel afraid. He was glad that he had come through it, but at the same time he felt sure that it had been a comparatively easy one. Now his job was to find the CO.

Several Swordfish were streaming south from the target, the last of which was flashing the letter 'A' on its wing lights. That would be the CO. He must have stayed behind to watch the operation. He informed Holy of the CO's position and settled down to plot a course to the carrier.

The flight back was uneventful and it was a cheerful and noisy group that met in the operations room for a debriefing, and a hungry one that assembled in the wardroom for their special post-operation breakfast.

Chapter 10

Benghazi

The stay in Soudha had been a short one, just sufficient time for the Fleet to oil up from a hastily acquired tanker. Bill Hewitt had stood entranced on the quarterdeck of *Peregrine* as the ship rounded the high plateau of Akrotiri Peninsula and entered the steep-sided harbour. At school, Bill had studied classics and had been interested in Greek and Cretan civilisations. He remembered now the stories he had read of the Minoan civilisation, particularly the ancient Minoan town of Knossos. He had stared broodingly as the ancient land swept past, a land used to conflict and the sword and now again endangered. Again he thought how one day he would return in his own boat and explore these ancient harbours.

A small village occupied the head of the harbour, but there had been no opportunity to explore it. Now they were again at sea, sweeping south westwards towards Benghazi, three hundred miles away. At dawn the next day, the squadron was to attack the port of Benghazi. Bill no longer feared the unknown. He had learned how impersonal was the war in the air, and now his feelings about the operation were ambivalent. He hated the thought of bombing and destroying and yet at the same time looked forward with anticipation to the thrill of taking part in a hazardous mission.

At present he was about to participate in a far from dangerous operation. His aircraft, B – Baker, was already lined up on the flight deck. Clipping on his safety strap, his arms resting on the sides of the open cockpit, Bill waited for the affirmative from the bridge.

Anti-submarine patrols were routine. He had already flown one and knew the drill. You took station fifteen miles ahead of the Fleet, patrolling a line about fifteen miles long across the direction the Fleet was going. There would be wireless silence unless contact with a submarine was made. Navigation was visual and the pilot had little to do but maintain a height of about a thousand feet and stay roughly on course. All three crew would devote their attention to lookout, Bill occasionally making sweeps with his binoculars. The patrol lasted for two and a half hours and was deadly dull. The CO in 'Abel', whom they were relieving, was already circling the carrier.

The affirmative flag was up. A green light was flashed from the bridge. The chocks were withdrawn. They were off.

As they passed over the round-down, the engine gave a heart-stopping splutter, and faltered. Holy Temple fought desperately to keep the plane aloft, putting his nose down and allowing gravity to build up speed, but there was little response from the engine. A crash was inevitable. Bill gripped the sides of his cockpit tightly and braced himself.

Holy knew he had to get out of the path of the monster behind him, so he jinked his plane to port, pulled on his joystick and let the tail wheel hit the sea first, so that he pancaked on to the water. The aircraft came to a splashing halt, throwing the crew forward in their seats. Bill had anticipated this and had braced himself against the forward bulkhead. Not so PO Black, the air-gunner. He was facing aft and his head had jerked back, hitting the bulkhead and leaving him unconscious.

With the weight of the engine, a full fuel tank and the two

depth charges, the aircraft was beginning to sink. The massive bulk of the *Peregrine* was only feet away, the ship's torpedo bulges brushing the aircraft with the foam of their passage.

'Get out quickly, Bill, she's going down,' came the cry of Holy Temple. 'Make sure you release the dinghy.'

'Blackie's knocked out,' shouted Bill. 'I need help.'

Holy clambered over the bulkhead separating him from his observer, who was already freeing Black's safety harness. Water was lapping the cockpit as pilot and observer hauled their TAG out of his cockpit and into the self-inflated dinghy, which Bill had released. Whilst Bill tended PO Black, Holy fended off the dinghy, which turned round and round in the wash of the carrier.

On the deck of the carrier the Captain had acted promptly.

'Emergency turn to starboard,' he called. 'Stop engines. Sound one blast.'

The prompt action had brought the bows of the carrier round just enough to brush the ditched aircraft further to port.

'Signal *Heron*, "Aircraft in the sea. Assistance required".'

Heron, *Peregrine*'s attendant destroyer, had already observed the accident and had increased speed.

Aircrew from the goofers' platform rushed to the port side to watch the drama unfold. They saw Holy and Bill lift the unconscious Black into the dinghy and paddle away from the aircraft. They saw the wave from the carrier spin the dinghy round and almost capsize it as Holy and Bill fought to keep it upright. They watched the way slowly come off the *Peregrine* and the *Heron* rush up and stop alongside the dinghy. A small cheer rang out as the three occupants were lifted aboard the destroyer.

Meanwhile Bolo hurried to the bridge.

'Range another aircraft for the A/S patrol,' said Wings.

'"C" is on standby,' said Bolo. 'I'll get them in the air as quickly as I can.'

Bolo immediately had them piped on the Tannoy.

'D'ye hear there? 999 Squadron range C – Charlie. The aircrew report to the operations room.'

Bolo waited anxiously on the bridge, quietly discussing the accident with Wings. A light flashed from *Heron*.

'Signal from *Heron*, sir,' said the PO signalman, addressing his Captain. '"Three crew rescued. Pilot and observer unhurt. Air-gunner has concussion, not serious."'

'Thank God!' exclaimed Wings.

'Send a signal, "Please transfer all crew to *Peregrine*, and thank you",' the Captain told his signalman.

Within a quarter of an hour of the accident, the crew of the stricken aircraft had been transferred, and C – Charlie had been ranged on deck and was flying off. The CO in A – Abel, who had witnessed the accident and had remained on patrol, was now returning, ready to fly on.

As soon as Lieutenant Commander Simpson landed, he sought out Bolo and together they made their way to the sick bay. PO Black had regained consciousness and was talking somewhat ruefully to his pilot and observer.

'I've kept them all here for observation,' the PMO informed Simpson. 'Temple and Hewitt have recovered well and they're showing no signs of aftershock. Black has a large bruise on the back of his head, but he'll be all right in a few days.'

'Good. I'd like to have a word with Temple. Is that okay?'

'Use my office. I'd like to keep him and Hewitt in the sick bay for twenty-four hours for observation.'

'What happened, Holy?' said Simpson as soon as they were comfortably seated, with coffee provided by an SBA.

'Well, sir, as we neared the end of the flight deck the engine just lost power. The speed dropped and the plane felt heavy and unwieldy. I knew we were going in, so I coaxed the plane over to port to get out of the path of the carrier and put her down. I got a little more manoeuvrability out of her by putting the nose down and gaining a bit of speed. Just before we crashed, I pulled the nose up and let her sink tail first on to the sea. I didn't have time for much else.'

'Have you any idea what caused the engine failure?'

'Not really, sir.'

'Any ideas, Bolo?'

'It could have been scraper rings going because of sand in the engine at Dekheila. It might be water in the petrol. *Peregrine* took on a new load at Alex. It might be loss of compression or loss of oil pressure, though that would be unlikely if the daily inspection was carried out properly. I'll look into that.

'Holy did very well to get his aircraft clear of the carrier and pancake it. That probably saved their lives.'

'Yes, it showed quick thinking. Well done, Holy!'

'Thank you, sir.'

Holy Temple flushed with pleasure at the approval shown by his CO and Senior Pilot.

'I'd like to have a word with young Hewitt now,' said the CO as they joined the other two at Black's bedside.

'I just wanted to say, Bill, that you did very well in rescuing Black. You showed coolness and courage in staying with the aircraft to release him and, with Temple's help, getting him into the dinghy. It was in the highest traditions of the Navy.'

'You can say that again, sir,' murmured PO Black.

In the hangar, Bolo checked B – Baker's engine log-book with Tom Stillson, the Chief Air Artificer. The daily inspection had been carried out correctly. Bolo talked to the aircraft's fitter and rigger. They were devastated by what had happened. Bolo became convinced that the crash was not caused by faulty maintenance.

'There's nothing else for it, Chief, you'll have to drain all engines and check for water or dirty fuel and check all scraper rings.'

'We'll get on to that straight away, sir,' said Stillson. 'Is the raid tomorrow morning still on?'

'Can you check the aircraft, refuel and arm them with bombs in time?'

'I think so, sir. All the lads will turn to.'

He turned to the group of mechanics and fitters who had been crowding round to hear what was said.

'Right, then. Come on, you load of loafers. Let's be having you.'

He proceeded to give instructions and soon the hangar was humming with activity. The 999 Squadron maintenance crews had no intention of letting the side down.

The time was 0400 and the first aircraft was taking off. Fourteen Swordfish had been ranged on deck for the combined operation on Benghazi. The briefing had been clear. Eight aircraft of 999 Squadron would dive-bomb, attacking ships in the harbour and port installations. Under cover of this attack six aircraft of 998 Squadron would lay mines in the harbour entrance. The remaining three aircraft would be responsible for the early A/S patrols.

The CO of 999 Squadron had briefed his men. Biddy Bidwell in F – Fox would drop flares, with Andy Andrews in H – Howe as back-up. Hank Phipps in G – George would join him in the first sub-flight as replacement for B – Baker. The CO's sub-flight would attack installations and anti-aircraft batteries and any ships alongside the mole. Bolo's sub-flight would seek out any ships at anchor in the harbour. Aircraft of these two sub-flights would each carry two five hundred pound bombs, two two hundred and fifty pound bombs and eight incendiaries. 'F' and 'H', the flare-droppers, would each carry four two hundred and fifty pound bombs.

A crescent moon gave sufficient light for Bolo to see the shadowy shapes of the aircraft around him. Somewhere astern was the other squadron. The coast of North Africa was now ten miles off and the CO had waved away the flare-droppers. Carrying a lighter bomb-load, they could travel faster and get behind the port to drop their flares for the arrival of the main bombing force.

Bolo stared intently ahead, but could see nothing of the enemy coast. Then he saw his leader's wings waggling. This was the signal they were waiting for and the aircraft responded by breaking into their two sub-flights and forming line astern.

Now the line of surf marking the coast could be seen and flashes of gunfire and tracers began to show ahead. That would be aimed at the flare-droppers, now getting into position. The squadron was at seven thousand feet, approaching the coast rapidly in a shallow dive.

Six incandescent balls lit up the harbour to reveal the jumble of buildings on the mole, with a tanker alongside and, in the middle of the harbour, a large passenger ship, no doubt a troop carrier. Two destroyers were moored close to the troopship. A second line of flares followed the first. Anti-aircraft fire was now intense, though indiscriminate. The buildings erupted in flame and smoke as the CO's bombs hit, followed soon afterwards by a huge explosion on the tanker.

It was Bolo's turn.

'Going down,' he said calmly into his intercom.

Lights, ship and sea chased each other as Bolo half stalled and half rolled into his dive. His mind was devoid of everything but the ship, now looking enormous, that lay beneath him. His aircraft was rocked by shell-bursts, but he was scarcely aware of them. Nor did he notice the lines of flaming onions arrowing towards him.

Five thousand feet. Four thousand feet. Three thousand. A slight aileron turn to line up with the bridge of the trooper. Two thousand. One thousand. Now. He pressed the tit, releasing his four bombs.

'Bombs gone,' and then he was away, diving, twisting and turning to avoid the close-range weapons of the destroyers.

Killer Compton in L – Love saw the explosions on the deck of the troopship and decided to go for the nearest destroyer. Snowball Kennedy could see the destroyer over his pilot's head as he braced himself against the bulkhead that separated him from Killer. They were in a good position. Killer must surely hit the target.

Then a burst of tracer came from the destroyer straight at them. Killer's reaction was immediate. With a quick flick, his aircraft side-stepped the tracers whilst he continued his dive towards the target. Fighting the crushing effects of gravity as Killer pulled out of his dive, Snowball observed the bombs burst alongside the destroyer. A near miss. That last burst of tracer had affected Killer's aim.

Bolo regained some height as he watched the effects of the bombing. The troopship was listing to port. The tanker had blown up. A destroyer appeared to be in difficulties. The port installations were damaged, but not destroyed; he still had his incendiaries and was already making for them. Another aircraft got there before him and a great wash of flame came from the damaged buildings. Flying at a thousand feet, he could feel the heat as he dropped his incendiaries into the middle of it.

Then he saw further bomb-bursts on the troopship and another explosion on the destroyer. A Swordfish passed him in the opposite direction and another crossed his bows. It was time to get out.

Snowball had seen no sign of the mine layers, but he assumed they had gone in unobserved under the cover of the bombs. Killer, disappointed with missing the destroyer, had

114

followed his CO's instruction and with a shallow dive almost into the heart of the flames had planted his incendiaries fairly in the middle of the largest building.

Now as Snowball looked back, the whole port area seemed to be ablaze. In contrast, the darkness ahead was intense. He had given a return course to the carrier to Killer but now, taking a backbearing on the fire, he was able to adjust it accurately. The attack had taken place in darkness, but the aircraft were due back at the carrier at 0600, after dawn had broken.

Half an hour later, the air was suffused with light as the sun's rim appeared. With it, Snowball could see other aircraft, all going the same way, home to *Peregrine*. One of the aircraft, fairly close to him, still had its bombs attached.

'Killer,' he said. 'Can you see the aircraft on our starboard side? He's still got his bombs on. Can you close him?'

'By God! You're right. We'll go and have a look.'

They could see, as they closed, that the aircraft was M – Mike. At the same time they saw Bolo Hawkins, in K – King, close up on the other side. Bolo was indicating by hand-gestures that Mike's bombs had not been released.

Bing gestured back that he knew about the bombs, pointed to his switch and gave a thumbs-down sign.

So it was a malfunction.

Bolo gestured to Bing to climb higher, dive and try dropping his bombs again, pulling out sharply.

Bolo and Killer followed Bing as he climbed to three thousand feet. They watched him dive and pull out. The bombs were still attached.

Forming up on 'Mike' again, Bolo indicated that Bing should throw his aircraft about with his switch pressed, to try and shake the bombs loose.

They watched 'Mike' as Bing went through a crazy performance trying to release his bombs. It was of no avail. They were now nearing the carrier and Bolo saw Harold

Lloyd, Observer of 'Mike', flashing with his Aldis lamp to the carrier.

The carrier acknowledged Harold's request for instructions and told him to wait. Then the reply came. It was left to the pilot to try to land on the carrier or ditch as he felt best.

Bing discussed the problem with his observer and TAG.

'They haven't come off so far,' he concluded, 'and I've tried everything to shake them off. I don't see why they should come off when we land. In any case I'll leave them on "safe".'

The others agreed to stick with him and Harold signalled the carrier that they were coming in to land. All the aircraft except for 'Mike' and 'King' had landed-on. Bolo had decided to stay with 'Mike' to give Bing support.

He watched as Bing approached the carrier. He had throttled back. His hook was out. Good lad, he was remembering his drill. Time stood still. Statuesque, the batsman held his arms out straight. Then they crossed as 'Mike' touched down, heavily. With horror Bolo watched the port two-fifty pound bomb thud on to the deck and roll to one side. The Swordfish came to a halt. The bomb was rolling back with the motion of the ship. It had not gone off.

Two figures leapt from the catwalk and pounced on the bomb. One at each end, they carried it bodily to the side of the carrier and dropped it overboard. It did not explode. Bolo let his breath go in a long sigh and prepared to land-on.

The operations room was full of noisy, excited young men, most of them wanting to talk at once. Bolo and his observer, Dicky Burd, were the last to arrive. Immediately, Wings called for silence, and the debriefing began.

The raid on Benghazi had been a success: the troopship in the harbour had been left in a sinking condition; one destroyer was sunk; the tanker alongside the wharf had blown up; and the installations alongside the harbour-offices, warehouses, even gun sites – had been flattened. The mine layers had successfully laid their mines across the harbour entrance, so more damage could be anticipated. All aircraft had returned successfully. The careful writing out of detailed reports began.

The CO called Bolo over to him.

'The two men who took care of the bomb,' he said. 'They were naval airmen, Hapwell and Rawlings, part of your maintenance team. The Captain is going to recommend them for gongs, probably the DSM.'

Bolo pictured the two men, Hapwell, young and eager, and his oppo, Tiny Rawlings, large and tough, the artist who had painted Old King Cole on his aircraft.

'Can I tell them, Boss?' he asked.

'Yes. That's why I told you – I thought you'd like to be the one to do it.'

Bolo made his way to the hangar, where the fitters and riggers, already working on the returned Swordfish, checking, rearming, refuelling, stopped work to gather round him for news of the raid. Briefly, he told them of its success and saw their faces light up with pleasure.

'Now,' he said. 'Where are those two rapscallions, Hapwell and Rawlings?'

The two men who had been standing at the back of the crowd were pushed forward.

'I hear you've taken on a new job,' he said, 'bomb disposal.'

The two men grinned sheepishly.

'What made you do it?' Bolo enquired.

Rawlings answered: 'When this little twerp, Hapwell, ran forward, I knew he couldn't handle it on his own so I went with him to help.'

'He took the heavy end, sir,' said Hapwell, 'while I took the tail. It wasn't half heavy.'

'It was well done, both of you And now you'll be pleased to know that you are both to be recommended for the DSM.'

Hapwell's young face flushed with pleasure. Tiny Rawlings stood, mouth agape in disbelief.

'It wasn't even armed,' he said. 'What will my old mum think?'

Bolo left the crowd thumping the two men on the back and showing their approval. The awards would do much for the squadron's morale, which was already high.

Before he reached the wardroom, action stations sounded.

'Enemy aircraft approaching. Attack imminent. Take cover,' blared the Tannoy.

Bolo hurried to the boat deck, where he could observe the action from beneath the shelter of the flight deck. The Italian response to the raid on Benghazi had been swift and deadly. Nine SM 79s, high-level bombers, were almost overhead at a height of fifteen thousand feet. They had approached out of the sun and, with no British fighters airborne, had a clear field.

The guns of *Peregrine*, the battleship *Ramrod*, and the escorting cruisers and destroyers put up a tremendous barrage. One Italian aircraft spiralled down, out of control, and crashed astern of *Peregrine*, leaving four parachutes descending slowly. The remaining aircraft seemed immune. Miraculously, they continued through the forest of shell-bursts until they were almost overhead. Then Bolo saw bombs leaving the leading aircraft.

Peregrine had increased speed and was turning to port, but she was an old ship and slow to turn. Bolo saw the splashes of the bombs rise high in the sky alongside *Ramrod*. Then he heard the crump of bombs on the other side of *Peregrine*. *Peregrine*'s turn had saved her from a direct hit, but she tilted heavily to starboard as the bombs burst close alongside.

Bolo's first thought was for the aircraft. He rushed back to the hangar, meeting the CO on the way.

Fortunately most of the Swordfish tethered firmly to their

ringbolts, had remained undamaged. G – George, however, had broken one of its fastenings and had slewed round, cannoning into H – Howe. Bolo saw the broken tail plane of 'G' and the broken wings of 'H' where they had collided. There was a danger of fire and already Chiefy had a team of men standing by with extinguishers.

Bolo, whose responsibility as Senior Pilot was for the aircraft of the squadron, took over control. Quickly, using tail-jacks and manpower, he had the aircraft pulled back to their proper positions and re-tethered. Petrol tanks had not been ruptured, so the fire hazard was receding. Next, he sent for the Ship's Air Engineer, and with Chiefy, the three men began to assess the damage. They could repair the planes aboard ship. Bolo hurried to the bridge to make his report.

There he found the Captain with Wings, the ASO, and the two Squadron Commanding Officers. They were pleased to have his report, but the ship's situation was grave. The Ship's Commander arrived on the bridge with the Engineer Commander to report the damage done by the near miss.

'Undoubtedly a dockyard situation. Plates weakened by former near misses now show serious buckling.'

With six hundred miles to go, the situation was grave, but not impossible.

'We can maintain a speed of twenty knots,' reported the Engineer Commander.

'That means a day and a half back to Alex,' said the ASO, 'with the possibility of more air strikes on us.'

'Or submarine attacks,' the Captain observed. 'What is our aircraft state, Wings?'

'In 998 Squadron, all aircraft are available, but 999 Squadron are down to six for the time being. We have two Gladiators available for air defence.'

'Right! We'll have two aircraft on patrol throughout daylight hours today and one fighter airborne. Can you manage that?'

Wings glanced towards Bolo and received an affirmative.

'Aye, aye, sir. I'll double up the aircraft. As 998 are on A/S duty today, will your squadron be able to take over late this afternoon, Simpson?'

'Yes, sir. We have enough aircraft to see the day out.'

'We'll continue with A/S patrols tomorrow morning until we're close to Alexandria,' said the Captain. 'I'll ask for RAF fighter support from dawn tomorrow. We shall be near enough to their aerodrome.'

'Very good, sir,' said Wings. 'I'll take the first patrol, Bolo,' he continued. 'Can you be ready to relieve me in two hours?'

'Yes, sir.'

'Good!' He turned to the ASO, 'Have them range one Gladiator and two Swordfish. Take off in fifteen minutes.'

In the late afternoon, there was one further attack by six SMs. Wings was on patrol and immediately dived into the group of enemy aircraft, shooting one down and damaging another. At the same time the Fleet put up a huge umbrella of defensive fire. The Italians had no stomach for the fight and dropped their bombs well out of range.

The following day a message was received from the RAF confirming the destruction of port installations, tanker and destroyer and reporting that the troopship had also sunk. Moreover, two small merchant ships and a destroyer had also sunk in the harbour entrance, effectively blocking it. The mines had also been successful.

At noon, having flown off all her aircraft to Dekheila, the Fleet steamed into Alexandria Harbour.

Chapter 11

The Western Desert

For the first few days at Dekheila the squadron was stood down. G – George and H – Howe had been repaired before flying off; B – Baker was replaced. Lieutenant Commander Simpson allowed his aircrews to relax and recuperate until all aircrews were pronounced fit for flying duties. Under Chiefy's guidance all aircraft were given a thorough overhaul, with special attention being given to the electrics, particularly the bomb-release mechanisms.

The only flying required was for test flights, which were carried out each morning. Swimming or a siesta was favoured in the afternoon, with sometimes a visit to the Sporting Club in Alexandria for a game of squash. In the evening most of the officers took the liberty bus to Alexandria for a visit to the Cecil, or a cinema, or a nightclub. By the end of the first week the CO realised that his flying-crews were getting restless and he was relieved when operational orders for the squadron arrived.

It was the seventh of November. All aircrew were assembled in the squadron office to hear the news. The CO began with a preamble about the state of the war in the Middle East.

'The Italians have met with a spirited resistance from the Greeks and their invasion of Greece has been halted. In Egypt they are massed at Sidi Barrani, ready to march on

Cairo and Alexandria. It is on these two fronts that we will have to concentrate over the next few weeks.

'*Peregrine* will be in dry dock for a month for repairs. This does not mean,' he continued, noting the hopeful looks on the faces of his young colleagues, 'that you will be going on leave. Far from it.

'Two aircraft are to be detached for special duties with *HMS Illustrious*. They will be joined by three aircraft from 998 Squadron. The remainder of our squadron are detailed for operational duties in the Western Desert in support of General Wavell's Army.

'Going to *Illustrious* will be A – Abel, with myself, Lieutenant Sandiford and CPO Cutter, and F – Fox, with Lieutenant Bidwell, Sub Lieutenant Weston and PO Jarman. The remainder of the squadron, with Lieutenant Hawkins in command, will fly to a forward base at Fuka and operate from there.

'Maintenance crews and stores will leave in a convoy of lorries at dawn tomorrow. "Abel" and "Fox" will leave at mid-morning to join *Illustrious*. The rest of the squadron will leave later for Fuka.'

A babel of discussion followed the CO's address and questions were fired at him.

'What kind of operations in the desert?'

'I don't know. Lieutenant Hawkins will be told when you get there.'

'Will it be daylight or night operations?'

'Almost certainly night operations, so don't forget to eat your carrots.'

Laughter greeted the sally.

'What will *Illustrious* be doing?'

'Your guess is as good as mine.'

The CO batted defensively as the questions were bowled at him, and gave nothing away.

The remainder of the day and half the night were spent in

feverish activity, as stores and tool chests, bombs and ammunition, and four-gallon cans of petrol were loaded into the lorries. At dawn the next day the convoy of lorries set off. By 1100, *Illustrious* was at sea and A – Abel and F – Fox were taking off to join her.

Bolo felt strangely forlorn as he surveyed the remains of the squadron. Some observers and most of the TAGs had departed with the convoy, leaving room for a few maintenance crews to service the aircraft and fly in their places.

If Bolo had thought of Dekheila as a desert aerodrome, he found Fuka to be little more than a desert strip. Nearly two hundred miles nearer the Italian lines, to the west of Alexandria, it consisted of a runway with a windsock and a number of tents for living accommodation. As they approached, Bolo noted a small group of RAF Hurricanes and a Blenheim parked to one side of the runway.

The heat of the desert engulfed Bolo as he stepped from his aircraft. Hapwell and Rawlings, cheerful as ever, were there to greet them and take charge of the aircraft as Bolo and Dicky Burd made their way to the large mess tent. There, Bolo introduced himself to Wing Commander Barker, who was Commanding Officer of the station. Wing Commander Barker explained what was required of the Fleet Air Arm squadron.

'The Italians are massing their tanks and armoured cars at Sidi Barrani,' he said, 'ready for the march on Cairo. Wavell isn't ready yet to go on the offensive and it is necessary to keep the Italians quiet for at least a month. Italian reinforcements are arriving via Bardia and Tobruk. We have got to prevent the build-up, so your primary target will be the shipping in both of these ports. Your secondary target will be ammunition and fuel dumps and armour concentrations at

Sidi Barrani. As far as we can, we shall provide up-to-date information on all three target areas, but I leave it to you to organise your operations.'

Dinner that night was a simple meal and the mood of the squadron was sober and serious. Dicky Burd and Holy Temple were the only officers present who had participated in an earlier desert operation and they were quietly talking about it to a group of interested colleagues. Dekheila had provided some experience of tented living but nothing like the primitive conditions in the desert at Fuka.

After dinner, Bolo and Dicky Burd strolled along the foreshore, discussing the situation.

'I think we'll divide into two sections,' said Bolo. 'Each section can do a night's operations if required and then stand down the following night.'

'That's a good idea,' Dicky replied. 'When we were operating from the desert before, we found three or four aircraft were quite adequate for each raid.'

'I think I'll keep my sub-flight together,' Bolo continued, 'but add G – George. Hank Phipps and Dorrie Dorrington are both lacking experience and I'd like to have them under my wing.'

Dicky agreed. 'Who is going to lead the other sub- flight?' he added.

'I think Holy Temple is the obvious choice. After you, he's the next most senior officer. Do you think he can cope?'

'Yes, I'm sure he can. He's already shown resourcefulness.'

'What about his observer, Midshipman Hewitt? Should we put Knocker White or Harold Lloyd as observer with the section leader?'

'No, I think we should leave the crews as they are. They're just beginning to establish confidence in each other. Bill Hewitt is an excellent observer. Sandy told me that he was placed in the first six of his course, so his training was shortened by a month. He's very intelligent, and that business with the ditching shows that he has grit and determination. He's maturing rapidly. I think he can be left to navigate his section.'

'Right. That's it, then. We'll take the first operation tomorrow night. The RAF photographic Hurricane is doing a run over Bardia and Tobruk and we'll decide which port to attack when we see his pictures.'

Back in the mess, Bolo found the remainder of the squadron talking quietly. He explained the disposition of the two sections that he had discussed with Dicky and gave an indication of the likely targets. There would be a briefing in Bolo's tent for 'A' flight at 1700 the next day. Bolo asked the observers to have a word with their air-gunners, who would also attend the briefing. He asked the pilots to check their aircraft security and let their maintenance crews know what was going on.

That night Bolo found his tent so hot that he decided to sleep out in the open. Lying on his back, wide awake, he gazed up at the firmament above. The stars were huge with an intense luminosity that he had never before been aware of. They seemed to beckon his soul into outer space, and he thought how insignificant he was in the universe. At the same time he felt a yearning within him to reach out to something he could not define.

Gradually his thoughts crystallised on Joyce. The desert, the stars and the firmament had awakened in him a spiritual need that in a strange way could be expressed in an emotional and physical link with Joyce; Joyce and himself, two inhabitants in the countless millions on Earth, two spirits hundreds of miles apart, yet connected now in his imagination. Would Joyce be thinking of him? Could their spirits be linked in their thoughts of each other? Was it possible that a child created by physical union might possess a spirit that came from joining the parents' spirits?

A child! A family! Marriage! A home! At last, as these

familiar concepts ran through Bolo's mind, he knew what he wanted. With Joyce, life for him would be complete.

He remembered now the occasion on his last leave when he had driven with Joyce to Devil's Dyke to see the sunset. They had found a flat space backed by a rock, where they had sat, with Joyce leaning against him. Joyce had told him about her mother, how much she missed her. She had described the family life, how much it meant to her. Bolo had not known it at the time but the seed had then been sown, the seed of family life. Subconsciously this had germinated in Bolo until it now blossomed into his need of Joyce and his desire for a family.

He himself had been an only child and never close to his parents. They had been well on in years when he was born. He had looked on Corny Wilde, Joyce's father, as his own father. That, he thought, was probably why at first he had thought of Joyce as a young sister. It had taken this experience of the desert stars to put the pieces in position and complete life's jigsaw.

Again he thought of Devil's Dyke. Joyce and he had watched the sun set and then had sat in companionable silence as the sky changed from gold to orange to red to black. They had watched the stars come out as he was watching them now. Then Joyce was physically present and part of his experience. Now in his thoughts she was again present and even more part of his experience.

The stars; Joyce; a family; with these competing thoughts he fell asleep.

The next night was pitch black. There was no moon. At 0400 hours, strung out behind Bolo, in echelon formation were the other three aircraft of his section. They were crossing the Gulf of Solum, for Bolo had chosen to take the direct route across the sea to avoid alerting the enemy. This was the natural choice for the Fleet Air Arm. They were more at home with dead reckoning at sea than with map-reading over land.

The section was approaching Bardia obliquely from the east. Dicky Burd had just informed Bolo that the enemy coast was fifteen miles ahead. Their height was seven thousand feet. Bolo's plan was simple. Ten minutes from the ETA he would increase speed and draw ahead of the others. He would release flares over the harbour to illuminate any ships present. The other aircraft, when they saw the flares, were to act independently, and bomb any vessels they could see. Bolo would circle round and follow the others in.

Killer Compton in L – Love was enjoying himself. With Bolo detached, he was now in the lead and this appealed to him. At five miles, he put his nose down slightly to build up speed for the run in and, looking round, he saw the others following.

'There go the flares,' exclaimed Snowball.

Killer saw the six balls of flame ahead descending slowly on their parachutes. Beneath them the harbour lay revealed, with a cargo ship alongside the pier and three or four others dotted in the harbour.

'Going down,' he sang out, and without hesitation put his nose down.

Steeper and steeper became his dive as he singled out the ship alongside the pier. Desultory anti-aircraft fire was started, which Killer ignored. Away to his right he could see the familiar flaming onions. He dived to eight hundred feet before releasing his bombs and making a tight turn to port and away out to sea.

'Good show,' shouted Snowball.

Killer saw that he had scored a direct hit on the ship, which had burst into flames. His immediate attention was taken up by the steep sand cliffs on either side as he made his escape at sea level.

127

Behind him Bing Crosby approached his target in a professional fashion. He had seen Killer's bombs burst and had decided to take one of the ships at anchor. Knowing that he would not have room to turn inside the harbour, he dropped his bombs at fifteen hundred feet and escaped over the cliff tops. A near miss.

Hank was next in and with a whoop, like Killer he bombed at eight hundred feet and continued down to sea level. It was nearly his undoing. The sand cliffs surrounding the harbour were six hundred feet ahead and it was only by the tightest of turns and thanks to the marvellous manoeuvrability of the Swordfish that he was able to avoid disaster.

Bolo saw the aircraft just avoiding the cliff as he took his own aircraft in. Like Bing Crosby, he took a professional view. The harbour was too small for a turn at sea level and he decided to drop at fifteen hundred feet and escape over the cliffs.

The last flare had just gone out as he made his run in. Hank's target was burning and in its glow he could see the outline of another cargo vessel. He noticed that it was down to its lubber line, so it was fully laden. As he drew nearer, in the dim light he saw tanks on the deck.

With clear, precise movements, he lined up his aircraft and released the bombs, two five hundred pound and two two hundred and fifties. Pulling out at fifteen hundred feet, he saw the bombs explode across the bridge and the lurch of the ship as the bombs struck.

By now searchlights were weaving across the sky and the anti-aircraft barrage was fierce but indiscriminate. Twisting and turning, Bolo dodged the searchlights until he was safely in the blackness out to sea. Then Dicky Burd gave him the course for Fuka.

The next night was the turn of the second section. The target was Tobruk. Midshipman Bill Hewitt felt strangely relaxed as he sat in his observer's cockpit waiting for Holy Temple. Holy, his pilot in B – Baker, was revving up his engine against the chocks and brakes. The airframe was juddering with the controlled power of the Pegasus engine. 'Baker' was the leading aircraft of the section, which would fly in a vic formation of three.

The ditching in the last *Peregrine* operation had had a profound effect on Bill. When 'Baker's' engine had faltered on take-off, his heart had faltered with it as he faced death. Surviving the crash had left him shaken but with a feeling of strength and power as he set about rescuing his air-gunner. Jobs had to be done – rescue PO Black, release the dinghy, paddle away from the aircraft, fend off the carrier, manoeuvre alongside the *Heron* – and he had done them without a moment's thought for his own safety.

Since joining the Navy he had developed rapidly. The clever but shy schoolboy of eighteen had found himself at St Vincent, the naval training base, bedding down in a hut of twenty fellow observer trainees, men mostly older than he and many of them outgoing and boisterous. Bill had never been away from home. His county grammar school had not prepared him for Service life. At first he was embarrassed by the men sleeping all around him and even more by the open showers. Never before had he paraded his nudity. And he was shocked by the coarseness of the language of the lower deck.

He threw himself into the work of the course but felt lonely on his off-duty days. He particularly enjoyed the marching and counter-marching that seemed to be an obsession with the Navy. He liked the precision and timing as the squad turned and wheeled across the parade-ground.

As the course developed, Bill began to open up. Dishing up meals or clearing away, squeegeeing or polishing the floors were all physical activities that he could share with others. He liked Sunday Parade and the march to chapel for the service.

Bill had been a regular churchgoer and for the year before joining up he had been a member of the church social club.

There he had learned to dance and, because of his sense of timing, to dance well. Perhaps this was why he enjoyed the counter-marching.

Greenwich had been a culture shock to him. There he had had to come to terms with bow ties and taxis, with being saluted and called 'sir'. His natural ability, within a framework of modesty, impressed his more discerning colleagues and he began to form tentative friendships. Dorrie Dorrington was one of his particular friends. From a very different background of wealthy family and public school, Dorrie had occupied the bed next to Bill at Vincent. Their friendship had developed as the course progressed and Dorrie had quietly steered Bill through some of the more difficult moments at Greenwich.

Now Bill was responsible for navigating the sub-flight to the target a hundred and fifty miles away. Only a month ago he would have questioned his ability to do this. Now his ability was buttressed by his new-found confidence.

Men mature rapidly in wartime when they are on very active service, and Holy was no exception. He was a different man from the raw officer who had taken part in the raid on Tobruk only three months before. Still quiet and mild of manner, he now displayed determination and leadership forged in the heat of action. With a wave to his accompanying pilots he released the brakes and rolled forwards. 'Hatters' Dunn in C – Charlie was on his right and Andy Andrews in H – Howe on his left. The three aircraft took off in formation and were soon climbing out to sea.

A light had been left on at the landing-strip and Bill used this to take a backbearing and check his drift. Now he gave a small adjustment to the course that would take them across the Gulf of Solum and then across the desert to Tobruk. Holy's plan was to approach Tobruk from the landward side, where they would be least expected. As in the earlier flight, on nearing Tobruk he would fly on ahead and drop flares to illuminate the targets. Again they were after shipping which the RAF reconnaissance had revealed to be in the harbour.

They crossed the coast between Bardia and Solum and struck out into the desert to the south of the coastal sand dunes and cliffs. The darkness of night was intense and Bill could sense the immensity of the desert beneath him. Away on his starboard side he could see the occasional dimmed lights of a vehicle on the road from Tobruk to Solum. He was navigating by dead reckoning, but he found the vehicle lights a confidence-building back-up to his navigation.

For the Swordfish it was a long flight. At a climbing speed of seventy-five knots and a cruising speed of eighty knots, it would take them nearly two hours to complete the outward leg. There would be no time to hang about, for their total endurance was little more than four hours. Bill must locate Tobruk quickly. There was no room for mistakes. Apart from the lights of vehicles, they had seen nothing of the ground beneath them. Holy, once Bill had given him a course, had selected a particularly bright star to steer by. This was easier than steering by his compass and probably more accurate.

The flight seemed a long one to Bill as his straining eyes peered into the darkness.

'We are now fifteen miles away,' he said into his intercom. 'Steer 315 degrees.'

This would bring them directly over Tobruk from the south. Holy hand signalled his sub-flight and turned on to the new course.

'Target ten miles,' said Bill.

He began to have worries. How accurate was his navigation? Where exactly was Tobruk?

It was exactly where it should be. At five miles anti-aircraft fire began to appear ahead of them and Bill knew his main task was accomplished. Now it was up to Holy.

Giving his sub-flight the pre-arranged signal, Holy put his nose down and forged ahead. His speed built up to 130 knots. The barrage ahead was now intense. Tobruk had suffered before and had made preparations. Shell bursts spattered the sky and flaming onions soared skywards in inverted cones. As they approached, searchlights came on, fanning the sky. It looked as if nothing could get through.

Then Holy spotted a gap between the searchlights and he made for it. Below him the harbour was illuminated by the searchlights and flaming onions. This was the moment.

'Flares gone!' he called, making a violent turn to starboard to avoid a searchlight sweeping towards him. The flares hung suspended across the sky, illuminating all below. A bunch of explosions in the middle of the harbour was followed by another alongside a tanker. Those would be from Hatters and Andy.

'Going down now!' he exclaimed.

Bill felt his stomach rise towards his head as the aircraft went into a steep dive. Above the pilot's head he could see the cargo ship – about five thousand tons.

'Bombs gone!'

The weight of gravity as Holy pulled out made Bill sink to his stool. Then the bombs burst, right across the cargo ship, which exploded in flame and smoke.

'Let's get out of this,' shouted Holy, as he put the nose down, skimming the sea below, clear of the shell-bursts and flaming onions.

PO Black sprayed the ships with his Lewis gun as they passed and then they were clear. After ten minutes flying on a north-easterly course, Holy dropped a flame float and started circling, flashing the letter 'B' on his navigation lights. This was the pre-arranged signal, and soon the shadowy shapes of the sub-flight aircraft appeared, one on either side, formating on his wing tips.

Bill had prepared a dog-leg course to avoid the bend in the coast north of Bardia, and wearily the three aircraft began the long flight home.

'How's the fuel, Holy?' asked Bill. They had been flying for nearly four hours and petrol must be low.

'Probably okay for another fifteen minutes.'

Bill looked anxiously ahead. They were approaching the coast at an angle and the scenery all looked much alike. Bill could not be sure whether they were to the east or to the west of Fuka. The early morning haze did not help.

'I can see a Verey's light just to port,' shouted Holy.

Bill looked out over his pilot's head and saw a second red light. Thank goodness! Bolo must have realised the problem and was sending up a helpful signal. Within minutes the aircraft had landed on the airstrip and were taxiing to their bunkers.

During the following week the squadron carried out another raid on each of the ports, scoring more hits on the ships at anchor. Then the RAF reported the harbours empty. No doubt the Italians were channelling their replenishments through ports further west, beyond the range of the Swordfish.

On the twelfth of November news came of a big raid on the main Italian port of Taranto. Battleships and cruisers were reported sunk. At the same time the RAF reported much activity at Sidi Barrani. Were the Italians about to move out? On the fifteenth, Wing Commander Barker sent for Bolo. His face was grave as he showed him the RAF reconnaissance photographs and told him what was wanted. The pictures showed a large number of tanks and a wire compound to one side.

'Those are fuel drums inside that compound,' he said, pointing them out. 'We must delay their attack for another fortnight, and the only way I can see to do it is to destroy their fuel. Yours are the only bombers available, but it will have to be a daylight raid. Can you do it?'

This was not an easy one for Bolo to answer. Beyond Sidi Barrani, at Bardia, was an Italian fighter station.

Modern Macchi fighters were stationed there and a day-light attack at Sidi Barrani would almost certainly entice them out. At their slow speed, in spite of their fighter evasion tactics, the Swordfish would be vulnerable.

'Can you give me a fighter escort?' he replied.

'We've six Hurricanes here now. We'll put them all up.'

'Right. I'll put up the whole squadron and hope for the best.'

The two officers planned the attack. The Swordfish would leave half an hour before dawn and attack at first light. Because of their much greater speed, the Hurricanes would leave twenty minutes later and get to the target at about the same time. The Swordfish would dive-bomb from six thousand feet. The Hurricanes would patrol at ten thousand.

The news was not received with great enthusiasm by the rest of the squadron. The older officers remembered the attack on Rhodes when Italian fighters had shot down four out of the nine aircraft. Admittedly there had been no fighter cover then. Surely this would make a difference.

As dawn was breaking next day, the squadron approached its target, just outside Sidi Barrani, in two sub-flights, one of four aircraft and one of three. The operation was timed to arrive when there was sufficient light to illuminate the target, so the sun had already risen when it appeared beneath them. Searching with his binoculars, Dicky Burd spotted it first. He saw the concentration of tanks with the wire compound alongside. His binoculars showed him the drums, hundreds of them, stacked inside. Leaning over Bolo's shoulder he pointed them out.

'Right! Going down.'

The squadron had already formed line astern and there was no point in wasting time. There was no sign of the fighter escort. The Swordfish were each armed with six two hundred

134

and fifty pound fragmentation bombs and six incendiaries. Bolo saw his bombs burst fairly in the centre of the compound and this identified the target for the following aircraft. One after the other, ignoring the flak, the Swordfish dived down, releasing their bombs at a thousand feet, and soon the fuel dump was ablaze with a massive column of smoke rising into the sky. Some of the bombs overshot and landed amongst the tanks, where they did considerable damage.

Killer Compton was just leaving the target area when he heard the urgent call from Snowball.

'Fighters approaching from ahead and they aren't ours.'

Killer looked up and saw the squadron of nine Macchis fanning out for their attack.

'Where are the Hurricanes?' he shouted. The squadron was in a hopeless position. They had not had a chance to re-form after the attack. Each aircraft was on its own.

'Enemy fighter approaching from starboard beam,' Snowball shouted 'Corkscrew starboard. Go, go.'

Snowball's voice was calm as he gave the order and L/A Gibbons had ranged his Lewis gun on the enemy fighter. In turning into the fighter approaching from starboard, however, L – Love presented a perfect target to another fighter, on the port side. The Swordfish shuddered as a shell burst against the engine, and Killer gave a cry of pain as a shell fragment entered his thigh. The propeller stopped. The Swordfish plunged earthwards.

Another fighter was coming from astern.

'There are the Hurricanes,' shouted Snowball.

The four Hurricanes came screaming down, straight into the nine Italians. The Italians immediately broke off the attack on the Swordfish and turned to engage the Hurricanes.

Killer had got his aircraft under control. With no bomb-load and no propeller, it was gliding down towards the

135

desert, with Killer nursing it to get as far from Sidi Barrani as he could. He clenched his teeth and ignored the pain in his leg. The road to Alexandria was beneath him and the easterly wind was reasonably good for a landing.

'Stand by!' he shouted into his intercom.

Snowball braced himself. Killer had put his nose down a little to increase speed and manoeuvrability and at the last moment he drew the stick hard into his stomach. The plane sank on to the road, making a good three point landing.

An Italian fighter was diving at them, chased by a Hurricane. Quickly the crew evacuated to a sand dune beside the road, where Killer made a tourniquet of two hand-kerchiefs to stem his bleeding. At last the skies seemed as empty as the desert – except for an Italian armoured car racing towards them from Sidi Barrani, about three miles away. They could clearly see the dust trail it set up.

'We've had it, sir,' cried L/A Gibbons.

'No we haven't, by Christ. Look there,' said Snowball.

Coming back towards them from the Fuka direction was a Swordfish. The three men waved.

'Wait there,' shouted Snowball.

He ran to the stranded Swordfish, and taking the Verey pistol fired into the petrol tank. The Swordfish was quickly a mass of flames.

'That will stop them getting hold of our IFF," he said.

It was Bolo who was returning. Making a tight turn round the stricken aircraft, he side-slipped on to the road and came to a halt opposite the three men.

'Jump in,' he called.

They wasted no time. The armoured car was barely a mile away. Dicky Burd and Snowball helped Killer into the observer's cockpit, whilst L/A Gibbons clambered into the air-gunner's cockpit. It was a tight fit.

Bolo was already pointing towards Fuka and away from the oncoming armoured car. With a roar, he opened up his throttle, and with the machine-gun bullets from the armoured car kicking up the dust behind him, he tore away from them to freedom.

The crews were in a grim mood when they assembled in the mess tent for debriefing.

'What happened to our escort?' Bolo demanded.

'Just as they were about to take off they were bombed by the squadron of Italian fighters that attacked you,' said Wing Commander Barker. 'Two of our Hurricanes were damaged and the start was delayed. I'm very sorry about it, but there wasn't a lot we could do.'

Bolo visualised the situation and realised the RAF had done very well in the circumstances.

'Well, apart from Killer's misfortune, they arrived in the nick of time. All our other aircraft got back safely, thanks to your blokes.'

'You made a right mess of the fuel dump,' said the CO of the Hurricanes. 'When I left, the whole dump was blazing furiously.'

'In that case, if anyone's got some beer, we'd better have a combined forces party tonight,' said Bolo, a sentiment with which all concurred.

Chapter 12

Taranto

The next morning Bolo was greeted with a message recalling the squadron to Dekheila. They were to be replaced by 998 Squadron for the next fortnight. It was a weary but triumphant party that arrived back at Dekheila, where their CO and the *Illustrious* detachment awaited them. After congratulating them on their efforts in the desert, Lieutenant Commander Simpson told them about the Fleet Air Arm triumph at Taranto. Later, Bolo heard the full story from Sandy Sandiford.

Killer Compton had been brought back from Fuka in one of the Swordfish, and an ambulance from the Royal Naval Hospital had come to fetch him. Having satisfied himself on that score, Bolo felt free to relax. Sandy joined him in his tent after dinner for a quiet chat.

'The *Peregrine* contingent had a good reception on *Illustrious*,' he said, 'and then we were given the news. The combined force of twenty-one Swordfish was to make a night attack on Taranto.'

'That must have shaken you.'

'I think the *Peregrine* aircrews had a slightly different view. Perhaps because we have more experience of operations than the *Illustrious* aircrews we were aware of the danger. I reckoned that we would lose a third of our aircraft, and some days after the operation we heard that the C-in-C had expected fifty per cent casualties. But in spite of our aware-ness of the danger, we were all determined to do our best.

'The *Illustrious* crews were quite bucked by the idea. They were so keen to be in on the operation that one crew, who crashed into the sea in the morning and were picked up by a cruiser, persuaded the cruiser's captain to have them flown back to *Illustrious*, and then managed to join the raid in the spare Swordfish.

'The operation was set for the night of the eleventh of November, and we were briefed that afternoon.

'An RAF photograph, taken that morning and flown out to *Illustrious*, showed six Italian battleships at anchor in the Mar Grande, the outer harbour, and several large cruisers and many destroyers in the Mar Piccolo, the inner harbour.

'There were to be two strikes, one of twelve aircraft, followed an hour later by the second of nine aircraft.

'The plan for both strikes was similar. Half the aircraft would be armed with torpedoes and would make for the battleships; the other half, armed with bombs, would dive-bomb the cruisers. Two of the bombers were armed with flares to illuminate the harbour. Our role was to lead a sub-flight of the dive-bombers, made up of *Peregrine* aircraft.

'At 2030 we began flying off. We were a hundred and seventy miles from Taranto, and the Fleet intended to turn southwards after the second strike was flown off. Because of these distances we'd all been fitted with long-range tanks. These were unarmoured aluminium containers that filled the observer's cockpit. So we didn't carry air-gunners, and observers had to man the W/T and the guns as well as navigate. I couldn't help thinking about the petrol tank only an inch or two from my back with no armour protection. What would happen if it were struck by a bullet or a shell didn't bear thinking about.

'Conditions were good when we took off. The wind was moderate; the moon was three-quarters full; and there was a

139

filmy haze of cloud that gave us some cover. The cloud, however, presented us with a problem. We had formed up easily enough round a flame-float, about eight miles away from the Fleet, but some time later, as we climbed above four thousand feet, the cloud became denser. We had been flying in very loose formation, but now we couldn't see our leader.

'The Boss closed up and I tried to see through the haze with my binoculars. Our sub-flight was with us but we saw no sign of the others. The Boss decided to continue on the prescribed course and I began navigating seriously. I had kept a note of courses and speeds, and now I plotted these on the chart.

'Just before 2300, I saw flak ahead. We learned later that this was aimed at one of the torpedo aircraft, which had also become detached. The pilot had increased speed to catch up with the others and arrived ahead of the rest of us. It was quite useful really because it showed us exactly where the port was. There were no searchlights and these were strangely absent throughout the operation. Finding Taranto was only the beginning of our problems.

'At the briefing we were told that the port was heavily defended with guns and an anti-aircraft balloon barrage. I think the barrage balloons worried us more than the guns. The guns were pretty fierce, with shell-bursts, tracers and flaming onions, but we could see these. The balloons we couldn't see until the flares were dropped. Then we could see the odd one illuminated against the light of the flares.

'We came in at eight thousand feet. I saw the CO of the *Illustrious* squadron diving into the centre of the Mar Grande, followed by two planes in his sub-flight. It seemed impossible to me. Guns were blazing all round him and he was heading into the centre of them, straight for the barrage balloons round the battleships. I saw him pull out, straighten up and then go into the sea in a ball of flame. But he must have released his torpedo and scored a hit, because we saw one of the battleships burst into flame.

'By now we had our own problems. We just couldn't see the damn cruisers. The mole they were supposed to be alongside was all in shadow. The parachute flares illuminated the battleships but they did nothing for us. Then we saw a balloon dead ahead of us, and another beyond that. It was every pilot for himself. The Boss managed to dodge the balloons and get through to the north. This was clear of balloons but full of flak. We still hadn't spotted the cruisers. Then, as we flew north of the mole, we saw them, a long line of ships, cruisers and destroyers mixed up, stern on to the mole. It was a lovely sight.

'The Boss did a tight turn and then put his nose straight down. A lot of flak was coming up from the ships below and it was very bumpy. He let his bombs go at fifteen hundred feet, then went on down to sea level. The others must have been close behind us for there were bomb-bursts all along the line of ships.

'By now, I think, the Italian Navy had gone mad. They were firing horizontally and hitting each other and merchant ships in the harbour. You could smell the cordite. It was an utter shambles.

'The Boss didn't fancy going through the balloons again, so he turned round and went out northwards, round the top end of the Mar Grande and out to sea. When I looked back it was the biggest fireworks display I have ever seen.

'It was a long haul back over the sea – two and a half hours – but we had company. Biddy Bidwell came up on our starboard side and formed up on us. It wasn't so bad. We were able to pick up the *Illustrious* beacon at twenty miles and we arrived back at 0130.

'One by one the Swordfish returned and to everyone's amazement only two aircraft were missing. At the debriefing the full picture emerged. In the first strike the battleships *Cavour* and *Littorio* were hit by torpedoes and some hits were scored on the cruisers and destroyers. The flare-droppers bombed an oil-storage depot and the seaplane base, which they set on fire.

'In the second strike the *Littorio* was again hit with torpedoes; so was another *Cavour*-class battleship, the *Duilio*. The RAF photograph taken the next day showed the three battleships sinking or aground and two heavy cruisers listing to port and surrounded by oil.

'We had a wonderful fry-up that morning, when we returned, but we weren't too happy at repeating the raid on the following night. Fortunately, the staff thought enough damage was done, and the Fleet retreated south.'

'How did you feel during the raid itself?' Bolo asked.

'Well, you know how it is. I was so busy watching out for the cruisers, warning the Boss about the barrage balloons I saw, and looking out for our own aircraft to avoid that I didn't think or feel much. It was all go. There was no time for thinking or feeling.'

'The Taranto operation has put half the Italian battlefleet out of action. That's just what the C-in-C wanted. He stands a much better chance of getting his convoys through now,' said Bolo.

'Yes. And I hear that you and the boys had a go at the Italian supply lines at Bardia and Sidi Barrani.'

"That went well. We hit some of their ships in harbour and blew up a fuel dump. I'm sorry about Killer Compton. He was hit in the leg by an Italian fighter and his plane was shot down, but fortunately we managed to rescue him.'

Typically in those few undramatic words, Bolo described the tempestuous events of the past few days.

"I'm going to visit Killer in hospital tomorrow,' said Bolo. 'Will you come?'

Sandy agreed and they planned to catch the liberty bus the following afternoon.

Killer was sitting up in bed, chatting to a pretty nurse, when the two officers arrived at the hospital. He was sharing a pleasant room with one other officer, an Army captain wounded in the desert. Killer was delighted to see his two colleagues and quickly introduced the girl.

'Meet Ann,' he said. 'She's a VAD attached to the hospital.'

Bolo studied the girl as he shook hands with her. She was young, about Killer's age, and, like Killer, a little below average height. Soft and yielding, even cuddly, Bolo thought.

'This is the guy I told you about, Ann,' said Killer. 'He landed alongside us in the desert and took us out of the jaws of death.'

'And how are you, Killer?' Bolo asked, avoiding any reference to heroic rescues.

'Not too bad. It's only a flesh wound and the doc thinks I'll be out in a week. It's been worth it so that I could be here and meet Ann.'

'Not so fast, young man,' said Ann, laughing. 'He's not been here a day,' she added, turning to Bolo and Sandy, 'and he's already asked me to go dancing with him.'

'And will you?' said Killer.

'I'll think about it.'

With that, Ann left to attend to her other patients.

'Do you know how long it will be before you're fit for flying duties?' Sandy asked.

'I asked the doc. He reckons I can have a week off to recuperate after I leave hospital. That means I shall be back to torment you in about a fortnight's time.'

'We'll put the red carpet out,' said Sandy.

'What about your VAD? Are you serious about asking her out?'

'Never been more serious in my life! I like her. I'm not sure about the dance. Dancing isn't my strong point. Maybe when she trips over my feet I can blame the gammy leg. But there are other things we can do. I bet she looks super in a swimsuit, so maybe we'll go bathing. I'm sure she'll agree it will do my leg good.'

Killer wanted to know all about Taranto. After Sandy had told him, the two officers went off, leaving Killer to his bed and his VAD.

By the end of the week *Peregrine*'s repairs were completed and she came out of dry dock. Word had come through that Italian frogmen, with miniature submersibles such as they had used at Gibraltar, were planning to attack the capital ships in Alexandria Harbour. The younger officers of 999 Squadron were called upon to form a rota for defensive patrols.

On his first spell, Midshipman Bill Hewitt found himself on duty on *Peregrine*'s foc's'le. He had the middle watch, twelve to four in the morning. Towards the end of the watch, Bill found it hard to keep awake. He had been searching intently all through the watch, sweeping the vicinity of *Peregrine* with his night glasses and sometimes checking the surrounding area of nearby battleships. But it was difficult to maintain concentration and once or twice Bill felt his head nodding. He pulled himself up with a jerk, and took a turn round the deck to wake himself up.

He knew how important the lookout was. The Italians at Gibraltar had shown how they had mastered the technique of sitting astride their submersibles with special breathing apparatus, submerging, and approaching their target by stealth in the middle of the night. They had attached limpet mines to the bottoms of their targets and retreated as stealthily as they had come, leaving the mines to detonate perhaps an hour later.

The shipboard lookout was a last defence. Bill had just stopped himself from nodding off for the fourth time when he became aware of a rustling presence all around him.

144

Immediately alert, he produced his torch and shone it down over the side of the ship. There was no sign of intruders. The faint noise continued and Bill, listening intently, suddenly realised that the noise was overhead. He shone his torch upwards, and caught in the beam was a rat, huge with staring eyes. It began to move along the girder. Bill moved his light sideways and saw the next rat, and the next – a line of them disappearing into the darkness. There must have been a dozen of the huge creatures, moving quietly along the girder and disappearing through a hole at the end of it.

Bill shuddered and switched off his torch. In his mind's eye he could still see the eyes of the rats overhead, staring at him through the darkness. Not for one minute did he feel sleepy again. He spent the remainder of his watch pacing the deck, with one eye on the water and the other on the girders above. It was not uncommon for old ships such as *Peregrine* to be infested with rats. They may even have come aboard when the ship was in dry dock and were now finding their way about.

Two nights later, Bill found himself involved in the other half of the night watchkeeping duties. He was in charge of the ship's motor-boat. With a small crew, his task was to patrol the harbour, dropping small depth charges indiscriminately at irregular intervals of roughly fifteen minutes. The object was to discourage submerged would-be intruders. If one were very close, the shock from the detonation would be enough to stun him and bring him to the surface. He would feel the shock waves even at a distance, and hopefully be frightened off.

Bill felt very close to the war as he patrolled through the dark night, even closer than when flying. He found himself peering at the water, looking for the unseen foe. He thought what brave men they were who ventured on such operations. Nothing, he felt, would ever induce him to go under water.

He enjoyed handling the boats. All the midshipmen were given spells of duty, in harbour, in charge of a cutter or a whaler or a motor-boat. Like the other midshipmen, Bill learned to manage the bucket steering on the cutter and the twin engines on the motor-boat. He liked the surge of power on the motorboat as he opened the throttles, and the quick manoeuvring by using one engine astern and one ahead. Although it was frowned on, Bill's favourite ploy was to race towards the ship's gangway, turn the boat sideways on, using gear and throttle control, and come to a sliding halt broadside on to the ship against the gangway.

By the end of November, *Peregrine* was still in harbour and Killer was nearing the end of his sick leave. He had arranged for a party of his colleagues, Bill Hewitt, Hank Phipps, Dorrie Dorrington and himself, to meet four of the girls from the hospital, organised by Ann, at the Sporting Club of Alexandria. It was a laughing, carefree party that met at the swimming pool. Killer's bandage had been reduced to a mere elastoplast and he was walking easily.

The boys were sitting at a table, wearing bathing trunks, when the girls came out of their dressing-room. Their eyes widened as the girls joined them and there was much appreciative banter. The girls looked most attractive in their swimsuits and sun-tan.

'Come and sit by me, Ann,' Killer said. 'I'm a poor invalid and need looking after.'

'You're as much of an invalid as that he-man there,' said Ann, laughing, and pointing at a young Adonis about to plunge into the water from the high diving board.

'Do I really look like him?' said Killer, preening his short and rather ungainly body.

They all laughed, as they rose to take their swim.

'I can't walk to the pool with my gammy leg,' cried Killer, pulling Ann towards him. 'I need your support.' He put his arms round her shoulders, leaning on her heavily.

'Be off with you,' she said, laughing, and, shrugging him off, she ran lightly down to the swimming pool and dived in.

Killer followed her with a whoop and a running dive. He seemed to have forgotten his disability.

The boys and girls had a thoroughly happy time, and over their iced coffees taken on the splendid, marbled terrace, they agreed to meet in the evening and go to the Carlton Hotel for dinner and dancing. They had formed natural pairs and the boys were very content with life, their war experiences forgotten.

At seven o'clock that evening, the eight young people gaily made their way to the table for eight reserved by Killer. The boys were wearing their smart mess undress with bow ties and cummerbunds and the girls were in evening dresses.

Again, Bill wondered what was happening to him as he fingered his bow tie. His partner, Janet, was slim and gracious, with a fresh complexion, blonde hair and deep blue eyes. Her father was a stockbroker and she had joined the VADs as soon as she was old enough, volunteering for overseas service. She told Bill that her uncle was a Commander in the Royal Navy and when war started she felt she wanted to help the men on active service. Nursing in the Royal Naval Hospital had given her this opportunity and she was content with her life.

Bill found her very relaxing. She had an easy manner and soon broke down his reticence and had him talking about himself. He told her how he had always been torn at school between love of sport and love of study, between physical challenges and mental challenges. Even now, with the intense physical demands made by flying on operations, he often found himself relaxing with his books. He had brought twenty books with him and was at present reading through Shakespeare's plays.

Killer's approach to Ann was more forceful. Walking to the Carlton, he had firmly taken her arm and placed it beneath his own. At first Ann had drawn back defensively, but then with a shrug she had accepted the position. She found Killer strangely attractive. On the face of it he had an elfin and mischievous quality that she found amusing, but occasionally in the odd remark, she detected a latent seriousness. Killer was particularly serious when he discussed the war and its effects on England. He was well aware of the danger of an invasion.

'If Hitler invades, we have the choice of going back home and fighting him to the death in England, or making our base in one of the dominions, say Canada, and fighting on until we defeat him. If I had a wife or a girl friend in England, I'd want to go home and defend her. Not having one, I think I can do more for England in the Navy.'

For a moment, the curtain was drawn aside, and Killer allowed a glimpse of his real self. He told Ann how he wanted to be a doctor, to heal not to wound. There was no point, he said in thinking of that until Hitler was defeated. He would do whatever it took to bring that about.

The next minute he was commenting on the people around them and joking light-heartedly about jellabahs and yashmaks.

Dorrie Dorrington had made a happy match with Pam, a brunette interested in folk music. She had always wanted to be a nurse and had chosen the VADs so that she could serve abroad.

Hank was well away with his redhead. In no time the two were arguing hammer and tongs and thoroughly enjoying themselves. Both were outgoing, forceful, energetic characters, enjoying life in the present and not worrying about the future. Hank told Maggie about his father's ranch, mechanised now – they hardly ever used horses. Maggie recounted tales of her father's Devon farm, rounding up the sheep on horseback, the sheepdip, haymaking, taking the cream to cool in the cubby on the river.

Killer was the first to ask his partner to dance. Awkward as always on the dance floor, he was not aware that it was only Ann's nimbleness that avoided disaster. He had a solemn look on his face as he plodded through the slow waltz, but Ann made him look better than he was. Light on her feet and very supple, she gave grace to his clumsiness. Killer enjoyed himself immensely. He loved the feel of Ann's soft body against his own and the way she yielded as he thrust forward. She made him feel like a good dancer.

Hank and Maggie might well have been dancing a barn dance. They seemed to be in step, but their rhythm was not that of the waltz. Still talking nineteen to the dozen, they cut a swathe through the couples on the dance floor and saw the other dancers moving away from them like corn cut by a harvester.

Dorrie's rhythm was perfect. His tall, willowy figure moved easily between the other couples and Pam was a perfect foil. They danced with almost a professional ease, enjoying the rhythm and the movement.

Janet had been wondering what this serious, rather gauche boy would be like on the dance floor. She herself was a good dancer and enjoyed dancing. She need not have worried. Bill danced a dragging, hesitant waltz that matched the tempo perfectly. His movements were long and slow and he led forcefully. A dreamy look came into Janet's eyes as she yielded to the music. Neither of them spoke a word. Their bodies, just touching, gave her a sensuous thrill as they moved into a reverse turn. Not once did Bill falter; not once did he seem in danger of collision on the crowded floor. As the music ended, they remained stationary for a moment, locked in each other's arms as they let the dance fall away. Then Janet gave her partner a wondering look as they made their way back to the table.

The evening was a huge success. The girls responded to the needs of the boys; the boys replied with courtesy and consideration; and it was a happy party that returned to the VAD's quarters for their goodnight kisses.

Chapter 13

Tripoli

The next day *Peregrine* put out to sea. The Second Division of the Battlefleet, consisting of *Ramrod, Peregrine* and supporting destroyers, was westward bound. The two Swordfish squadrons flew on shortly after the Fleet left harbour and at eleven o'clock were grouped round the Tannoy speakers for the Captain's customary address.

'As a result of the Taranto raid,' the Captain said, 'the Italian Battlefleet has left Taranto and retreated to Naples. They are no longer a threat to us in the Eastern Mediterranean. Presently we are covering a convoy from Alexandria to Malta. At the same time, the C-in-C is taking the opportunity of returning the battleship *Ramilies* and other heavy units to Force H at Gibraltar. The First Division of the Battlefleet, including *HMS Illustrious,* is north of Crete, attacking the Dodecanese Islands, in support of the Greek defence against the Italian invasion of their country.

'We shall make an attack on Tripoli, which is now used by the Italians as the main supply port for their army in Africa. As a result of the operations of our squadrons in the Western Desert, Tobruk and Bardia have been made inoperable and the Italians have had to rely on the longer supply lines from Benghazi and Tripoli.

'After we attack Tripoli we shall turn northwards to meet a convoy from Gibraltar to Alexandria. This convoy will contain tanks and reinforcements for General Wavell's Eighth Army and enable them to go on the offensive.

'Whilst we are no longer under threat from the Italian Fleet, we still have enemy planes and submarines to worry about. When we are within striking distance from enemy airfields we shall maintain a fighter patrol during daylight hours. Anti-submarine patrols will be carried out throughout each day. The Italians are keen to avenge Taranto, and their submarines will be out in strength looking for targets.'

The Captain concluded his speech with a word of approval to the squadrons for their participation in the Taranto and Western Desert operations.

Hour after hour the Fleet moved westwards at an overall speed of thirteen knots, the speed of the convoy that was out of sight to the north of them. Anti-submarine patrols began at dawn and ended with dusk, Swordfish taking off every two and a half hours. Endlessly the planes patrolled fifteen miles ahead of the Fleet, searching and searching but seeing nothing but the empty sea.

Bolo took this opportunity to write his letter to Joyce. Sitting at his desk after dinner the first night at sea, he found it extraordinarily difficult to begin. He stared at the picture of Joyce in front of him and tried to re-create the images he had formed in the desert. Instead, a picture of Joyce at Lee-on-Solent came into his mind.

It was the Easter of 1940. Training had been stood over for three days and Bolo had nothing to do. A telephone call from Joyce had brightened his day considerably. He remembered now how he had gone to the telephone vaguely expecting trouble – perhaps his father was ill. Then he had heard Joyce's clear, fresh young voice.

'Hello, John. Guess who.'

He had recognised the voice immediately and he remembered vividly the surge of pleasure that had run through him.

'I'm down from university and at a loose end. Any suggestions?'

Bolo was duty officer on Sunday and unable to get away from the air station. He explained this to Joyce, but added, 'I'm free today and on Monday. Can you come here?'

'Yes, I can. Can you arrange some digs for me?'

'I think so. There's a retired music critic, Dan Pritchard, here, who's been very friendly. He gives music recitals on his gramophone to those of us interested. I'm sure if I asked him, he'd put you up. Can you come here today?'

'Yes. I'm free now. I could catch the two o'clock train and be with you by four.'

'Good. I'll meet you at the station.'

Bolo enquired after her father, Corny Wilde, and learned that he was in good health, then rang off, thoughtfully. How best could he plan the weekend? They could have dinner at the Blue Boar and afterwards, if Dan Pritchard were agreeable, listen to some of his records. On Sunday he was on duty at the station, but he was sure the CO would allow him to invite Joyce to lunch. Perhaps he could show her round the station. After all, it was a training station. There was no secret equipment.

Then a new thought entered his mind. Would he be allowed to take Joyce up in the Proctor? Again he felt sure the CO would agree. It could be written off as an aircraft test. Joyce, of course, would have to sign a 'blood chit' so that the Navy could disclaim responsibility if there were an accident.

Bolo remembered now the excitement that had pervaded him, how he had eagerly pursued his plans. Dan Pritchard had been wonderful. He and Joyce had immediately taken to each other and Mrs Pritchard had treated Joyce like a daughter. Bolo remembered the evening starting with their meal in the Blue Boar. Not even the limited fare had spoiled the meal.

Joyce had spent most of the meal talking about her life at Cambridge. Many of the dons had been called up and most

153

of the students were either women or very young men. The social life was quiet and Joyce had thrown herself into her studies. Bolo recalled now how animated and attractive she had been as she described her introduction to Donne and the metaphysical poets.

> I wonder by my troth what thou and I,
> Did, till we loved.

What had Bolo done in life before he met Joyce? Now it seemed to him that he had been in love with her from the first time he met her.

Dinner had been followed by Brahms' Fourth Symphony. Dan and his wife occupied the armchairs, leaving the settee to Bolo and Joyce, and Dan gave a brief introduction to each movement, so that Bolo caught the mood of the symphony and felt the power of the music. Bolo was stirred by the seven chords of the opening movement. With the haunting music of the slow movement, Joyce nestled against his shoulder and Bolo lay back contentedly, his arm round Joyce, responding to the music. Even now, he could hear the quiet voice of Dan, showing him what to listen for, the powerfully emotive music, and he could feel the softness of Joyce's body, curving into his, and smell the scent of her so close to him.

If Saturday had been Joyce's day, Sunday was Bolo's. Bolo, as officer of the day, was in charge of the small ceremony of colours and Joyce was watching. Bolo had always enjoyed Navy ceremonial and he marched with pride as he led the guard off the parade ground.

Joyce joined him in the wardroom for breakfast and was an immediate success with the officers. She responded to their banter and laughed at their witticisms. It seemed to Bolo that everyone liked Joyce, and he remembered now how proud he had been of her, and that without realising it he had treated her as his own.

After breakfast, Bolo took Joyce to see the hangars and the aircraft. He showed her the Sharks, old prewar biplanes that were their main training aircraft. He allowed her to climb into the Walrus, the strange amphibian with a pusher airscrew, now carried extensively by battleships and cruisers as their spotter/reconnaissance aircraft. She sat next to Bolo in the co-pilot's seat whilst he demonstrated how the controls worked, and she showed great interest and understanding in everything he described.

Joyce was amazed when Bolo took her to the Swordfish. She could scarcely believe that this was the front-line aircraft of the Fleet Air Arm and would carry out dive-bombing or torpedo attacks against capital ships at sea or in harbour. She had a lively imagination and she shuddered at the thought of young men going into battle in canvas aircraft.

Lastly, Bolo came to the Proctor, his surprise for her. A neat, small monoplane with two seats in front and two behind enclosed in a comfortable cabin, it was the first aircraft that Joyce thought looked at all modern.

'I hope you're not airsick, Joyce,' said Bolo. 'We are going up in her tomorrow.'

'We? You mean me as well as you?'

'Would you like to?'

'Try to keep me away!'

Joyce flushed with pleasure and excitement at the thought of flying. She had never been up before and the thought of sharing Bolo's world was very appealing.

At lunch, Joyce was impressed with the splendour of the wardroom and the service by Navy stewards. Her own background was modest, and wartime Cambridge had little more than basic service and basic food to offer. Here at Lee the rations, although limited, were served up with a wealth of style and tradition associated with the Navy.

Again, Joyce was the centre of a group of young officers, both in the ante-room over drinks and in the wardroom at lunch. She was surrounded by laughter and gaiety and the war was a long way away.

The next day, dressed in a suit of white overalls that Bolo had acquired for her and equipped with her parachute harness, Joyce sat expectantly next to Bolo. They were at the end of the runway. She admired his professionalism as he went through his pre-flight check, and held on to her seat as he prepared to take off. The ground raced past and she was scarcely aware of it when they were airborne.

Now Bolo was able to show Joyce his world. Riding high above the clouds, she admired their fleecy whiteness. She was impressed with the deep blue of the sky, bluer than she had ever seen it. Far below, the sea looked flat, lined with tiny waves like the furrows of a ploughed field. Bolo pointed out how the larger swell of the sea ran counter to the direction of the waves.

Bolo showed her the aerodrome, now a toy, ten thousand feet below. This was his world, a world of sky and billowy clouds, sunshine and space, and freedom. Joyce enjoyed every minute of it and when they landed she showed her thanks with a spontaneous kiss.

Bolo thought of that kiss now. He had laughed at the time, and dismissed it as girlish enthusiasm. Now he wondered. In the mess, Joyce was very much the woman, admired by the men. Was Joyce possibly in love with him? Well, there was only one way to find out. Bolo's forthright manner asserted itself and he wrote quickly.

My Dearest,

You may be surprised by the title, but this is how I think of you. I have recently returned from a spell in the desert and this has opened my eyes wonderfully. I believe I have always treated you as a kid sister, although I don't think of you as such.

156

My dear, you are my sun and my stars. You are all the world to me. I think of your touch – and your voice, of your hair against my cheek, of your soft lips on mine. I think of you watching the deer in the New Forest, climbing the Devil's Dyke, flying with me in the Proctor. I think of you listening to music, talking of poetry, laughing and gay, sad and serious. You are my life.

More I would say, but only when I hear that you return my love.

I cannot tell you how eagerly I await your reply, my darling,

With all my love,
John

On the second day out, 999 Squadron was ordered to mount a parallel search of seven aircraft. Holy Temple in B – Baker was the extreme right-hand aircraft of the search. Bill Hewitt, his observer, had laid off a course to starboard of *Peregrine* with a first leg of forty-five miles before turning on his search track. Thirty miles along the first leg, he was sweeping the horizon with his binoculars when he saw faint whirls on the surface of the sea, just to starboard of their course.

'Ships at Green one-oh,' he told his pilot. 'I think they must be the convoy.'

'Right! I'll continue on this course,' said Holy. 'Keep your eyes peeled for submarines.'

As they drew nearer, the whirls resolved themselves into ships, three columns of large ships with a protective screen of destroyers. The centre column consisted of large warships and the other two columns were merchant ships. The largest of the warships started flashing to them.

Bill picked up his Aldis lamp and acknowledged the flashing.

'Message from *Ramilies* asking for the position of *Peregrine,*' he told his pilot.

Consulting his chartboard, Bill quickly worked out the position and flashed a reply. To aid Bill, Holy had circled the battleship's column. As B – Baker passed down the line of ships, Bill could see men on the merchant ships waving and cheering. The presence of a Swordfish meant that a strong naval force was close by and this would be reassuring to the sailors below.

Ramilies flashed a thank-you and Holy directed his aircraft back on to the second leg of their search. The contact with the convoy provided a welcome break in the routine of a search flight, most of which were dull affairs, with routine navigation, wireless silence and constant searching by all three crew.

Bolo was not on the search party. Wings required him for fighter patrol. *Peregrine* had added a third Gladiator to its fighter flight, manned by Peter Rawlings, a lieutenant in 998 Squadron. The three Gladiators took it in turn to provide the overhead patrol.

He had relieved Peter and climbed to a height of fifteen thousand feet. Circling the Fleet and keeping an alert lookout all round him had become second nature. He flew the machine instinctively, without conscious thought.

Suddenly, his earphones crackled and the voice of the Fighter Direction Officer broke in on his thoughts.

'Bandits approaching from the port beam, about five miles away. Angels five.'

Bolo quickly spotted them, six Savoias coming in, line abreast, for a torpedo attack.

'Tally-ho,' he called, putting his nose down into a steep dive.

The Savoias had been diving to sea level, and were two miles from their target when Bolo flashed down at them in a beam attack. The fleet anti-aircraft barrage had stopped.

First one enemy plane then another and another were caught as Bolo swept through them, spraying each with his machine-guns. In moments the enemy raid deteriorated into a riot. One plane had gone in and another had retreated with smoke pouring from one of its engines. The remaining four dropped their fish at extreme range and turned away from the Fleet.

Bolo watched them go. His role was to protect the Fleet and he knew that another attack could materialise as quickly as the first. None of the ships had radar and the defences relied purely on a visual sighting. Bolo saw the capital ships turn towards the torpedoes, which passed harmlessly down the sides of the carrier as *Peregrine* combed their tracks.

'Hello Red two. Can you maintain patrol for another half-hour?'

That was the FDO calling up Bolo.

'This is Red two. Affirmative.'

'Climb to fifteen thousand and patrol over the Fleet.'

'Wilco. Over.'

'We shall land you on when the search party returns.'

'Roger. Out.'

So passed another routine day at sea. The night, however, was by no means routine. Both squadrons were to carry out a night attack on Tripoli, one of the most heavily defended ports in Italian North Africa.

Briefing for all crews was at 2000, after an early dinner, when both TBR squadrons assembled in the briefing-room. Wings addressed them first. The main objective of the operation was to destroy or damage merchant shipping in the harbour.

'Tripoli,' he said, 'has become the main supply port for the Italian forces threatening Egypt. Your task is to destroy what shipping you can in the harbour and put the port out of action: 999 Squadron will attack ships and port installations,

159

and under cover of this attack, 998 Squadron will lay mines in the harbour entrance.

'Take-off is at 0400, tomorrow morning.'

He was followed by the Air Staff Officer.

'The latest RAF pictures,' he said, 'show a number of ships lying alongside the mole, with others anchored off, waiting to unload. On the mole are cranes and sheds used for the unloading.

'Each member of 999 Squadron will carry six two-hundred-and-fifty-pound GP bombs and eight incendiaries. You will approach the target at eight thousand feet. Your main task is to hit the ships with your bombs and the port installations with your incendiaries. Your commanding officer will brief you on the attack.

'Then 998 Squadron will follow 999 Squadron and endeavour to lay their mines whilst the defences are engaged with the bombing squadron. You will come in low, at sea level, and drop your mines in the harbour and just outside the harbour entrance. Each of you will carry two mines.

'The timing is important. Tripoli has a good aerodrome and fighter squadrons are known to be there. We cannot risk a daylight raid. At the same time, we are not yet geared to night deck-landings.

'Both squadrons will be ranged on deck, with 999 Squadron flying off first, followed immediately by 998 Squadron. The ship will then be in position eighty miles due north of Tripoli. The Fleet will steer north at twenty knots to meet the eastbound convoy coming from Gibraltar. Your distance back to the carrier will be about one hundred and twenty miles. It will just be daylight by the time you return.'

Lieutenant Commander Simpson was the next to address the squadron.

'I shall drop a flame-float eight miles south of the carrier and circle at one thousand feet so that you can form up on me. We shall proceed in the usual squadron formation of three vics of three, climbing at seventy-five knots to eight thousand feet. I shall flash the letter "A" on my navigation lights and keep them flashing until we reach attack height, when I shall switch off. From then on your only help will be exhaust flames, so maintain a tight formation until we close the target, when I will give the order to form line astern.

'On that order, Lieutenant Hawkins, in K – King, and Sub-Lieutenant Crosby, in M – Mike, will break off, increase speed and make for the landward side of the harbour to drop flares. Hawkins will go in first, dropping flares at intervals of a quarter of a mile. Five minutes later Crosby will follow him. Hawkins and Crosby will bomb independently after dropping their flares.

'Midshipman Compton, in L – Love, will close up astern of C – Charlie and Lieutenant Bidwell will close up with his sub-flight on L – Love.

'I shall endeavour to drop my bombs and incendiaries on the mole to create a fire. That will give you an aiming point. Remember, the principal target is shipping. If you can, drop your bombs on ships and your incendiaries on the shore installations.

'The flares should give us illumination for about ten minutes. That should be time enough for everyone to drop their bombs and for 998 Squadron to drop their mines.'

The CO of 998 Squadron followed Lieutenant Commander Simpson, giving his squadron a careful briefing on the mine-laying operation.

It was pitch dark when Bolo and Dicky Burd walked out to their aircraft. The time was 0345. There was no moon. PO Mercer was already in the aircraft, waiting for them.

Since nightfall, the hangar had been the scene of intense activity. After the earlier search and the day's A/S patrols all aircraft had been thoroughly checked. Armourers had been busy checking guns and loading the aircraft with mines or bombs. An air of intense but suppressed excitement had run through the men, and the banter between aircrews and ground crews had betrayed controlled nerves.

Now all was ready. The two squadrons were assembled on the after end of the flight deck, with wings folded. Shadowy figures moved as fitters gave up their cockpits to the pilots and helped them to strap on parachute harnesses. Observers quietly climbed into their own cockpits and stowed chartboards and navigation equipment. Ground crews stood by to manoeuvre aircraft into position and unfold the wings. The Flight Deck Officer stood motionlessly waiting for a signal. A green was flashed from the bridge and he gave the order to start up. Starter motors whirred to an increasing pitch and eighteen Pegasus engines roared into life. The pilots opened their throttles to test their engines, holding their aircraft in check with chocks and brakes. Cockpit drills were completed. The squadrons were ready.

Slowly the great carrier turned on to its new course, dead into wind. An illuminated wisp of smoke at the forward end of the flight deck was blowing straight down the deck. The time was 0400. On the bridge, Wings flashed a green to the waiting aircraft. At a signal from the Flight Deck Officer, A – Abel started rolling forwards, quickly building up to flying speed. Before he had left the deck, B – Baker was wheeled into position, its wings unfolded and locked, ready to take off. The pilot was given the signal to take off and as soon as he started rolling, C – Charlie was wheeled forwards. And so it went on. One after the other the shadowy planes rumbled forwards until all eighteen were airborne. The ship was strangely quiet as the aircraft disappeared into the night.

As 999 Squadron were now well trained, they had no difficulty in forming up. Dicky Burd informed Bolo that his sub-flight was closing up on him, whilst Bolo formed up on the starboard quarter of the CO's flight. The operation was completed without fuss and soon the squadron was climbing steadily as it made its way south.

At eight thousand feet the CO adjusted his throttle and pitch to maintain a cruising speed of eighty-five knots and switched off his navigation lights. The darkness was almost tangible as Bolo felt his way forwards. The exhaust flare of B – Baker, to starboard of A – Abel, was a mere flicker of blue. 'Abel' itself was almost invisible. Keeping closed up required all Bolo's attention. His two sub-flight aircraft were tucked well in behind his wings, and Dicky Burd watched them rising and falling gently as their pilots strove to maintain position. The slightest error or lack of concentration could cause disaster. Time stood still.

After an hour's flying, the CO gave the pre-arranged signal.

'Time for us to go, Bolo,' said Dicky.

Bolo broke away to starboard, taking M – Mike with him and, putting his nose down slightly, built up a speed of 120 knots.

'Tripoli is five miles ahead,' said Dicky.

Bolo peered, but could see nothing. Suddenly a search-light came on, two miles away on the starboard bow, then another and another until a ring of searchlights fanned the sky. Bolo turned towards them. In their reflected light he saw the harbour beneath him, with the mole stretching away, lined with ships. Guns were firing now, their shell-bursts making his aircraft stagger like a punch-drunk fighter. Flaming onions were piercing the sky in their inverted cones, as multi-barrelled guns opened up. He was past the harbour. It was time to drop the flares.

'Steer east,' called Dicky. 'Start dropping flares – now.'

Dicky watched as the flares burst into incandescent flame at quarter-mile intervals until a string of eight bright lights descended slowly on their parachutes.

'There go the Boss's bombs,' he shouted as flame and

smoke erupted below them. Sheds were soon alight, illuminating the mole, with ships alongside. Bolo saw that groups of three or four ships, were rafted together: some were barges, loaded with stores; others were larger merchantmen, some with tanks on deck.

Then came more explosions below as other aircraft followed their leader. Ack-ack was fierce now, though indiscriminate. The scene was macabre: dozens of searchlights fanning the skies; shell-bursts and purple smoke; incendiaries fired in all directions; a plane silhouetted momentarily against a searchlight; and over all the slowly descending flares.

The second string of flares had been dropped when Bolo went in.

'Going down,' he said in his measured voice. He could see the raft of barges beneath him, five in all. He dropped his incendiaries as he crossed the mole and kicked his aircraft round in a spiralling turn to line up on the barges. His aircraft shuddered as close-range flak hit the wings. Still he kept going until the barges were large in his sights. At five hundred feet he released his bombs and had the satisfaction of seeing them fall across the line of barges. He continued down to sea level, turning to starboard. Now he was underneath the shells and the bullets and sneaking out through the harbour entrance to sea.

Sandy Sandiford was pleased with himself. The lights of the flares ahead of him showed that his navigation had been spot on. It was the CO's turn now. Taranto had given Sandy enormous confidence in the Boss. It had shown Lieutenant Commander Simpson to be what he was, a mature, confident, thoroughly professional naval officer. Now the Boss pressed on steadily, ignoring the increasing ack-ack. Into the harbour he went, making straight for the mole. He must have assessed the situation immediately, for without deviating he went into his dive and Sandy could see the port installations on the mole revolving above his pilot's head.

'Bombs gone!'

Sandy felt the judder as the bombs were released and then the CO was pulling out in a violent corkscrew turn. Behind him he saw the buildings burst into flame. The barges and ships alongside were revealed in the glare. As they passed down the mole and out to sea, CPO Cutter sprayed searchlights and machine-gun nests with his Lewis gun.

Holy Temple had followed his CO into the attack. Bill Hewitt found himself mesmerised by the scene. The flares, the fire, the shell-bursts, the flaming tracers created a scene out of Dante's *Inferno*. Which level of hell was this? Bill knew there was nothing he could do to help. He was in the hands of his pilot and he was glad his pilot was Holy Temple. Holy was cool and professional, picking his target carefully, twisting and swerving to avoid searchlights and flak, and dropping his bombs across the merchant ships.

Killer Compton was fourth in the line-up. He went in fast in a screaming dive and when he pulled away his bombs had not released.

'I'm going round again,' he called, and Snowball knew Killer was fully recovered from his injury and was himself again.

It seemed impossible for Killer to get round and gain height, but this he did, using all his undoubted skill to avoid disaster. He climbed to two thousand feet and made a shallow dive at the mole, releasing his bombs at five hundred feet. This time the bombs came away and added to the destruction.

Bing Crosby was the last to go in. He was no longer the jittery, nervous officer of the first raid, on Tobruk. Action had matured him, had steeled his nerves. Following Harold Lloyd's directions, he dropped his flares competently above the line of Bolo's flares just before they went out. He was now on his own. Ships and buildings were well ablaze. Anti-aircraft fire and searchlights were directed horizontally as the Italians sought to bracket the departing aircraft and Bing was able to approach his target unmolested. He picked a troopship at the extreme end of the mole and, in an almost leisurely fashion, planted his stick of bombs across its stern.

The raid was over. The mines were laid. All the aircraft had got away safely – but not unscathed. Dawn found them straggling across the sky as pilots wearily made their way back to the carrier.

Now it was the turn of the observers. Each was responsible for his own navigation, his task to find a moving target, a hundred and twenty miles away, in the faint light of dawn.

Slowly they came out of the darkness, some of them limping. The CO's aircraft had been hit by the fragments of a nearby shell-burst. Killer's tail plane was damaged and Bolo had a dozen bullet holes in his wings.

However, they were safe, and a weary but jubilant squadron sat down to the traditional breakfast. Tripoli would be out of action for many days.

Chapter 14

In Support of Wavell

The day before *Peregrine* was due to return to Alexandria she received a signal from the C-in-C.

'*Peregrine* squadrons to be disembarked to Dekheila for operations in the Western Desert.'

The sea and the sand! Bolo thought how amphibious the squadron was becoming. One set of operations at sea, with A/S patrols, searches and attacks against shipping, with the ordered life of the carrier, cabins and bathrooms, regular meals served by stewards in the wardroom, and excellent hangar facilities for maintenance, was followed by another set of operations in the desert, with rough living in tents, scratch meals, sand and grit in your food and in your engine, and primitive maintenance.

A further signal ordered 999 Squadron to fly from Dekheila to a forward base from which they would carry out the first week's operations in support of General Wavell's offensive. They would be relieved by 998 Squadron at the end of a week.

Repairs to the damaged aircraft had been completed, the maintenance crews again working at maximum pressure. Bolo, as Senior Pilot, was responsible for the maintenance of the squadron aircraft and he drove himself and the maintenance crews remorselessly. He was encouraged by Tom Stillson, who never seemed to take time off for sleeping or feeding, and by the cheerful support of fitters and riggers like Bailey and Rawlings, his own crew. The mainplane of A – Abel, the CO's aircraft, was removed and replaced; the holes in the wings of Bolo's Swordfish, K – King, were patched up with canvas and doped; the tail plane of L – Love, Killer's Swordfish, was also replaced. All the aircraft were given an overhaul, engines serviced, controls and electrics checked, guns, all of which had been fired in the recent operation, removed and serviced, ammunition replaced. Bolo and Chiefy were determined to have the aircraft on top line for whatever desert operations were required.

A great change had come over Dekheila since Bolo had first known it. As he followed his CO's sub-flight in to land, he could see the new control tower at the end of the runway. The runway itself had been reinforced by steel mesh. The Royal Navy had taken over the Egyptian barracks on the airfield and renamed the air station *HMS Grebe*. The Fleet Air Arm squadrons now had the full use of brick-constructed buildings, with a wardroom and cabins for the officers and dormitories and mess decks for the men. Buses, renamed liberty boats, ran into Alexandria at regular times. The day was organised into watches, the same as on the *Peregrine*, and a free afternoon was called a 'make and mend'.

On their first afternoon ashore 999 Squadron was given a make and mend and Killer took the opportunity of telephoning Ann.

'Can you come dancing?' he asked.

A long pause was the response.

At length, 'Well, I'm off duty tonight. I'll come if I can bring a friend.'

'That's okay by me. Who's the friend?'

'Janet. You met her at the Sporting Club.'

'I remember. She was Bill Hewitt's partner. I'll ask him if he'd like to come, too.'

Within a few minutes, Killer reserved a table at the Carlton

Hotel and sought out Bill Hewitt, who agreed to make up the fourth. This was a time to throw off the cares of war. Killer meant to enjoy whatever Alexandria had to offer. He had something to celebrate. The day before they left the *Peregrine* had been his twentieth birthday and consequently the end to being a midshipman. He had been prepared for this and had brought gold half rings and sub lieutenant's epaulettes from Gieves with him in *Illustrious*. His steward had worked wonders, removing the purple patches from the lapels of his uniform and sewing the rings on the arms.

Adjusting his bow tie and giving his lapels a flick to remove an imaginary speck of dust, he turned to Bill.

'How do I look?' he asked.

'Like a midshipman who has just been promoted to sub lieutenant. I can see the cream on your whiskers.'

Killer offered a gentle swipe at his friend as the two of them hurried out to catch the liberty bus.

They called at the hospital and greeted the girls dressed in their evening gowns, Ann in powder-blue tulle and Janet in honey-coloured satin, then rode in a gharry through the ancient and distinctly Middle Eastern streets of Alexandria. The Egyptian doorkeeper, in white jellabah and red fez, greeted them, and they were aware of the glitter of the tables, the soft lights of the restaurant and the quiet music as they were shown to their table. The table Killer had booked was close to the dance floor. As Bill helped Janet into her chair, a quick vision of his home in North London, a terraced house in a poor street, flashed across his memory and was gone. He had come a long way since then.

Killer, influenced by his promotion, was in full swing, entertaining and amusing as he chattered to the two girls. Bill was in a quieter mood, as if under a spell, drinking in the new experiences. He brightened with the table-talk and began to enjoy the meal. He did not trust himself in the choice of wine and left that to Killer, who, though his

169

knowledge was little more than Bill's, dealt with their order confidently. They all enjoyed the floorshow, the singing and the dance routines. However, it was when the ballroom-dancing started that Bill came into his own. He danced with both of the girls and they enjoyed dancing with him. Gradually, under the influence of the food and the wine, the small talk and the dancing, he became intoxicated with the atmosphere and let himself float along as if in a dream. In the last waltz the lights were turned down, and Janet pressed herself closer to him, following his lazy, sensual steps. Bill became intensely aware of the sexual attraction of the girl, the scent of her hair, the soft breasts, the curve of her stomach and thighs enclosing him. He felt his manhood rising and becoming hard against the girl and he became embarrassed and drew away from her.

Janet sensed his unease. She realised that although he was intelligent and clever, in experience and sophistication he was young, even innocent for his age, and this had endeared him to her. Gently she pulled him forward until again their bodies touched. Bill began to relax and enjoy the sensation and his dancing became even dreamier. Janet laid her cheek against his, and in the darkness he kissed her hair, as the dance drew slowly to a close.

Bill retained his dreamlike state throughout the journey back to the hospital, leaving Killer to take charge. Killer had enjoyed his evening, carrying the party with him. Expertly he dealt with the waiters and the cloakroom attendants, the doorman and the gharry driver. It was a good night for him. He was now a sub lieutenant. He had enjoyed good company and a good meal. He was very attracted to Ann and she seemed to respond to him. Life was good.

Bill wondered whether he could kiss Janet goodnight. Surreptitiously in the gharry he had tucked Janet's arm in his own, and had felt the soft swell of her breast against it. In the dark shade of the shrubs outside the hospital door he covertly noticed Killer boldly taking Ann into his arms. And then it was all so simple. Without any volition on his part he found Janet in his arms, her mouth against his. He felt the tentative thrust of her tongue against his lips and then he surrendered himself to the embrace.

Wing Commander Barker greeted the CO as soon as he landed at Fuka and invited him with his senior pilot and senior observer to drinks in his tent. Fuka had changed since Bolo was last there. As with Dekheila, a steel mesh had been laid down to reinforce the runway, and more bunkers for aircraft had been built. Some of them were occupied by a squadron of Wellingtons and two squadrons of Hurricanes that had been flown in on the trans-African route from Takoradi on the Gold Coast.

When the CO, Bolo and Sandy were ensconced with their drinks in the wicker chairs the airstrip now boasted, the Wing Commander told them his news.

'The convoy from Gibraltar you escorted brought guns, tanks and armoured cars for General Wavell's offensive,' he said. 'This is to commence at dawn the day after tomorrow. Your squadron is to be used in a softening-up process. Each night, before the dawn operation begins, the Army has asked for one of your aircraft to overfly the enemy lines at Sidi Barrani, dropping one bomb every ten minutes precisely. With nine aircraft you can maintain the bombardment for nine hours, say from 2000 to 0500 the next morning.'

The naval officers looked at each other in consternation. The CO spoke for them all.

'That's a tall order. One aircraft flying over enemy lines for an hour! What targets will they be dive-bombing? A single aircraft will be shot out of the sky.'

'They won't be dive-bombing and they won't be attacking any targets. The idea is to circle around Sidi Barrani at their

171

maximum height and drop a bomb from that height any-where on the Italian lines. Just imagine what it will do to the enemy. All night long, precisely at ten-minute intervals, a bomb will come hurtling out of the sky. They will all know that it will hit their lines somewhere, but no one will know where. Just imagine what it will do to their morale.'

'It will certainly keep them awake,' said Simpson. 'But isn't the risk too much for my boys?'

'It isn't so risky as you think. The Italians have no search-lights at the front and no night fighters or radar in the vicinity. Your Swordfish will be flying at, what, ten thousand feet overhead. They can fly off into the desert or out to sea for five minutes and come back to drop their bomb.'

'All right, we'll give it a try. When do we start?'

'Tomorrow night. Wavell's offensive will begin the next morning.'

Lieutenant Commander Savage allowed his squadron time to settle in in their billets and to check the picketing and servicing of their aircraft, then he called a briefing meeting in the mess tent for 1500 hours.

A curious and somewhat apprehensive group of pilots, observers and air-gunners assembled for the briefing.

'The Fleet Air Arm has been asked to do some odd jobs,' the CO began, 'but this one is the oddest.'

He then went on to tell them about the night's operation.

'I shall start the proceedings at 2000,' he concluded 'and you will follow in squadron order.' He gave the floor to his Senior Observer.

'Each aircraft is on his own in this one,' said Sandy. 'Each observer is responsible for the timing and accuracy of the bombing. We are approximately eighty miles from the target. You will take off an hour and a quarter before your first bomb is to be released – that will allow time to climb to ten thousand feet. Your navigation must be spot on. There is little moon tonight and what there is will probably be obscured by clouds, so you will have no landmarks to guide you. This will be good for us, but it needs exact navigation from the observers and accurate steering from the pilots.

'Immediately you have released your last bomb, you will set course for home. As soon as we hear you over this airstrip the landing-lights will go on. Wireless silence will be maintained throughout the operation. The name of the game is "stealth".'

It was a dark night, with a bleak wind blowing sand across the runway, as Bolo watched the winking lights of A – Abel disappear over the desert. Bolo pulled his scarf closer round his neck and made his way over to B – Baker, which was being fuelled by its maintenance crew. C – Charlie stood nearby, with mechanics working on its engine under subdued arc lights. The remaining aircraft stood waiting in a line that disappeared into the darkness.

Bolo shivered. This was one of the most difficult tasks the squadron had undertaken. In all previous operations there had been a sense of fellowship, of shared danger. On this operation, as Sandy had said, you were on your own, and Bolo's thoughts were with A – Abel as he made his way back to the mess tent.

In A – Abel, Sandy was concentrating on his task. Since Taranto he had great confidence in his pilot. The CO was flying most carefully. Whenever Sandy glanced at the compass or speedometer he saw that the Boss was dead on course and exactly maintaining the required speed. As the altitude increased, the temperature dropped. In the open cockpit he was glad to be wearing his Sidcot suit with the stuffed inner suit and his fleece-lined flying-boots. Even so, he shivered and huddled well down on his stool to make himself warmer.

'Ten thousand feet,' came the voice of the CO.

'Right! Maintain a speed of eighty knots. We're fifteen miles from the target.'

Sandy peered over the sides of his cockpit at the blackness beneath. Not a thing moved. Not a light betrayed any glimmer of the enemy. Sandy could see the hunched figure of the CO in front and the silent, shadowy figure of CPO Cutter in the TAG's cockpit, absorbed and concentrating on his wireless set. They were in a world of their own.

Where was the enemy? From the briefing, he knew that the enemy line, east of Sidi Barrani, stretched for ten miles from the coast southwards into the desert. A – Abel was approaching this line obliquely from the south-east.

'Target five miles.'

Sandy sounded more confident than he felt. If this were an enemy harbour, anti-aircraft fire would have started by now from ships and port defences. From the briefing, he knew that the enemy lines consisted of trenches and earthworks where Italians would be waiting for their advance on Egypt. Behind them would be lines of tanks and armoured cars ready to press forward when the offensive began. Where were they? The time was 1959. In one minute they were due to drop their first bomb. Where was the enemy?

A shell burst a quarter of a mile away to starboard, suddenly and dramatically. Then another and another, until all along the line flashes marked the position of the enemy troops.

'Bomb gone!'

The CO had started the long night's work. Sandy saw the bomb-burst below, a brighter flash than those of the guns. To the north, searchlights were suddenly switched on, a dozen of them quartering the sky aimlessly.

'Now we know exactly where we are,' cried Sandy as he took a bearing of them. 'Those are the searchlights surrounding the harbour.'

The CO directed his Swordfish away from the enemy lines before turning back. The searchlights were still searching, fruitlessly, giving him an accurate position. The enemy guns, however, began to falter and then die away completely.

174

At 2010 the CO dropped his second bomb into the black void beneath him.

The flash beneath heralded another outburst of firing, which started below them and proceeded along the enemy line until the whole front was firing. The harbour particularly had a brilliant display, with shell-bursts and flaming onions and no doubt close-range ack-ack.

A – Abel was well away, back over the desert, with its occupants enjoying a ringside seat of the spectacle.

Again the firing died away and again the CO turned back over the enemy lines. At 2020 he dropped his third bomb and again firing started up all along the line. Each time they dropped a bomb the firing recommenced, only to fade after a few minutes.

'There's no doubt about it,' said Sandy, after the last bomb had gone, 'we may not be hitting anything but we're certainly keeping them awake.'

'Yes, that is the objective,' the CO commented. 'I'm going to hang around south of the enemy for ten minutes to see that B – Baker follows up.'

Sandy carefully noted the position where 'Abel' was circling, well clear of enemy gunfire. At 2100 an explosion flared across the sky ten miles to the north of them.

'Good!' said the CO. 'Holy Temple is on the ball. Now we can leave for home.'

As they turned eastwards, Sandy thought of the thousands of British and Commonwealth soldiers assembled just north of their flight path, waiting for the big offensive at dawn. Was their bombing having a useful effect? Did the Italians know that an offensive was building up? Sandy had always been a student of strategy. As they flew back across the desert he thought of the events of the past month, the early desert raids on Bardia and Sollum, the attack on Tripoli, the convoy of men and arms for Wavell's army, the build-up of the RAF at Fuka, and now their softening-up operation.

Great events were taking place. Britain sorely needed a victory: was this about to happen and change the course of history?

He glanced at his watch. The time was 2150. Behind him Holy Temple would be dropping his ten-minute bombs. Somewhere nearby, Hatters Dunn in C – Charlie was passing in the opposite direction, to maintain the all-night pressure on the Eyeties. His tired eyes caught the glimmer of the lights ahead.

'The landing-strip is about seven miles ahead,' he said to his pilot.

'Good show, Sandy, and well done!'

Bolo was waiting for the CO on his return. Leaving Chiefy and the maintenance crew to deal with the aircraft, he walked with the flying-crew of 'Abel' to the mess tent, where the remainder of the squadron were waiting.

'What was it like, sir?'

'How did you make out?'

'Was there much flak?'

A chorus of questions greeted the CO and Sandy as they entered the mess.

'First things first,' said Bolo, pouring out drinks.

'Well, chaps,' the CO began, sipping his drink, 'it's not too bad. There was lots of flak, but most of it was nowhere near us. A bonus of this operation is that the Eyeties are using up a good deal of their ammunition without much chance of hitting anything.'

He then explained his tactics, how each bomb had raised a storm of flak all along the line, only to die off and be renewed when his next bomb was dropped. Most of the time he had spent circling outside the range of their guns.

Sandy explained how the flak had given away the enemy positions and how the searchlights at the harbour had given him his position. A method of carrying out the operation had developed and this was to be followed by all aircraft.

It was Biddy Bidwell's turn to take off in F – Fox, and the CO walked with him to his aircraft.

'We appreciated your advice, Boss,' Biddy said as they made their way. 'I think there were a few stomach flutterings – probably fear of the unknown. Now we know what to expect, everyone is happier.'

'Well, have a good flight, Biddy. I'll stay up tonight to see this through. We can always rest during the day.'

Throughout the night the bombing continued. Aircraft after aircraft, bomb after bomb, the operation was relentless. By the time Bing Crosby dropped his last bomb, dawn was just over the horizon. They had been told to return on a line across the desert, ten miles from the coast. They had scarcely turned inland when the desert to the north of them erupted. Hundreds of guns had opened up on a pre-arranged signal. The desert was alive with the flash of firing and thousands of shells poured on to the Italian lines. General Wavell's offensive had begun.

As they crept eastwards, the crew of M – Mike felt awed and humbled by the spectacle below them. Thousands of men were locked in a bloody war of attrition. Already, the Italians were opening up in reply. How eager were they for the fight? Had 999 Squadron's operation had any effect on them? Bing Crosby and Harold Lloyd and Leading Airman Davy discussed what they were seeing all the way back to their base.

Chapter 15

Capture

Bill Hewitt felt and looked very tired as he prepared to take off. The squadron had been in the desert for six days and this was his third operation; only one more and they would be relieved by 998 Squadron. Would he find the energy to dance? He thought of Janet and the Carlton and they seemed a very long way away.

He thought, too, of the momentous events of the past week. From their first attack the British and Indian divisions had fought with spirit and determination, driving the Italians back. The Seventh British Armoured Division had pushed its way forward round the rear of the retreating Italians and had reached the sea, cutting off the Italian forces in Sidi Barrani. With the help of a naval bombardment, the Army had inflicted severe losses on the Italians and the resistance of those caught in the pocket had crumbled. Hundreds of guns, tanks and armoured cars had been captured and thousands of Italians taken prisoner.

The remaining Italian troops, still a formidable force, were retreating westwards to Bugbug and Sollum. They were putting up a strong resistance. In their first two bombing operations at Sidi Barrani, the night bombing by 999 Squadron had had a considerable effect on the Italians who, wide-eyed and weary by the morning, had had to face an unstoppable foe. The set positions had been breached. The war was now more fluid. The Italian Army had begun to regroup near Bir Sheferzen, south of Sollum, and 999 Squadron was again called in to assist.

The CO had left an hour before Holy Temple was ready to take off. Bill was occupying the TAG's cockpit, facing aft. He could feel his head pressing against the auxiliary petrol tank in the observer's cockpit. This was the same type of unarmoured aluminium tank the Fleet Air Arm had used at Taranto. The distances now were too great for the normal endurance of the Swordfish, so the auxiliary petrol tanks had been fitted. As well as navigating, Bill would have to maintain a wireless watch. He expected to be airborne for at least five hours, cramped and cold in an open, unheated cockpit. At ten thousand feet in winter, even in North Africa, the temperature would drop to freezing-point.

'All set?' came Holy's voice.

'Ready and willing! ' Bill replied, shrugging off his gloom.

They were off. The outward journey was uneventful. Holy climbed slowly to ten thousand feet, following the road from Sidi Barrani to Sollum. Even at night-time evidence of the aftermath of battle could be seen. From time to time they passed vehicles with dimmed lights, either singly or in convoy, moving westwards. Other convoys, probably containing prisoners or wounded, moved eastwards. At Sidi Barrani lights in the harbour showed that the port was being restored to use. As they approached Bir Sheferzen the lights diminished in number and then ceased altogether. They were now in darkness. Bill knew their target was between Bir Sheferzen and Sollum but he was not sure of the exact position. They were only ten miles away and there was no sign of activity. He began to worry about his navigation.

'I can see a bomb-burst ahead, about eight miles,' called Holy.

'That must be the CO's last bomb. Make for that position.'

Not another light showed. The Italians had learned their lesson. They were not giving anything away.

'Nine o'clock coming up. Stand by. Drop.' In a tense voice Bill gave his instructions.

'Bomb gone.' Holy's voice was steady.

Bill looked over the side at the blackness beneath him. Then he saw the flash of the bomb, faint and insignificant. It was as if they were bombing a continent – dropping a bomb on Africa.

The Italians made no reply to the attack and Bill could only assume that they had hit nothing significant. Were they even over the enemy lines?

The second and third bombs had a similar effect. Holy did not even bother to leave the vicinity. He circled round where he was. No one was firing at him.

The fourth bomb was different. It burst with a tremendous explosion and a huge sheet of flame. They must have hit an ammunition or petrol dump. The effect was immediate. Guns opened up all round them and they were caught in an intense barrage of bursting shells. The Swordfish rocked violently from nearby shell-bursts, and Holy threw it into a violent corkscrew dive to escape. He had no chance. A shell burst close by and the engine stopped, hit by a fragment. A splinter from the same shell just missed the auxiliary tank, but clipped Bill's shin. He uttered a cry of pain and felt for his leg. The Sidcot was in shreds and his hand came away wet and sticky with blood.

'We've had it,' cried Holy. 'Get your parachute on.'

Bill felt for his parachute, clipped on the bulkhead beside him. It was in pieces.

'No go, I'm afraid, Holy. My parachute's had it.'

A long pause that seemed all the longer for the strange silence of the aircraft. The plane was gliding down, engineless, still under Holy's control.

'Stay put. I'll try to land the damn thing. I'll get rid of the two bombs first.'

Bill felt the twitch in the plane as the bombs were released and the angle of glide became less steep.

'We've got one chance,' cried Holy. 'I'm going to land near that fire. There might be a road and there is some illumination. Strap yourself in and hold tight. If we do land, get out quickly in case she blows up.'

'Okay, Holy. Good luck.'

Bill's voice was surprisingly calm. Death was just round the corner, but he did not give it a thought. He watched Holy bring his aircraft down in a spiral round the glare of the fire. At first the flak became more intense, and then died away as if the Italians had realised that the plane was no longer a danger.

The wind was whistling through the struts. Bill had forgotten the pain in his leg. He had forgotten the petrol tank in front of him as he faced forward and watched the approaching flames. Five thousand feet; four thousand; three thousand; two thousand. Still nothing but flames. One thousand. And then Bill saw the gleam of tanks and cars reflected in the flames and the figures of running men. And there was the road, stretching below them with nothing on it.

Holy brought the plane round in a stomach-churning turn, side-slipped and was pulling back on his joy stick, yards above the road. Then they were down, with the flames to one side of them, Holy braking sharply.

'Out as quick as you can,' Holy gasped.

Bill unhooked himself from his safety strap, unplugged his gosport tubes and clambered over the side, collapsing in the road. Holy was quickly after him, dragging him to one side, away from the aircraft. Bill could see the uniformed men converging on them. Holy had retained the pistol they were each equipped with for desert operations. Pulling it out now, he aimed deliberately at the auxiliary tank. His aim was good. The aircraft exploded in flame. Then he turned to face their captors and proffered his pistol.

The two British officers were ringed by a crowd of armed men. One of them, an officer by his uniform, stepped forward and took the pistol. The men were talking excitedly but they did not appear to be threatening.

Holy gestured towards Bill, lying beside him.

'This officer is wounded – leg – hit by shell.'

In the darkness he was illustrating his words with body actions. A torchlight from one of the onlookers cut the darkness and illuminated Bill's leg. It looked a mess – the leg of his Sidcot and the top of his flying boot were torn and covered in blood. Bill himself looked white and drawn. There was a gasp from the crowd and renewed muttering, but the sound was gentle, even sympathetic.

'I – get – help,' said the officer, speaking his words carefully.

A messenger was sent off and a few minutes later a stretcher party appeared. One of the orderlies carefully cut away the clothing and cleared up the wound, applying a rough dressing. He fixed a tourniquet to stop further bleeding. Some of the onlookers appeared to want to touch Bill's shoulder as if to identify themselves with the wounded Britisher. Then Bill was carried off to a hospital tent whilst Holy was escorted to a marquee.

Holy found himself taken before a colonel, seated at a table with an army captain on either side of him. Politely he was asked to sit down.

'Would you like a drink?' the colonel asked, in good English, offering a brandy bottle.

Holy nodded his assent.

'What is your name and rank?' the colonel asked.

'Sub Lieutenant Temple RN.'

'And your unit?'

'I am not allowed to tell you.'

'But you are Fleet Air Arm. I can see that from your wings,' said the colonel, pointing to the wings on Holy's sleeve.

'Yes, sir. I am Fleet Air Arm.'

'And your aircraft was a Swordfish.'

There was little point in denying this. The wreck of the Swordfish was there for all to see.

'Yes, sir.'

'You did very well at Taranto. Are you from *Illustrious*?'

'I am not allowed to say, sir.'

'Very well. Why do you bomb us, one bomb every ten minutes?'

'I am not allowed to say.'

'Do you come from an aircraft carrier?'

'I am not allowed to say.'

'Very well. I respect your silence. You will join a party of prisoners and be taken back to Tripoli. From there you will be taken to Italy.'

'What about my observer, Midshipman Hewitt?'

'Midshipman? How can he be flying on operations. He is only a boy.'

'He is nineteen, sir, man enough to do a good job. Will I be able to see him?'

The colonel nodded. 'I will arrange for you to see him as soon as the doctor has finished.'

'Thank you, sir.' The interview was over and Holy stood up. Surprisingly, the colonel also rose to his feet and offered his hand.

'I was in England for five years,' he said, as he shook hands. 'I learned many English ways.'

'That explains why your English is good, sir.'

When Holy was taken to the hospital tent he found Bill sitting up in bed, with his leg swathed in bandages. He looked surprisingly cheerful.

'How are you, Bill?'

'Not as bad as I thought. The wound is only superficial – it looked worse than it was. Some of the skin has gone and there's a small nick in the shinbone. The doc thinks I'll

183

be walking tomorrow. Would you like some coffee?'

Holy nodded.

'Gino, Gino!' Bill called.

A grinning sick-berth attendant, dressed in a white smock, approached the bed.

'Coffee, Gino. Café for my friend. Two cups.' Bill illustrated what he wanted by drinking an imaginary cup of coffee.

'Si, signor. Caffè.'

Gino hurried away.

'He doesn't speak English,' said Bill, 'but he's very friendly. In fact they are all friendly, considering what we're doing to them.'

'I found the same thing,' said Holy.

'It looks as though we've had the war,' Bill said, sadly.

'I'm not so sure of that,' said Holy. 'I've got an idea or two. Hang on to your helmet and your gosport tubes. You may need them.'

Bill looked at Holy, but before he could speak Gino returned with two coffees.

'Thank you, Gino,' began Bill.

His words were cut short by a loud explosion, not far away. Gino threw himself beneath a bed.

'That's the third I've heard,' said Holy. 'It must be Hatters Dunn. He's the next one over the target.'

'It makes me jump each time I hear it,' said Bill. 'I'd hate to be in the Italian Army with this going on.'

'Well, you'll have to put up with it, at least tonight. Tomorrow they're taking us back to Tripoli in a convoy of prisoners.'

The next morning Holy and Bill found themselves joining the party of prisoners. Some were officers; most were soldiers. There were about fifty all told. Voices betrayed their origins, British, Australian and Indian. About half of the prisoners were wounded. Guards, carrying rifles or light

184

machine-guns, shepherded them towards three waiting lorries. About sixteen men with two guards mounted each lorry. An armoured car contained more guards.

Holy took a last look at B – Baker as he passed the Swordfish. The nose was still intact, but the after end of the aircraft was a shambles. The precious IFF was completely destroyed. Beyond the aircraft were the remains of a petrol dump. Bits of tin strewed the ground, with charred wood everywhere. There was no sign of any petrol.

Holy made sure he was next to Bill as they climbed into the lorries and set off to captivity. Their first stop for the night was at Bir el Gubi, an oasis in the desert. The men were tired and thirsty. The open trucks gave no protection from the glare of the sand or the dust of the desert. Some of the worst wounded were moaning with pain and discomfort.

The prisoners were herded into a wire compound that had been prepared for them, and two guards patrolled the wire fence all night, their rifles at the ready. Holy's eyes were everywhere, looking for a means of escape.

'If we're going to get out of this, Bill, we've got to do it sooner rather than later. It's a long walk back to our lines. Do you think that you can make it?'

'I'm certainly willing to try. Anything is better than captivity.'

'Be prepared for anything. If we get half a chance, we'll take it.'

Their chance came sooner than Holy expected. The next day, the convoy of lorries was passing alongside some steep sand hills. Holy could see an armoured car coming from across the desert. Probably an escort, he thought. Suddenly the armoured vehicle opened up with machine-gun fire. An order was given in Italian and the Italian armoured car turned to face the intruder whilst the guards urged the prisoners to leave the trucks and take cover by the sand cliff.

'It's a long-range army patrol,' cried a British Army captain. 'I've heard of them but never seen them. They range far behind the enemy lines, looking for trouble.'

'This is our chance, Bill,' said Holy urgently, pointing to a depression in a corner by the sand cliff. 'Lie down in the depression and I'll get some of the army lads to cover us up with sand. Use your gosport tubes as an air tube.'

The Army captain quickly understood what Holy had in mind, and whilst the Italian guards were facing outwards, firing at the enemy patrol car, he had a dozen men scooping sand with their hands over the two naval officers, until they were both completely covered. He arranged the gosport tubes so that only an end of each was showing, and these he hid beneath lumps of hard sand. The area was sufficiently scuffed by the feet of the prisoners to disguise any marks left by the movement of sand.

The action ended as suddenly as it began. The British armoured car turned fast on its tracks and disappeared into the desert. The Italians hurriedly waved their prisoners back into the trucks and set off once more to the west. It did not occur to them to count their prisoners.

For Bill, the half-hour underground was a time of torment. At first he found no difficulty in breathing: the gosport tube was most effective; but he had a terrible feeling of claustrophobia. Any minute he expected a heavy foot to tread on his face and cut off his air supply. His eyes and mouth were tightly closed. His nose was filled with sand. He found himself gasping for breath and had to force himself to breathe evenly through his mouth and give the tubes a chance. He wanted above everything to push upwards and break free. His leg gave him a burning sensation and he began to feel a rising hysteria. How long could he hold out? He gritted his teeth and brought his nerves under control. He felt the shake of the sand as the prisoners moved away. Then there was silence. He waited. He must not break out too soon – before the Italians left. He could not trust himself. He must leave it to Holy.

The agony ended when he felt the movement next to him and Holy's hand, brushing the sand away from his face.

'We've made it, Bill,' said Holy, pulling his friend free. 'All we've got to do now is to walk back to Sidi Barrani. Do you know how far it is from here?'

Bill thought for a moment and pictured his last chart.

'I would guess about a hundred miles,' he said.

'Well, we'd better get started,' Holy exclaimed.

It was hot, but not too hot. As it was mid-winter the sun was low and sometimes obscured by cloud. Encouraged by Holy, Bill tramped eastwards, limping as he went. His leg was painful and felt hot and inflamed, and he was becoming thirsty.

Holy picked a route that followed the sand hills. 'If we see any suggestion of the enemy, a dust cloud for instance, we can make for the hills and hide.'

They found signs of the enemy's presence. At one place they came across what must have been an enemy camp. Amongst the litter, Holy found an empty wine bottle.

'We'll keep this,' he said. 'It might come in handy.'

The sun reached its zenith and began its slow decline – slow for the two airmen as they plodded slowly eastwards. The horizon shimmered emptily ahead of them. Behind them their erratic footsteps told their own tale. Bill was finding it increasingly difficult to steer a straight course. His leg was on fire and this had probably caused his body temperature to rise. He was sweating and his shoulders were bowed under the strain.

He made no protest, however. Mostly, he followed two paces behind Holy, staring at Holy's feet. His mind began to wander over past events. Janet featured strongly in them. Janet and the Carlton dance floor. As he walked, his steps seemed to take on the pattern of a dance step, a slow foxtrot.

He thought of Janet in his arms, dancing with him as if she were part of him, Janet responding to his need and relaxing him, Janet's softness against his hardness, Janet in the darkness responding to his kisses. Janet.

Bill thought of his home and his strict upbringing. His parents were Catholics, his mother a devout one. Bill himself had served at the altar at mass every morning in the years before joining the Fleet Air Arm. He wanted to make love with Janet, but he knew he would not. He no longer attended mass, but his experience in the Catholic Church had given him a strong sense of right and wrong, of moral responsibility. Sex was the sublime act of love and belonged only where love was lasting, where it could be blessed by marriage and family. This was how Bill had been brought up and the bonds of his upbringing were too strong for him to break.

Janet came from a wealthier background. A stockbroker's daughter was far beyond Bill's humble expectations. He was living on his midshipman's pay and this was, almost all of it, required to pay his mess bills. It was only long spells at sea or in the desert that allowed him to save the money for an evening out. How could he ever meet Janet's expectations?

As he struggled with the journey and with his emotions, Bill felt a subtle change come over him. His mind cleared. He would not give way to his physical pain. He would not give in to his emotional stress. Strength flooded through him and his shoulders straightened. He was at a low point. Things could only get better.

Just before dusk Bill was jerked into full alertness by Holy's shout.

'What's that ahead?'

Bill raised his head and gazed at the hump, indistinct in the half-light. They approached cautiously and found it to be an abandoned car. Holy jumped inside and pressed the starter. There was no life at all in the battery. Never mind there might be life for them under the bonnet. Yes, the radiator had some water left in it.

Carefully filling his wine bottle, Holy offered a drink to Bill and then himself. They drank slowly of the life-giving fluid and refilled the bottle as soon as they had emptied it.

'We'll spend the night here,' said Holy. 'We can drink more water in the morning and there is enough in this radiator for one more refill.'

Holy chose a spot in a hollow by the sand cliff where they were unable to see the car.

'If we can't see the car,' he said cheerfully, 'no one will be able to see us.'

Bill sank on to the soft sand, exhausted by the long march and his injured leg. His spirits were high, however, and he was confident they would reach safety. He was content to rely on Holy's leadership. They had come through the crash off *Peregrine*'s deck and the forced landing yesterday, and they would escape from their present predicament. He talked over the situation quietly with Holy until darkness covered the desert. Then he fell asleep.

The next morning both men felt refreshed and ready for the day. They finished off the water in the wine bottle and Holy refilled it with the last of the water from the radiator.

'How far do you think we've come?' Holy asked.

Bill was still the navigator, as far as he was concerned.

'I shouldn't think we averaged more than two knots, and taking out our rests we walked for about five hours. I would say we covered ten miles.'

'I doubt whether we can manage more than fifteen miles a day in our condition,' said Holy.

'That means about six more days' march,' said Bill.

'Right. We've drunk well here, so we'll ration the water from now on. We'll try to make the bottle last two days and hope to find some more on the way.'

'We can make for Bir Sheferzen. There's a well there

and with any luck it might now be occupied by the British Army.'

In the event, they did not have to wait so long. British long-range patrols were out in force and they were picked up by one on the second day of their march. Bill was the first to spot it.

'Take cover,' he shouted, pointing at the approaching cloud of dust.

As it drew closer their keen eyes both spotted the Union Flag flying.

'It's one of ours,' cried Holy, running out on to the track and waving his arms.

The armoured car slithered to a halt beside them and a young army lieutenant jumped out.

'Hello, chaps. What are you doing here?'

'Are we glad to see you!'

The exclamations were shouted simultaneously as the naval officers ran forward and grasped the hand of the soldier.

'We've got a problem,' said Holy and pointed to Bill's leg.

'Right. We can deal with that. Fortunately, we're at the end of our patrol. We'll run you back to camp.'

It was a tight fit as Bill and Holy squeezed into the back of the patrol car. They endured the good-natured banter of the soldiers with pleasure and when one of them asked where their boat was, Bill replied, 'Waiting for the tide to come in!'

Within a few hours the patrol car had delivered Bill and Holy to the airfield at Sidi Barrani, now occupied by the British. Although 998 Squadron had replaced 999 in the desert operation, the CO immediately made a Swordfish available to fly the two officers back to Dekheila. By eight o'clock that night Bill was in the Naval Hospital having much-needed treatment to his leg.

Chapter 16

Cairo

In the early hours of the morning Bill awoke suddenly, hot and sweating. He had been dreaming, a mixed-up dream of explosion, fire, captivity and an endless trek across the hot sand. A cool hand was on his brow and a cool voice was talking to him, calming him.

'You've been running a temperature, but it has started to fall now. I'll give you something to make you sleep.'

It was Ann, Killer's girl friend. He was in the same ward Killer had occupied, the same bed, the same nurse. Bill was glad to be with friends and thankful for the cool, wet cloth with which Ann was wiping his forehead and face. His leg was throbbing. A cage had been made over it, to keep the weight of the blanket off, but he was restless and disturbed. Under the influence of the sleeping-pill and Ann's soothing caress, his eyes became heavy and he faded into a heavy and dreamless sleep.

He awakened late in the morning, feeling much better. His temperature was normal; the throbbing in his leg had stopped; he was propped up against soft pillows with a breakfast tray before him; and Janet had come to visit him. He felt shy and awkward in her presence, not wanting to be seen as an invalid in bed, but Janet's first words put him at ease.

'Hello, Bill. How's my wounded hero?'

191

Bill approved of Janet's smile and the sound of her voice and the light kiss on his forehead.

'I don't know about hero. I feel more like a baby, propped up in this bed.'

'We know about your escape from the Italians. All the girls think you're a hero. In fact we've become very fond of the Fleet Air Arm.'

'That's Killer's influence,' said Bill. 'He started the trend by coming here first. I hope it doesn't develop any further. We don't want any more wounded heroes.'

Janet laughed and decided not to tease Bill any further.

'I have to go,' she said. 'I'm on duty in another ward.'

'Will you come and see me again, Janet?'

'Of course I will. Now you just lie there quietly and get better.'

Bill's next visitor was the doctor. The nurse on duty carefully unbandaged his leg and Bill was able to see what had happened. A couple of square inches of skin had gone and his shin was exposed, showing some roughness where the shell had grazed the bone. It did not look too bad.

'The problem,' said the doctor, 'is that on the shin where there is little flesh the skin takes a long while to heal. We'll let nature take its course, but it means rest and strict bed for you, I'm afraid.'

And that is what Bill had to submit to over the next few weeks. Ann attended him when she was on duty and Janet came to see him when she could, but after three days Bill was removed to a building on the outskirts of the city, where visits were few and far between.

Casualties were increasing in number as the actions in the Western Desert and the Aegean developed, and the Naval Hospital was required for the newly wounded. Those recuperating from earlier wounds were sent to the auxiliary hospital, where Bill was now fretting. He had been encouraged by visits from his friends, Holy Temple and Killer

Compton, Hank Phipps and Dorrie Dorrington, and by senior officers, the CO and Bolo, and Sandy Sandiford, who came with Snowball Kennedy.

They brought him the books he had requested and he spent much of his time reading. He longed for more visits from Janet, who had visited him with Ann, but the two girls were now working overtime dealing with the influx of casualties and had little time or energy for much else.

Then the visits of his friends suddenly stopped and Bill assumed, correctly, that *Peregrine* had gone to sea. He felt very much alone and rather sorry for himself, particularly on the thirty-first of December. He was sharing a ward with a marine officer who was recovering from a chest wound and was uncommunicative. Bill had been two weeks in bed and his wound showed no signs of recovering. What a way to spend New Year's Eve! Bill thought of the previous New Year's Eve. He had been on leave from his observer's course and had joined many of his old friends at the church social party. The Social Club was where he had learned to dance and the party had been a fancy dress ball. He remembered the fun and the laughter, the dancing and the games.

The time was ten o'clock. Bill's companion was asleep. The hospital had settled down to night routine. Bill's morale was at a low ebb. Suddenly a thought came into his mind and he acted on the impulse. His leg was bandaged and under control. He climbed carefully out of his bed and walked to the wardrobe. He was tottering on his feet, but determined. He found his uniform and other clothes and quickly dressed. The ward was on the ground floor and the window was open. Climbing through it, he made his way slowly through the grounds to the street. His departure seemed to have gone unnoticed. He hailed a passing gharry and had himself driven to the Carlton, where he was able to obtain a table. For New Year's Eve, the Carlton ballroom was remarkably empty. The Fleet must be out, Bill thought.

Somehow, the Greek dancing girls had lost their lustre. The gaiety and laughter of Killer and Hank and Dorrie were missing. Bill sat huddled over his drink. This was a mistake. He had thought to recapture the atmosphere of yesteryear, or of the last time he had been in the Carlton, but it was the people not the place that gave the atmosphere.

Gloomily, Bill thought about leaving.

Suddenly he felt a hand on his shoulder and, looking up, saw a man of about fifty years smiling at him.

'My name is Socrates Agussi,' he said. 'My wife and I thought you looked very lonely. Perhaps you would like to join us at our table.'

He pointed to a table by the dance floor, where a pleasant-looking middle-aged lady was smiling at him.

'That is very kind of you,' Bill said. 'I'd love to join you. My name is Bill – Bill Hewitt.'

He shook hands with Socrates Agussi and went with him to the table indicated, where he was introduced to Lucetta, Socrates' wife.

'We thought you looked so unhappy,' said Lucetta, 'and no one should be unhappy on New Year's Eve.'

Bill explained about his wound and how, on the spur of the moment, he had left the hospital for a night out. He told the Agussis about his friends and how he had enjoyed the last party with them here at the Carlton.

Socrates and Lucetta were sympathetic and encouraging and soon Bill felt at home and at ease with them. They told Bill something of their own lives.

'I am Greek and my wife is Italian,' said Socrates, 'so you must not give any secrets away.'

Lucetta laughed.

'I do not like this war,' she said, 'and I hate Mussolini. He is a bad man.'

Bill commented on the good English spoken by his hosts. Each had a slight accent and Bill could detect the difference, but he could not place which was Italian and which was Greek. He told Lucetta how he had been captured and how well the Italians had treated him. Lucetta was very pleased. Socrates was greatly impressed by Bill's escape.

'I would like to be fighting for my country,' he said. 'All Greeks want to do that.'

He told Bill more about themselves. They owned a hotel, the Rialto, in Alexandria. They had had a son, Niki, but he had died soon after he was born.

'He would have been about your age,' Lucetta added, sadly.

Skilfully, Lucetta and Socrates brought Bill out of his black mood. Before the meal was over, he was talking animatedly about England, about Alexandria, but not about the Navy or the Western Desert. He managed to forget all about his leg. Socrates talked about his hotel and about life in Egypt. French was the lingua franca, spoken by Greeks and Italians and educated Egyptians. There were many Italians living in Alexandria and Cairo. The Egyptians felt neutral about the war, but many of them resented the occupation by the British.

Time passed quickly for Bill and in the early hours of the morning Socrates offered to drive him back to the hospital. He also offered a room in his hotel any time Bill was on leave or wanted a night away from his ship. Bill asked Socrates to drop him at the back of the hospital where he could make his way back to his room unobserved.

Getting in was just as easy as getting out. The window was still open. Bill's bed was as he had left it, with pillows humped underneath the blanket, suggesting a sleeping body. Bill put his clothes away and crept into bed. It had been an absorbing evening. Soon he was asleep.

Two weeks later Bill was still in hospital. The Fleet had returned and his friends had visited him. He learned of the advent of Germany in the Mediterranean War. *Illustrious* had

195

been bombed and nearly destroyed by German Stukas. Malta was under attack by German bombers. The war in Greece was now going badly for the Allies as German troops took over. But the Western Desert was still going well, though it was only a matter of time before the Germans were brought in to strengthen the Italians.

Bill was worried about his future. His wound was showing no sign of healing and had turned into a running sore. One day the surgeon made a special visit to see him.

'I'm afraid we're not winning with your wound,' he said. 'I think this climate is not conducive to healing sores. We may have to send you home to England.'

Bill was shocked.

'Is there nothing you can do?' he asked.

'Well, there is something we can try. A new treatment has been developed but it's still untried. It's in powder form, called sulphonamide. If you're prepared to be a guinea-pig, I'm prepared to try it on you.'

'I'll try anything to get back to my ship,' Bill exclaimed.

'You'll have to sign a statement that you understand that there are unknown risks attached to this treatment and that you are prepared to accept them voluntarily.'

The surgeon looked grave; nevertheless Bill did not hesitate. He enjoyed life in the Navy and wanted to get back to it, back to his squadron. He signed willingly.

The treatment was miraculous. Within a week, the running sore had dried up and a scab was forming. He was to be released from hospital. Had he any ideas for a fortnight's recuperation, to get strength back in his legs before rejoining his ship? He remembered Socrates, and his offer of a room in his hotel. A telephone call and it was confirmed.

Socrates and Lucetta made Bill very welcome at the Rialto, but both of them were involved in the work of the hotel and Bill found himself with time on his hands.

'I've often thought how interesting it would be to see

196

Cairo,' he said on the evening of the third day. 'No one in the ship has had an opportunity of going there. I have the time now, but unfortunately I'm on twenty-four hours' notice of recall.'

'I think something can be done about that,' said Socrates. 'I have a brother, Charlot, in Cairo. He lives there with his wife and daughter. I'll telephone him. We can have a fast car available, and if you are recalled we can get you back to Alexandria in a few hours.'

Bill was excited at the prospect and delighted when Socrates told him the visit had been confirmed. The man who greeted them when they drew up at a large house in a wealthy quarter of Cairo was older than Socrates, with greying hair and a rather stern-looking face. He introduced his wife, Helene, a Frenchwoman with delicate features and a pleasant smile.

'And this is my daughter, Louise,' he said, turning to the young lady standing behind him.

As she came forward to greet him, Bill found himself staring at a girl of about eighteen years with very dark hair, large eyes and a mischievous smile. She greeted him in French, but when he replied in English she immediately changed to that language. All the family, he learned, were multi-lingual, speaking Greek, French, Arabic and a fair English. Louise's English was attractive, with a French accent. After the formalities of introduction, it was she who took charge of Bill, showing him to his room and taking him on a tour of the house.

The family must be very rich, Bill thought as they mounted the wide staircase leading to a balcony that branched out on either side. On the walls of the balcony were portraits of men and women, some of Greek and some of French background.

Louise explained. 'My father was a Greek diplomat in France. When France fell, he brought my mother and me here where he would be nearer his younger brother. He still works for the Greek Government, but I do not know in what capacity. We are very sad at what is happening to Greece, my father's country, and what has happened to France, my mother's country.'

For a moment, a deep sadness crossed Louise's features, but not for long as she took Bill's hand and hurried him along to the salon 'where my mother holds her receptions'.

Dinner that evening was more formal than Bill was used to. Charlot was in a dinner jacket and Louise and her mother wore long evening dresses. Fortunately, Bill, with Socrates' advice, had brought a bow tie to go with his Number Five uniform.

The next day began a week of exploration and evening entertainment such as Bill had never expected in his wildest dreams. Louise was his guide. She was known everywhere and knew everybody.

The first day they spent exploring the Arab Quarter, finishing in the Khankalil, the Street of Gold. Bill was fascinated as he watched a craftsman beating delicate lines into a gold cigarette case and filling these lines with emerald, garnet and ruby dust. The street itself was straight out of fiction, cobbled, narrow, with buildings almost meeting overhead, and walls hung with carpets. The goldsmith's was a dark, small room off the street, lit with an oil lamp. The goldsmith was bent shortsightedly over his work, patiently punching the tiny holes that formed a line in the pattern.

Across the street was a diamond merchant, a seller of precious stones. Louise greeted him by name and introduced Bill.

'Midshipman Hewitt.'

'Mr Akmed.'

Mr Akmed bowed as he took Bill's proffered hand, and immediately rubbed his own hands together as if washing them. His smile was jovial and friendly.

198

'You like to see precious stones?' he said. 'I show.'

Bill hoped he would not be asked to buy – not on his midshipman's salary.

Akmed displayed his wares with flourish and panache. He showed Bill a diamond with a dull, off-white look and a smaller one with great sparkle. The smaller one, he explained, was more valuable. He showed Bill the many facets and how to look into the heart of the diamond with a magnifying glass and discover its real brilliance. He showed Bill two sapphires, one large and pale blue, the other much smaller and a glowing deep blue. Bill got the message. The smaller one was more valuable. Akmed showed Bill emeralds and garnets, moonstones and a spider stone, describing their qualities and telling of their histories. At the end of an hour he invited Bill and Louise to drink coffee with him, and Bill found himself with a tiny cup of very black, very sweet coffee.

'He didn't even ask if I wanted to buy one,' he said to Louise as they made their way to their next stop.

'He is a friend,' said Louise. 'Not everyone here wants to take your money. At least, not while I am with you,' she added mischievously.

In the next place an artist in leather was working. Bill watched him tooling pictures of ancient Egypt on to a wallet. It was all done by hand and with great skill.

Next to him was a wood carver. With great delicacy he was chiselling a rose pattern on a cigarette box. What a wealth of craftsmanship and artistry was here! Bill was enthralled.

That evening, Louise introduced Bill to her friends. All much of his age, they looked at him with awe, one who had fought battles in the air, who had been shot down and had escaped. Bill felt much older than his companions, but he enjoyed their company. They made him feel one of them, and when he danced with Louise he became the idol of the girls and the envy of the boys. Louise proudly took possession of him, her Englishman.

The main event the next day was a visit to Al Hazar, the principal mosque of Cairo. Louise took Bill there but she remained outside, while Bill removed his shoes and entered the imposing portals. He was impressed with the majesty of the building, the marbled floors and tiled walls. The huge, pillared hall was hushed, the quietness emphasised by the intonation of those at prayer, kneeling and kissing the floor.

The Moslem religion was a serious religion, Bill thought, with its own gravity and sense of the eternal. He felt uplifted in spirit. Already he had forsaken Roman Catholicism and adopted the Church of England. He wondered whether the exclusive nature of the world religions was justified. Perhaps each religion was a facet of the one religion, the worship of God.

On the fifth day, Louise had arranged to take Bill to see the Sphinx and the Pyramids. This was the climax of Bill's explorations. He had always been interested in ancient history and Charlot had been a mine of information about Egypt's past. He stood with awe in front of the worn face of the Sphinx, thinking of *Ozymandias,* and crawled with Louise into the heart of the Great Pyramid. He wondered at the workmanship of the pyramid and pondered on the methods of construction.

It was late in the afternoon when they had finished sight-seeing. Louise had a special treat for Bill. She had arranged for a guide with two camels to take them to a nearby oasis. It was becoming dark as they mounted the camels, but a full moon flooded the desert with pale light. Louise laughed at Bill's attempt at mounting the camel. Like all beginners, he was nearly thrown off by the unexpected straightening of the hind legs before the fore legs. But he was enchanted with the ride across the desert. How different this was from his last trek!

At the oasis, Louise took his hand and they walked together through the palms. She was enraptured by her young man. Sophisticated as she was, he was totally outside her experience. She had enjoyed showing him Cairo. She had shared his interest in the craftsmen, appreciating their work in a way that had never occurred to her before. She had been impressed with his deep sense of religion. She herself was a Roman Catholic, but not so strict as her parents. Most of all she had enjoyed dancing with Bill. She had responded to his lead and recognised his mastery.

With a sigh she sank to the ground, inviting Bill to sit beside her. Would this big, very male young man never recognise her need? Bill settled beside her, his back to a tree. He was very conscious of the girl's nearness and it seemed natural to him when Louise moved across and laid her head on his chest. The girl's lush hair brushed his face, soft and fragrant. He placed his right arm around her waist as she snuggled closer to him, and felt his blood stir as tentative fingers took his hand and guided it to her breast. He felt the firm, tender young flesh at his finger tips and instinctively cupped his hands.

This had never happened to him before and he was unsure how it would develop. He was not well versed in physical sex. He knew that his religion forbade it, except in marriage, and he would not go against his religious instincts. He thought of Janet, and for a fleeting moment wished that Janet was the girl with him. Then Louise turned her face upwards to him and kissed him on the lips, the full passionate kiss of her southern race. Bill felt himself responding and forgetting everything else in the ecstasy of the moment.

With another long sigh, Louise settled back in his arms, content. Bill relaxed, happy to enjoy the moment, savouring the palm trees and the desert, the moon and the lovely girl in his arms.

The movement of the camel caught his attention and he remembered, with a start, that they were meeting Louise's parents for dinner at the Mena House Hotel. The moment of enchantment was over. He pulled Louise to her feet and, full of joy and laughter, they mounted the camels and hastened back to the Pyramids.

The setting in the restaurant of the Mena House Hotel was rich with the glitter of evening gowns and jewels. Charlot and Helene looked on with approval as Bill danced very correctly with their daughter. What a splendid young couple, Helene thought as she watched them gliding past. She remembered her own youth and instinctively touched her husband's arm to share her feelings.

After the meal, Bill was quietly talking to Charlot when he became aware of the discussion going on at the next table to them. It was in French, a language that Bill understood well, although he did not speak it fluently. He put his finger to his lips and drew Charlot's attention to what was being said.

The four men at the table had been drinking heavily throughout the evening and were now talking about some Italian destroyers at Massawa in the Red Sea. One of them was a naval officer, visiting relations in Cairo. The gist of their conversation was that an Italian naval force was to attack the Red Sea port of Port Sudan.

'Do you know these men?' Bill asked Charlot.

'I know they are Italians. I can find out more about them.' Charlot, like Bill, was taking the conversation seriously.

They listened for more information but the men had stopped talking, as if they realised they had said too much, and were looking round nervously. A few minutes later they left the room and Bill's party continued to enjoy the evening.

Before Bill left Cairo, Charlot had obtained the identity of the four men and learned something of their background. One was an Italian officer, on leave from the Navy. The other three were known to belong to a strong anti-British group in Cairo. Bill determined to pass on his information to higher authority.

Chapter 17

HMS Peregrine

It was the beginning of February 1941 when Bill rejoined his ship. He stepped aboard *Peregrine* with a feeling above all else of homecoming. The midshipman's flat seemed roomier than he remembered it. Killer had moved out, after his promotion, to share a cabin with another sub lieutenant, and only four midshipmen were left. All of them were nearing their twentieth birthdays and Bill supposed that soon the midshipman's flat would cease to be used.

Dorrie Dorrington updated Bill on recent events. *Peregrine* had returned from another sweep in the Eastern Mediterranean, covering a convoy to Malta. *Illustrious* had been severely damaged by German Stukas and was on her way to America for a refit. One of her squadrons had taken on the role of desert squadron in the Western Desert. Both of *Peregrine*'s squadrons were now aboard.

Bill made his rounds to the squadron office, to the hangar and to the wardroom. Everywhere he was greeted with pleasure and he was deeply aware of the good fellowship that existed not only in his squadron but throughout the ship. Holy Temple took him along to see the replacement Swordfish for B – Baker. His fitter and rigger were working on it and they greeted him warmly. In the wardroom, at lunchtime, the squadron officers gathered round, congratulating him on his return. Bill basked in the sunshine of approval, but he knew there was a cloud on the horizon. He was worried about the secret he held. He must let the authorities know about the information he had overheard in the Mena House Hotel, but this would mean admitting that he had left Alexandria without permission and gone to Cairo. All would be well if he could keep his secret. No one need ever know. Socrates would never tell anyone and Charlot and his family were far removed from *Peregrine*.

Cairo, the Pyramids, Louise, they seemed to be very far away now, a different world from that of *Peregrine*. After lunch, Bill paced slowly up and down the quarterdeck pondering his problem. Eventually he made up his mind. He would see Commander (Flying) and tell his story. He knew he would bring trouble on himself, but his secret information must be passed on.

Wings was reclining at ease in an armchair when Bill knocked on his cabin door. He stood up courteously and with a smile invited Bill to take a chair. He looked curiously at the young man before him who appeared to be so worried and ill at ease.

'What can I do for you?' he said.

'Well, sir, it's rather difficult to explain. You see, whilst I was on sick leave, I went to Cairo!'

'You what?'

Wings was no longer smiling. His face was stern and forbidding.

'I went to Cairo, sir.'

'You went to Cairo! Do you know that is a court martial offence?'

For the next five minutes Wings blazed forth and Bill was left in no doubt what a heinous crime he had committed by breaking bounds. He felt very much like a fourth former at school, facing an angry headmaster. He almost wished he had never confessed.

'And why have you told me this?' said Wings when his anger had subsided.

Bill related what had happened at the Mena House. He told about the Italians at the next table and what he had overheard – the proposed attack on Port Sudan.

Wings sat very quietly through the recital, regarding Bill intently, as if testing the validity of what he was saying.

'My God! How extraordinary!' he exclaimed when Bill had finished. 'This could be extremely important. Port Sudan is our most important fuelling base in the Red Sea and the only one capable of coal bunkering. We still have coal-fired ships on that run. Leave it with me. I'll see that this information gets to the right quarters.'

As Bill was leaving, he added, 'I mean what I said about your irresponsibility in going to Cairo, but you've done well to come and tell me about what you overheard. I shall take no further action over your escapade.'

Bill left with a sigh of relief. He had been very worried for his future, particularly when Wings had torn into him. He had always thought himself lucky to obtain a commission in the Navy and he knew how proud of him were his mother and father. He did not want to let them down. And he had come to relish the lifestyle of the wardroom. He did not want to lose it.

Peregrine spent the next fortnight on her mooring, and life for the squadron took on a new routine. All the officers shared watchkeeping duties, the lieutenants as officer of the day, the sub lieutenants and midshipmen as junior officer of the day.

Wes Weston had taken over from Bolo the role of Squadron Sports and Recreation Officer and he organised a series of activities for the squadron, sailing in the cutter and whaler, deck-hockey, and badminton in the lift well. Also for the keep fit specialists there was an evening run, ten times round the flight deck, and morning PT under a marine sergeant. At short notice, the ship's officers were organising a wardroom party to which friends from outside the ship could be invited.

Bolo led the drive to get fit. For months, the squadrons had been on very demanding service. He felt jaded, and not at his physical peak. He particularly enjoyed deck-hockey because it was a team game, and he was captain of the squadron team. The ship's company was organised into a number of teams, and matches were played every afternoon. Bill Hewitt was not able to play because of his leg, but Killer Compton had recovered and resumed his place in the forward line. Holy Temple, Dicky Burd, Wes Weston, Hank Phipps and Andy Andrews made up the rest of the team.

The squadron's first match was against 998 Squadron officers. The game was fast and furious and no quarter was given. Almost the full length of the flight deck was used. The hockey sticks looked like walking-sticks with a flattened-out crook. The 'ball' was a puck. There were no fouls and almost no rules. The only defence against a stick raised too high was to dodge it, or block it with your own stick, rather like a sword fencer. Many bruises were suffered. You were forbidden to fall over the side of the ship.

Hank thought the game was crazy, but he loved it. Each half was a quarter of an hour, and by half-time, Hank, like the rest of the team, was gasping for breath. He had been running almost non-stop since the game started and 998 Squadron were one goal up.

'We go all out in the second half, chaps,' said Bolo. 'The other side may be one up, but look at them. They're like a lot of old men, nearly on their knees.'

'What about us?' gasped Hank. 'I'm on my knees,' and he sank dramatically on to the deck.

'Time,' called the referee after one minute's break. The

puck moved from one end of the deck to the other, chased by most of the contestants. The more expert players, like Bolo, flicked the puck rather than hitting it, and it was from one of these flicks that Killer hooked his stick around the puck and, running it half the length of the deck, hit it into the open goal. The game finished in a draw, leaving both teams exhausted.

Just as the flight deck had a hockey pitch printed on it, so the after lift was painted with a badminton court. The lift was lowered to hangar level and presented the perfect environment for badminton, free of draughts yet well lit by the open sky above. In harbour the badminton court was well used and had to be booked according to a timetable.

One afternoon, the CO, Sandy Sandiford, Bolo and Dicky Burd gathered in the wardroom for afternoon tea. They had just finished a game of badminton.

'How long are we going to stay here, in harbour, Boss?' asked Bolo.

'Probably another week. Now that *Illustrious* has gone, we're the only carrier left. We'll have to cover convoys to Malta and make sweeps into the Mediterranean. We have a problem, though.'

'You mean lack of fighters,' said Bolo.

'That, and lack of radar. Jerry with his Junkers 88s and Stuka dive-bombers is a different proposition from the Italians. We dare not go too near their bases in Greece or North Africa. We haven't the fighter defences. I think that's why we're stuck in harbour.'

'What about the Western Desert, Boss?' said Sandy.

'I don't think we shall be required there either,' said the CO. 'The *Illustrious* squadron has taken on that role and there are also Wellingtons and Hurricanes. I don't envy them. Jerry is bound to come in to support the Italians. I wouldn't fancy our chances in Swordfish against Messerschmitts or even Junkers 88s. I think the war is going to become more ruthless.'

'Let's hope they find something for us to do,' said Dicky. 'There's a limit to how far we can keep the boys happy with games and sport.'

'That's why the Commander is organising the party,' said the CO.

The party had been fixed for the following Saturday. Killer and Bill, who had maintained contact with their girl friends, had invited the four girls from the hospital to be their guests. On the night, Killer, Bill, Hank and Dorrie arrived at the hospital in two gharries to collect the girls. They were wearing white mess undress, with bow ties and cummerbunds, and all were animated and eager as they waited for the girls.

The girls arrived, flushed and excited, in their long dresses and cloaks. Janet looked stunning, Bill thought, in an ivory dress, a lacy top over a satin petticoat. She greeted him warmly. Killer greeted his girl with panache. With a bow he took Ann's hand and raised it to his lips. The others laughed.

'*Très galant!*' said Dorrie. French seemed the only language to use in describing it.

The pairs sorted themselves out, Ann and Killer with Janet and Bill in one gharry, and Hank and Maggie and Dorrie and Pam in the other. It was a happy, laughing group that joined the throng in the ship's motor-boat, to be taken out to *Peregrine*.

The wardroom and ante-room had undergone a transformation. The heavier furniture, armchairs and sofas, had been removed from the ante-room, to be replaced by occasional tables bearing vases of flowers. The wardroom had been equipped with extra tables to accommodate the guests, and the guest room was used as a cloakroom where the ladies could leave their cloaks and tidy up.

As the girls emerged from the guest room to greet the boys, a steward offered them drinks from a tray, wine, spirits or soft drinks. Other, less fortunate, officers of the squadron

208

soon joined them, so that the girls became the centre of a noisy, happy group.

The CO and Bolo came along to talk to them and greeted Ann and Janet, whom they had met in the hospital, as old friends. They were followed by Wings, and it was Bill who made the introduction.

'Are these young gentlemen looking after you?' Wings said.

He went on to tell them that, alas, the ship was unable to put on the parties of peace time, when the hangar was converted into a grotto and seamen dressed up as mermen – and mermaids, he added, laughing. Everyone then came in fancy dress, and a wooden dance floor was laid in the centre of the hangar.

'The hangar, at present,' he said, 'is full of aircraft.'

'May we take the girls into the hangar to see our aircraft?' Killer asked.

'I don't see why not, though I should wait till after dinner if I were you.'

As the evening progressed, more 999 officers came to be introduced until they had all met the girls. About half the officers had produced lady guests and there were several civic and fleet notables. The Captain had been invited and he appeared with the Rear Admiral (Aircraft Carriers).

A section of the marine band was playing soft, background music and gradually the volume of chatter increased to a point where it was difficult to hear what was being said. Everyone was laughing and talking at once, and everything that was said was humorous.

Just when Bill wondered where the party could go from here, the cymbals clashed and there was a complete silence.

'Ladies and gentlemen,' said the Chief Steward. 'Dinner is served.'

With talk and laughter, the crowd began to move into the

wardroom, the gentlemen offering their arms to their ladies and drawing chairs back for them to sit on.

Bill thought it was like something out of a book, but he was pleased and proud as he escorted Janet to her place.

The wardroom looked magnificent. The best silver and the Waterford glass were being used, three glasses to each place: white wine for the fish, red for the meat and the inevitable port glass for the Loyal Toast. Soon the meal was in full swing. The band continued to play background music. The stewards, all dressed in the costume of Nelson's time, served avocado mousse, followed by a fillet of sea bream stuffed with grapes. When the meat was due to be served, the marine band changed to a slow march and a baron of beef, carried by two chefs in costume and escorted by a team of stewards, was paraded slowly round the room amidst hand-clapping and cheers and laughter. Few would remember what was discussed: certainly not the war nor the Navy. But conversation rose and fell and rose again. Devils on horseback, a favourite savoury in *Peregrine*, was followed by an assortment of cheeses. The port was passed round the table.

It fell to Bill, the youngest officer present, to pledge the Loyal Toast. The officers remained seated.

'Gentlemen, the King.'

The Commander made a witty speech, in which he made it clear how much the officers had enjoyed having women aboard as their guests. He was followed by the Admiral's wife, who concluded, 'And from what I have seen this evening, *Peregrine* must be a very happy ship.'

The girls had enjoyed their meal. The group had been animated and the boys had been assiduous in looking after their needs. Their corner, farthest away from the Commander, had been a centre of lively conversation and laughter.

After coffee in the ante-room, the girls readily agreed when Killer asked them if they would like to see the planes. Bill took Janet's hand and led her through a maze of passageways and steps until they came to a steel door that opened into the hangar. Janet gazed with amazement at the scene.

The hangar was well lit and, as far as she could see, down its enormous length were Swordfish, with wings folded, tethered diagonally in lines.

'This is B – Baker, my aircraft,' he said. 'I haven't flown in it yet. It's a replacement for the one we crashed.'

'I had no idea it was so large,' said Janet. 'I've seen them flying over town and they always looked so tiny.'

'They're large enough to carry three men and a fifteen-hundred-pound torpedo.'

'It seems out of date – a biplane with an open cockpit.'

'It is out of date but I like it. Everyone that flies in them likes them.'

Bill helped the girl to climb into his cockpit and showed her his chartboard and his compasses and the safety strap to stop him falling out. He also showed her the air-gunner's cockpit with its wireless and Lewis gun.

In L – Love Killer had Ann seated in the pilot's cockpit and was showing her the controls. He allowed her to move the joystick and rudder bar, operating the ailerons and tail fin.

A group of mechanics had gathered in the hangar and Killer and the other officers took the girls over to introduce them. The men were delighted and took up the story of their aircraft and the men who flew them. Janet was impressed by the easy relationship between officers and men.

After the hangar, the boys took the girls up to the operations room and the rest-room, and then on to the flight deck, where they split into couples. The weather was kind to them. Although it was February, the night was warm and dry. Bill wandered along the flight deck, his arm round Janet's waist, pointing out the hockey pitch and the badminton court, the lifts and the arrester wires. He told her how the batsman brought the aircraft in and showed her where Bats stood. Just below was the catwalk and here in its shadow he took Janet into his arms for a long kiss. Afterwards they stood, Janet leaning against him, watching the glints of faint lights on the water. The shadowy shape of the harbour patrol passed them and Janet shivered at the thought of war and of Bill flying through the night on a bombing mission in his out-of-date machine.

It was time to go. The party had been a huge success. They rejoined the others in the wardroom, where the girls said their goodbyes to the Commander. Then with the boys escorting them they clambered into the motor-boat to be taken back to their everyday world of the hospital.

After bidding the guests goodbye, Bolo retired to his cabin, where he took out the letter from Joyce that had arrived with the day's post.

My Darling,

I was overjoyed to read your letter. How I have longed to read the words you wrote, to read that you love me as I have always loved you! I think I fell in love with you at our first meeting and my love has grown and grown until I am bursting with love.

I know you treated me as a young sister and I hated it. That time when we saw the deer in the forest by the pool, I leaned against you and I loved it. I cursed the aeroplane flying overhead that broke the spell. I loved our walks. When I lay in your arms listening to Brahms at your friends' house I was overwhelmed. When you kissed me I did not know how to hold back, I wanted you so much.

Dearest one, let us not waste more time. Let us get married as soon as you return, so that we can truly be together. I so long to have your next letter and to hear those sweet words from you, that you love me.

212

Bolo read to the end and then sat down and wrote quickly.

My Dearest One,

I have re-read your letter tonight and I cannot believe my good fortune. It arrived this morning in the convoy and after reading it I had to put it aside for a while.

The ship was giving a party and we had lots of visitors to drinks and dinner. Four of our young men brought four young girls from the hospital, much your age when I first met you. They are all nurses. The boys were proud of their girls and I could share their delight because I could think of you.

My darling, I know we are far apart, that you cannot be with me; but how I long to share my life with you, to talk to you, to hold you in my arms, caress you. I know now that we belong to each other. I agree with you. We must be married as soon as I return to England so that we can share each other fully.

It is strange, my dear. Two years ago I could never have seen myself writing a love letter, nor listening to music, nor reading poetry. It is you who has opened my eyes to poetry, to music and to love, and I find it easy and natural to describe my love.

Until I learned to love you I was incomplete. Together we make a whole, and until I am with you again I shall feel that part of me is missing. In some ways, I envied the boys with their girls this evening. But then I thought how deep our love is, deep enough for us to be able to wait until we can consummate it.

How I yearn for that time,

Darling of my heart,

John

213

Chapter 18

Sirocco

For the next month *Peregrine* was required for routine patrols in the Mediterranean. Troops and equipment from the Western Desert were being moved to Crete and Greece, which were under increasing threat from the Germans, and supplies transported to Malta, which had become a focus for air attacks against Italian and German convoys to North Africa. *Peregrine*, with *Ramrod* and a flotilla of destroyers, was engaged in covering these convoys, which crept along the African coast before making their dash for Soudha Bay or Malta.

The Italians had been driven back well beyond Benghazi by the Eighth Army, so the airfields of Bardia, Tobruk, Derna and Benghazi were in British hands and could provide fighter air cover for the fleet. *Peregrine*'s three Gladiators would be no match for a determined German attack, such as the one on *Illustrious*, and it was vital for the convoy to keep well clear of German airfields.

Peregrine's role was to provide anti-submarine patrols throughout the voyage and air searches in the dangerous area between Crete and Malta. After the Battle of Taranto the Italians had relied more and more on their submarines to harass the British convoys, and several warships and merchant ships had been sunk or damaged by their torpedoes.

214

Farther west the Italians were using Tripoli as the main port for reinforcements to their defeated North African Army, and increasingly throughout March for the build-up of a German Army led by a new leader, General Rommel. Italian cruisers were being used to escort these reinforcements from Sicily and southern Italy to Tripoli. *Peregrine* mounted regular searches in this area in the early morning and late afternoon.

Throughout the first convoy operation nothing was sighted. In the hangars the opportunity was taken to clear the last vestiges of sand from engines and airframes. The squadron settled down to the routine of the sea. An inner and an outer anti-submarine patrol was maintained, so, regularly, every two and a half hours throughout the day, two Swordfish were flown off and two landed-on.

Like most of the aircrews, Bill Hewitt enjoyed this routine. It meant usually a flight once a day with very occasionally a second flight. His leg was no longer troubling him. Sometimes his thoughts returned to Janet and, more rarely, to Louise, but he was content to throw himself into the work of the squadron, in the air, in the hangar and, since his return to the carrier, in the squadron office, where he had been made assistant to Dicky Burd, the Squadron Adjutant. Bill enjoyed his work in the squadron office. It made a complete contrast to flying.

His first task was to go through the squadron copy of *King's Regulations and Admiralty Instructions* and bring it up to date. Time spent at Dekheila and in the Western Desert had left Squadron Administration well behind in its programme. Each post brought many amendments to *KR and AI*, the Bible of all naval units. One such was a requirement that the tool kits of naval air mechanics and fitters should be inspected and checked. A new inventory of equipment was given and squadrons must check their own personnel. Bill was delegated by Dicky to look into this. It meant that he had to organise a tool-kit inspection with Bolo and liaise with Biddy Bidwell, the Stores Officer, on the question of kit supplies and replacements.

Above everything else, Bill enjoyed flying. He threw himself with renewed energy into the A/S patrols. No longer were they dull and boring routines, to be endured but not enjoyed. Since his capture and subsequent escape, war for Bill had become deadly serious. Every breaking wave might be the feather from a periscope, and Bill was determined that no submarine would get through while he was on duty.

It was on *Peregrine*'s second sweep into the Mediterranean, later in the month, that Bill had his opportunity. B – Baker had taken off with the CO in A – Abel for the dawn patrol. A – Abel was the outer patrol at fifteen miles' range and B – Baker was inner patrol at five miles.

The two aircraft had been ranged on deck in the dark, before dawn, and at first light *Peregrine* had turned into wind to release her aircraft into a hazy sky. The sea was a steely-grey as Holy climbed to one thousand feet, their patrol height. The CO had already departed for his outer patrol as B – Baker passed over the destroyer screen, a mile ahead of the capital ships. Bill was sweeping the sea with his binoculars. If there were a submarine in the vicinity, this was the most likely time to catch it. It would have been on the surface, charging its batteries, until dawn; then it would submerge and make a sweep of the horizon in the dawn light, before settling down to the routine of its patrol.

Suddenly, Bill caught sight of a flicker of white, the mere suspicion of a breaking wave. He focused his binoculars on it, and he clearly saw the periscope.

'Submarine green four-five, distance two miles,' he called to his pilot. 'Black, make a wireless signal to *Peregrine* in plain language, "Submarine bearing 030 from you, distance four miles." Get it off as quickly as you can.'

Holy was already turning to starboard.

'Dead ahead now, about a mile and a half,' Bill said to his pilot. He was standing up in his cockpit, eyes glued to binoculars, staring over his pilot's head. He must not take his eyes off the wisp of foam for fear of losing it.

'I've got it.' Holy's voice was jubilant. 'Going in now.'

The engine note rose as Holy put his nose down and opened the throttle. Bill watched the periscope anxiously. It continued on course. The submarine was making no attempt to dive. It could not have seen them; the captain must be concentrating on his attack on the Fleet. Thoughts tumbled through Bill's mind in rapid succession. He felt keyed up, his mind working rapidly.

'Don't forget to arm your depth charges,' he said. A timely warning.

'Have done.' A terse reply.

'Our message received by *Peregrine*,' came PO Black's voice. 'Message from Abel. "Coming to assist." Fleet turning away. Two destroyers coming in.'

The crew were working as a team. The pilot was concentrating on his attack. The observer was monitoring the submarine's movements closely through his binoculars. The TAG, his message sent, was able to watch the Fleet and give a running commentary on its movements.

Time almost stopped. Events proceeded in slow motion. Just before they reached the periscope, there was a disturbance on the water and the periscope disappeared.

'They've seen us,' called Bill.

'Stand by,' echoed Holy.

He was coming diagonally on to the course of the periscope's wake and was now only a hundred feet above the sea.

'Depth charges gone.'

Bill saw the splashes of the two depth charges just ahead of the periscope's wake, bracketing where the submarine must surely be. He felt the gravity as Holy pulled the aircraft round in a tight turn. Then he saw the two underwater eruptions where the depth charges exploded.

The crew waited anxiously, all eyes riveted on the disturbance.

'There she is.' It was the air-gunner who called first.

They watched as the black shape emerged bows up and then porpoised downwards.

'We've done some damage,' cried Holy. 'I'll drop a smoke-float to mark the spot.'

Whilst he did this, Bill took a bearing of the heading the submarine had been on in its brief appearance.

By this time, A – Abel was approaching, and Bill took up his Aldis lamp and flashed a signal to Sandy Sandiford, giving the course of the submarine when last seen. A trace of oil had appeared on the surface leading away from the smoke-float. He watched as the CO lined his aircraft up along the bearing and dropped two further depth charges.

The two Swordfish continued to circle the oil trace as they awaited the approaching destroyers. The two destroyers made a brave sight as they came in at over thirty knots, sending up huge bow waves on either side. As they approached, Bill saw the CO dive on to a spot ahead of the oil slick. He was indicating the submarine's position to the destroyers. The two destroyers worked together, and as the submarine turned desperately away from the depth charges of one, he was followed and bracketed by the other.

By the sixth depth charge pattern it was all over. Bill saw the heave of the sea caused by an underwater explosion, followed by a massive oil slick emerging with debris of all sorts mixed with it.

The destroyer's lamp winked.

Thank you, Bill read, *and well done.* It was all over.

An Aldis message came from A – Abel: *Resume patrol until relieved.*

Two days later the Fleet was on its return passage to Alexandria. The convoys to Crete and Malta had been delivered successfully, without interference from the Italian Navy. After the sinking of the Italian submarine, no further submarine attacks had been experienced. *Peregrine* and her escorts were some eighty miles north of the Libyan coast in an area that was safe from enemy air attack. It was nine o'clock in the morning and a parallel search was about to take off for the last time before the run into Alexandria.

Six aircraft of 999 Squadron were involved in the search, A – Abel, B – Baker and K – King to the south and L – Love, F – Fox and H – Howe to the north. The six aircraft would fly on diverging courses from the carrier's course until they were twenty miles apart, then steer due east until it was time to turn and head back to the carrier to arrive at 1130. The carrier would steer due east and maintain a speed of eighteen knots. This was the familiar, routine pattern. The search would cover an area about a hundred and thirty miles long and a hundred and twenty miles wide. With good visibility, anything on the surface would be picked up and reported by one of the search aircraft.

Before they left, Schooley had briefed them on the weather. Wind was slight, but increasing. Visibility was exceptionally good. The temperature was higher than usual for the time of year. The barometric pressure had started to fall.

'I'm not sure what it means,' said Schooley, 'but keep your eye on the wind. We could have a sharp rise.' Half an hour later, A – Abel had just turned on to its eastward leg, when Sandy Sandiford spoke into his intercom.

'Have you seen that lot to the south, Boss?' he said.

'Yes, I've been watching it,' said the CO. 'It doesn't look too good.'

They were looking at a huge black cloud, still some forty miles away. Above it, the sun shone a lurid red.

219

'I don't like the look of the sea, either,' said Sandy.

The placid sea of half an hour before had given way to a large swell. The heave of the sea looked menacing.

'There's something big pushing it,' said Sandy. 'I hope we're not in for a sirocco. It has all the signs, though – the excessive heat, the swell and that black cloud and red sky. This is the season for them.'

A sirocco, the dreaded wind feared by sailors and airmen in the Mediterranean. It built up over the hot North African desert, gathering dust and sand, and swept northwards at increasing speed until over the sea it reached storm force or more. The wind could reach a speed of seventy knots and waves could rise to a height of fifty feet.

The black cloud was approaching rapidly. Already the sea's surface was breaking up and Sandy could see the white horses increasing in number and in size. Taking a bearing of their direction, he estimated that the wind had risen to force seven from the south and was still increasing. He gave his pilot a twenty-degree course correction to the south to allow for the wind and increased it to thirty degrees as the wind increased.

'This is a sirocco,' the CO said a few minutes later. 'How far before we turn back?'

'We have fifty miles to go.'

'I think I'll turn now. We shan't be able to see anything once that lot hits us. Can you give me a course back to the carrier?'

Quickly Sandy drew a line on his chartboard. Allowing thirty degrees for the wind pushing them north, he gave his pilot a course of 315 degrees to steer.

'I'll try to pick up the ship's beacon and give you a correct course,' he added.

The cloud now was frighteningly close, black and solid and arching over them, from sea level to high above. The sun had been blotted out. Suddenly the cloud hit them, savagely, taking the aircraft with it. Sandy felt the sharp sting of sand hitting his face and he pulled his goggles down to protect his eyes. He found himself gasping for breath, breathing in sand particles.

'I'll try to climb above this, Sandy,' came the CO's voice.

Sandy heard the pitch of the propeller change and the note of the engine deepen as the CO opened his throttle to the full. Crouching low in his cockpit, he turned the knob of the beacon receiver. At first he heard nothing. Then A – Abel burst out of the sand cloud and into the open sunlight at five thousand feet. At the same time Sandy heard the blips; *Peregrine*'s signal was coming in clearly. He checked the beacon compass.

'I have the beacon,' he called. 'Carrier bears 322 degrees. Hold your present course. I'll give you a correction if the bearing changes.'

Below them the tossing sea could be seen dimly through the murk of the sand cloud. In the sunshine Sandy was able to clear the grit from his face and take stock. Everywhere in the cockpit there was sand. In the air-gunner's cockpit CPO Cutter was wiping his face.

'No signals from *Peregrine*, sir,' he said, catching Sandy's eye.

'No, and there won't be one,' the CO interrupted. 'We're within striking distance of long-range bombers from the Dodecanese Islands, and probably there are still submarines ahead of us. The Fleet won't break wireless silence and nor must we. I am concerned, though, for the safety of our aircraft, particularly those to the north. They could find it difficult to get back to the carrier against this wind.'

'Yes. To some extent, the wind is helping us,' said Sandy. 'But I'm worried about Andrews and Hampden in H – Howe. If they leave it too late, they'll have to face a wind of up to seventy knots with an airspeed of just over ninety knots. Their ground speed will be only twenty knots. They could be in trouble.'

The CO, Sandy Sandiford and CPO Cutter were a very experienced and mature crew. They were aware of the dangers of the approaching storm and had taken professional decisions to deal with them. In H – Howe the situation was very different. Andy Andrews, the pilot, was competent, but not gifted. His observer, Midshipman Hampden, was still quite unsure of himself. In the operations they had undertaken together so far, they had come through with remarkably few stress situations. Now they were about to face their biggest challenge.

The search had gone without incident. Both Andy Andrews and Hampers Hampden had noticed the disturbance in the sea without worrying about its significance. Ten minutes before they were due to turn on to their home track, Hampers had taken a wind that he found was now force five from the south. He realised that he had been using a false wind, probably for the past hour, and must be several miles north of his course. This did not worry him. He would compensate on the way back to the carrier.

Just before they were due to return, he made a final sweep with his binoculars. His eyes fastened on an object about fifteen miles away to the north-east.

He spoke into his gosport tubes.

'Andy, there's something about fifteen miles away, red four-five. What do you think? Shall we investigate?'

'When are we due to turn back to the carrier?'

'In about a minute.'

'Well, it will only take us about ten minutes to get there. We might as well go and have a look. I'll see if I can catch up a bit on the way back.'

Ten minutes later H – Howe was circling the object, which turned out to be a caique. Andy circled two or three times, and waved to the Greeks on the caique, who waved back enthusiastically. The caique was making heavy weather of the mounting seas, but neither pilot nor observer noted these signs.

'Give us a course back, Hampers?' Andy said.

Midshipman Hampden had already worked this out. Using a wind of force five, about eighteen knots, he gave his pilot the return course. What he did not realise was that the wind was now force seven and increasing, blowing him further north of his track. They had left the caique at eleven o'clock. By quarter past, all three occupants of H – Howe were aware of the growing menace to the south of them.

The same black sand cloud that had caused Lieutenant Commander Simpson to abort his mission and turn for home was now thirty miles south of them and approaching at a frightening speed.

'How far to the carrier?' Andy asked.

'About ninety miles.'

'That's all right. It will take us a bit more than an hour, but we've got plenty of petrol. We'll be a bit late back, though.'

'I expect the Captain will forgive us when he hears that we investigated the caique.'

What neither Andy nor Hampers understood was that the wind had pushed them far north of their plotted position and because of the observer's failure to appreciate its full strength, the wind was pushing them further and further north of the ship. By the time the full sirocco hit them they were in deep trouble.

Andy Andrews was frightened. He found himself fighting to control his plunging aircraft, blinded by the stinging sand, unable to see a horizon.

'What kind of weather is this?' he gasped.

'I think it must be a sirocco.'

Hamper's voice had risen. The fear in his voice echoed that of his pilot.

'You can get winds of up to seventy knots, blowing from the south. This must be sixty knots.'

223

He looked down at the violent sea beneath him and was terrified. He realised now that he had been underestimating the wind and must be many miles north of his estimated position. He was the navigator and he had made the error. He also realised that their effective speed southwards against a sixty-knot wind was only thirty knots. How far north were they? Would they have enough fuel to get back to the carrier? His mouth had gone dry and had an unpleasant taste of iron.

The TAG's steady voice came through his earphones. 'The beacon's working, sir. Perhaps you can get a bearing.'

Yes, that was it. Get a bearing and fix their position. He read off the bearing 220 degrees. God! They must be miles out. With this wind he would have to steer 200 to counter the effects of the wind – almost into the teeth of it.

'Steer two hundred degrees,' he told his pilot, a note of desperation creeping into his voice.

'Two hundred degrees. Right. I'm on instruments now. I can't see a thing in this murk.'

Just as Hampden's inexperience caused him to make a mistake with his navigation, so Andrews' inexperience showed in his judgment as a pilot. It did not occur to him to climb above the dust storm. At least there he would have been able to see, and he might well have found less strength in the wind. He would certainly have been buffeted less, thus saving precious petrol.

He continued to press southwards, fighting the wind and the sand. His eyes were shielded by his goggles and he had covered his mouth and nose with the mouthpiece of his gosport tubes. He had himself under control now. They had the ship on the beacon. It was just a matter of plodding on. What he did not know was that when they had picked up the beacon at 1130 they were over seventy miles away and on this course and with this wind that was two and a half hours' flying. They had fuel only for another two hours.

At 1230 the bearing of the beacon had shifted to 190 almost due south. They were now flying dead into wind. Andy was becoming tired. He had been fighting his machine with foot and hand controls, with muscles tensed by anxiety, and the strain was beginning to tell. He could not really see why they had not arrived. Was the ship really there? What if the beacon were giving a false reading?

Hampers was thinking along the same lines – although, now, deep down, he knew that it was his own error that had imperilled them. He worked at his navigation, re-checking his plot with the newly estimated winds and constantly checking the beacon.

At 1430 he knew they were not going to make it. They had been airborne nearly five hours and with the constant manoeuvring required by the storm there could not be much fuel left.

Andy Andrews confirmed this.

'Tank reading empty,' he said. 'Sorry, Hampers. I think we've had it.'

'What about sending an SOS? We can't be far away from the Fleet. Maybe the Admiral will send a destroyer.'

'You know there is wireless silence?'

'Yes, I know. But I don't think this situation was expected. No one else will fly in this weather. And we are only a day or so from Alexandria.'

'Okay, then. But wait until we're going in. Then give Roberts the word.'

Five minutes later, their time had arrived. The engine coughed and spluttered into life again.

'Going down, now,' shouted Andy.

'Get the signal off, Roberts,' Hampers called. L/A Roberts was ready. Quickly he tapped out the message in morse. *SOS, SOS, Howe ditching, Howe ditching, SOS, Howe –*

Andy put his nose down and watched the speed build up. The engine was still pulling – but coughing.

'My God! Those waves look enormous,' he cried. 'Hold on everyone!'

Stick back. Close the throttle.

An enormous wave reared up ahead of him. Andy had no power left in the engine. He pushed the throttle forward, but there was no response. The wave was overwhelming. Andy threw his arms protectively over his head as the Swordfish flew into the wave. It was like hitting a wall. All three of the crew died instantly. The Swordfish took only a few seconds before it, too, died, crushed and broken, to disappear beneath the turbulent waters.

Aboard *Peregrine*, Wings had watched anxiously as the aircraft returned. He had to give everyone a chance and, difficult as it was, he kept them circling round the carrier, waiting for the last. If the ship turned south into wind, it would make it even more difficult for the stragglers to find her.

One by one they appeared like ghosts in the half-light: A – Abel; then B – Baker; K – King and L – Love almost together; then, after a pause, F – Fox. Wings waited. He could not hold the others any longer in the deteriorating conditions. He reported to the Captain and *Peregrine* made the difficult turn into wind. The seas were very large. The stern of *Peregrine* rose and fell forty or fifty feet. One by one Bats brought them in, Lieutenant Commander Simpson waiting until last. At length the five aircraft were down and the Fleet resumed its course. The anti-submarine aircraft had landed-on and only H – Howe was missing.

Two hours later they received the broken SOS message from Howe.

A light winked from *Stalwart.*

'Message from Admiral, sir,' said the Yeoman of Signals. '"*Heron* despatched to search for missing aircraft. Advise anticipated bearing."'

Captain Bentley nodded to the ship's navigator, who gave the bearing to the Yeoman. His lamp blinked.

Sadly the group watched the destroyer depart on a northerly course. Wings felt in his bones that no crews could survive in that savage sea.

Chapter 19

Flight Down the Nile

It was a sad ship that returned to Alexandria. Neither Andy Andrews nor Hampers Hampden had taken a prominent part in the social and sporting life of the ship, but Andy had been with the squadron since the Italians first came into the war and Hampers was certainly missed in the gunroom. Only three of the midshipmen remained, Bill Hewitt, Dorrie Dorrington and Hatters Dunn.

The usual party celebrating a successful voyage was cancelled. No one felt like celebrating. The ship's company threw itself into the work of cleaning ship and the maintenance crews concentrated on cleaning the aircraft. Sand from the sirocco had penetrated everywhere and the ship, from water-line to top of the mast, was encrusted. Grit had penetrated in those aircraft that had been flying and engines were stripped and overhauled and cockpits thoroughly cleaned.

Bill Hewitt and Killer Compton managed to get ashore in the evening and call on their girl friends, but it was a quiet quartet that gathered at the officers' club, where they sat drinking and talking. The girls were good for the boys, gradually drawing them out until, at the end of the evening, they planned a full day together, the same group of eight as before, to start with swimming at the Sporting Club and end with dancing at the Carlton.

This meeting was never to take place. The next day it was announced that all leave was cancelled. There was to be a meeting of all flying-crews in the briefing-room at 1500 hours. No telephone calls could be made nor letters sent out of the ship.

Rumours spread throughout the ship. The buzzes were that the Italian Navy was out, that Crete was to be evacuated and that *Peregrine* was returning to England.

At 1500, the briefing-room was packed. Conversation died as Wings, flanked by the ASO and Schooley, took up his place, facing them.

'Gentlemen,' said Wings, 'we are about to embark on an unusual operation.'

There was a stir amongst his audience, who waited expectantly.

'What I am about to tell you is in the strictest confidence. That is why all leave has been cancelled. Our secret service has uncovered a plan whereby the Italians intend to attack Port Sudan and disrupt our operations in the Red Sea.'

Bill felt a flush spread over his face. Wings was looking directly at him and he was sure there was a meaningful smile on Wings' lips.

'At the present time,' Wings continued, 'a British Expeditionary Force is advancing through Eritrea and threatening the Italian port of Massawa. The Italian plan is for the flotilla of six Italian destroyers stationed at Massawa to break out, steam north and bombard Port Sudan, then scuttle themselves in the harbour entrance. Port Sudan is our main harbour in the Red Sea and our only harbour that has coal-bunkering facilities. At present many coal-burning ships are using that route and depend on refuelling at Port Sudan.

'Gentlemen, we have been given the honour of taking care of those Italian destroyers.'

He paused for a moment, letting the news sink in, then continued.

'It would take too long for *Peregrine* to get there via Port Said and the Suez Canal. It has therefore been decided that our two Swordfish squadrons will fly there direct. This means a flight of fifteen hundred miles down the Nile and across the desert, stopping every three hundred miles to refuel. The ASO will give you details later. At Port Sudan we shall be billeted in the Red Sea Hotel, which will become our headquarters.

'I am happy to say,' he concluded, 'that I shall be going with you. I shall pick up a replacement aircraft for "Howe" from Dekheila and join you when you leave the ship.'

The Air Staff Officer followed Wings.

'This is a complicated operation,' he said, 'so listen carefully. The Schoolmaster Lieutenant is handing out a set of maps to each observer. You will mainly be following river and railways, hence maps, gentlemen, not charts. You will be flying over some of the wildest desert country in the world, so don't lose touch with your leaders. First 999 Squadron will fly off, followed one hour later by 998 Squadron.

'There will be four stops en route where you will be able to refuel. After leaving the ship you will follow the road that runs from Alexandria and joins the Nile just south of Cairo.'

He waited for observers, with pilots looking on, to trace the route on their maps.

'Then you follow the Nile to Asyut, a small landing-strip where you can refuel. From Asyut you will follow the Nile to Aswan, cutting out the loop that goes to Qena. Again there is a landing-strip for refuelling. Again you will follow the Nile, to Wadi Halfa, where you will spend the night. Before the war Wadi Halfa was an established holiday resort and has an aerodrome. From Wadi Halfa you will strike south-eastwards across the desert, following a railway line, until you pick up the Nile again at Abu Hamed and follow it to Atbara. Again at Atbara there is an airstrip where you will refuel. From Atbara you will follow the railway line eastwards to Port Sudan.'

Shortly after dawn the next morning *Peregrine* was turning into wind, a few miles offshore from Alexandria. The eight aircraft of 999 Squadron were ranged on deck. Circling the carrier was Commander (Flying) in the new H – Howe. One by one the Swordfish took off and formed up on Lieutenant Commander Simpson in A – Abel. Wings completed the formation, taking H – Howe's place in the second sub-flight. At two hundred feet, in close formation, the squadron completed a fly-past, a salute to *Peregrine*, before turning off to begin the long journey to Port Sudan. Bill Hewitt wasn't the only one with a lump in his throat. When would they see the old lady again?

Mile after mile of desert, criss-crossed by dried-up watercourses, called wadis, broken by hills and sand dunes – Snowball Kennedy in L – Love, who before the war had been a reporter on a large provincial newspaper, surveyed the scene with his journalist's eye for detail. Older than most of his squadron colleagues, he had adapted to the ways of the Fleet Air Arm and had become accustomed to the youth and enthusiasm of his young pilot. He appreciated Killer's skill. More recently, perhaps because of the operations they had shared, or perhaps because of his promotion to sub lieutenant, Killer had grown quieter, seemed more mature. Perhaps the girl he had met, Ann, was having an influence on him. There was more to Killer than at first appeared.

The flight to Port Sudan appealed to him immensely, not only for the non-operational drama of the flight, but also for what it would reveal of the country they overflew. Below him the country had the flat appearance and colours of a gigantic map. Miles away to port he could see the green fields of the delta, steadily getting closer, and when they reached them he saw that it was cotton country. The line between desert and green belt was sharply defined, and as they approached the Nile the desert encroached more and more on the greenery until it was a mere strip. The squadron was flying at one thousand feet and Snowball could clearly see the sharp boundaries of the green belt not more than ten miles apart.

The squadron had split up into a loose pattern, hardly a formation. They were now following the Nile and navigation was simple. Snowball was able to study the terrain below. At his request, Killer descended to five hundred feet. The chart showed little but sand and wadis, flat and empty, to starboard, and sand hills to port on the far side of the Nile. Apart from a few villages and settlements along the river banks, there was no sign of human habitation.

It took two and a half hours to reach Asyut. Snowball had left Alexandria in cool March weather, but as he climbed out of the Swordfish the heat took his breath away, leaving him stifled and thirsty. Local mechanics very efficiently refuelled the aircraft, and after a brief spell he was glad to be airborne again.

The flight path followed the Nile, and Snowball saw that the riverbank was now dotted with numerous villages. As they flew overhead, people came out in their hundreds to stare at the aircraft. Sometimes he saw a felucca, with its single lateen sail, making up or down river, or trolling for fish. Twice he thought he saw a large dhow, probably used for trade. He had been hoping to see the Pyramids of Giza, but the flight took them across a deep bend in the river and Giza was passed fifteen miles to port.

As they approached Aswan the banks became more rugged, the river shallower and full of small, rocky islands. At Aswan itself, Killer flew low over the imposing cataracts. The deep, slow-moving waters of the Lower Nile had given way to the fast-moving torrents of the Upper Nile.

There were no mechanics at Aswan, just a pile of four-gallon jerricans of petrol. The flying-crews formed teams, passing the cans from one to the other and up to the pilot who was responsible for filling the fuel tanks in his own plane. The work was gruelling and in the heat Snowball, like the others, was tormented with thirst. He had finished his water-bottle and there was no fresh drinking-water on the airstrip. He was glad to get back into the aircraft and into the air.

The river had changed again. The narrow gorges of Aswan had given way to broad reaches, with fertile fields on either side. Temples and ancient relics abounded and, as they flew low over them, Snowball thought how he would like to come back one day and explore. He chatted with Killer about the places they passed until they talked themselves into silence, both very tired with the long flight.

At last they arrived at Wadi Halfa, where a pleasant surprise awaited them. The Wadi Halfa Hotel, where they were spending the night, was modern, with splendid rooms overlooking the river and baths or showers in each room. Perhaps the thing that most impressed Snowball was the first glass of cold, English beer with which they were greeted when they entered the hotel.

After a shower, Snowball and Bill Hewitt, with several of the officers, stood on a veranda and watched the sunset. The river was calm and slow, hardly a ripple on it. A flat-topped steamer with barges on either side was passing, the only moving thing. Quickly the great red ball of the sun fell and dipped below the horizon and the sky changed from ochre to orange, to red, to purple, its colours reflected and enhanced in the still water.

A great peace descended. The war was far away. Snowball sighed with contentment as he turned from the veranda and accompanied the others into the dining-room, where an excellent meal was served by silent waiters in immaculate white.

The squadron was not taking off until 1000 the next morning and Snowball did not want to miss an opportunity of exploring the village. Killer was checking his aircraft and unable to accompany him, but Bill Hewitt was willing. The two officers took the path along the river, past a group of moored feluccas, to where fields were being irrigated. Here they saw a kind of well supplied by water piped from the nearby river. A bullock, driven by an Egyptian workman dressed in a jellabah, was pushing a pole round and round the well. This operated a simple mechanical system whereby jerricans on an endless belt lifted water from the well and poured it into the irrigation ditch many feet above the Nile.

'Is this the famous irrigation system of the Nile?' said Bill.

'I suppose it is. It's primitive, but effective enough,' said Snowball.

The irrigation ditch stretched away from them to form a series of criss-cross ditches to perhaps a mile from the river. The small squares in between the ditches were intensely cultivated.

As they wandered into the village itself, they saw neat, well-kept houses made of baked mud, with thatched roofs. The streets were clean. Men in white jellabahs greeted them; women in yashmaks turned shyly away from them; children giggled and followed them, talking excitedly.

'What a contrast to the slums of Alexandria!' Bill exclaimed.

Their walk took them through the village back to the hotel. Here they found tennis courts, a swimming-pool and, of all things, a squash court.

'We live and learn,' said Snowball. 'I'd never have expected to find such a civilised place so far south in Egypt.'

'Egypt is an old country,' said Bill. 'Its civilisation stretches back much further than ours.'

'It's the mix that impresses, mud huts and irrigation by bullocks, and squash and tennis courts.'

At ten o'clock all aircraft had been checked and were ready. Because of the intense heat, the CO decided to fly at six thousand feet. The route left the Nile and followed a single-track railway across the desert to Abu Hamed.

'I'll go a bit higher,' Killer said, when they had settled on to their course; 'it'll be even cooler.'

At eight thousand feet the wind was in their favour and Snowball noted that at seventy-five knots they were able to keep up with the leader. Visibility in the dry air was unbelievable. The bearing on Jebel Kuror, a four-thousand-foot mountain that stuck out of the flat plain sixty miles to starboard, changed so slowly that their aircraft seemed hardly to be moving. To port was nothing but sandy hills, broken by crags and mountains.

Mile after mile they followed the railway line, dotted every thirty miles by an unmarked station known only by a number. This was their only link with civilisation and Snowball shuddered as he thought what would happen if the aircraft were forced to land. All the stations looked alike, with a single building, and only a mile from the line the terrain was so ravaged that you would be lost forever.

The Nile, when they rejoined it, was very shallow indeed. Many islands appeared in it and in places tall grasses grew right across it so that the river all but disappeared. At other times it showed up clearly, wriggling and writhing like a serpent.

At Atbara, 999 Squadron hastily refuelled and prepared to take off quickly, whilst 998 Squadron, arriving later, were to stay at Atbara for the night. L – Love would not start and Snowball watched anxiously as Killer checked his engine. The problem was a faulty plug and it was half an hour before they could take off to follow the squadron. Now Snowball felt very much alone.

Carefully he followed the railway line running eastwards from the Nile. They were flying over a flat, empty desert, most of it uncharted on the map, with only the railway line to guide them until they came to the mountain range guarding the coast. Snowball was grateful for his map and for the railway line that followed a series of passes and wadis through the mountains. Huge peaks and mountain ranges towered over them on either side, threatening and frightening. Killer flew through them steadily, countering the updraughts and downdraughts, and always following the track below.

At times it all but disappeared, and it was with great relief that Snowball saw the sea, twenty miles away. A short while later he saw what looked like four immense giraffes guarding a tiny village. As they approached, the village grew into a town and the giraffes became cranes on the harbour mole. They had arrived at Port Sudan.

The Red Sea Hotel, a large two-storey colonial-type building, was to be their home throughout their stay in Port Sudan. There were not enough rooms for the officers of the two squadrons, so the junior officers, sub lieutenants and below, would sleep on the roof. At first Snowball resented this, but after the first night he came to realise how lucky he was. The night was warm, with a dry heat. As he lay on his camp-bed that first night, with all his friends on similar camp-beds around him, and the countless stars, looking twice as big and three times as bright as he had ever known them, above him, Snowball felt happy and content with his lot – and ready for whatever the future held for him.

Chapter 20

Port Sudan

The next morning the squadrons assembled in one of the hotel lounges, which had been converted into an operations room. Here Wings addressed them and told them what would be expected of them over the coming weeks.

'As you know, the six large Italian destroyers based at Massawa, three hundred miles to the south of us, have been ordered to bombard Port Sudan and scuttle themselves in the harbour entrance.

'An RAF Blenheim patrol will search the area at dawn and dusk each day and report if the destroyers have left harbour. We will send a patrol of three aircraft each day to search the area north of Massawa, with 999 and 998 Squadrons taking it in turn to supply these search patrols. If the RAF report that the destroyers have left Massawa, the duty squadron will carry out a parallel search across the Red Sea as far as the Arabian coast. The other squadron will arm with bombs and stand by as a strike-force. The operation will start tomorrow, with 999 Squadron carrying out the first patrol.'

Life settled into an easy pattern for the Fleet Air Arm crews. The only operational requirement for 999 Squadron was one search patrol of three aircraft every other day. This left them time to relax and to explore the town.

They found that Port Sudan was little bigger than a

provincial market town. The harbour, with its wharves and cranes, seemed like an appendage, and the airfield was three miles away. The market was the real centre of the town, surrounded partly by colonial-style buildings with colonnaded fronts, rather like cloisters. In the deep shade of these cloisters were small shops of every kind, mostly Greek-owned but many of them managed by Sudanese.

Life proceeded at a very easy pace in this hot climate. Bill and Killer, on their first walk into town, found that because the atmosphere was so dry the heat was not oppressive. The town was very clean. The shopkeepers refused to bargain; you paid their price or you went without, and Bill and Killer found this strange after Alexandria. Of the people loitering in the streets, the Fuzzy Wuzzies, from a tribe in the south of Sudan, were the most interesting. They were tall, with ragged clothes and bare feet and carried an evil-looking knife, curved like a kukri. Their most prominent feature was the mass of jet-black hair, curled upwards and plastered in dried mud. This made them look seven feet tall.

'Did you see the film *The Four Feathers*?' Killer asked his friend.

'Yes. These must be the tribesmen that appeared in it.'

'They didn't need much make-up, did they?'

The two officers were soon aware of how small the town was and how closely the desert encircled it. This was emphasised when they saw a camel train coming into town from the desert.

A favourite rendezvous for all the flying-crews was the swimming-pool next to the hotel. Here, every morning, those not on duty gathered for an hour or two, swimming and sunbathing and lounging with a cool drink on the terrace. In the evening they had a choice of three clubs, the Red Sea Club, the Red Sea Sports Club and the Greek Club. The Greek Club was patronised almost exclusively by the Greek population, but the Red Sea Club boasted a good library, a good lounge and a billiard-room. The Red Sea Sports Club was popular for its dances and, encouraged by Bill and Killer, some of the younger officers soon found partners amongst the Greek girls.

Life for the squadrons had a strange, holiday-like atmosphere, consisting mainly of eating and sleeping, swimming and dancing and twice a week a film at the local cinema, probably one they had seen before they left England. The film show was held after dark in the open air. At the end of each reel, music was played while the film was changed, and once it broke down for nearly an hour. It was popular, however, and usually crowded.

The routine patrol was demanding, but only came once every five or six days. After breakfast three crews made their way to their aircraft and took off for Teklai, an airstrip run by the RAF, where they topped up with fuel, then on to the archipelago north-east of Massawa, where they split up and searched the islands. Sometimes they landed at Teklai for refuelling on the way back to Port Sudan. Altogether, the operation lasted about eight hours.

On the first of April the first sign of movement occurred. A sub-flight from 998 Squadron was on patrol when one of them sent a W/T message: *One enemy destroyer thirty miles north-east of Massawa. Laying mines.*

Half an hour later, a message came from the sub-flight leader: *Enemy destroyer has scuttled itself.*

When the sub-flight returned to Port Sudan, the full story was revealed. The destroyer appeared to be laying mines, but the first aircraft had not been sure. The other two aircraft had closed up and were preparing to bomb the vessel with the two bombs they carried when they saw the ship's company taking to boats. The ship began to settle in the water and within an hour had sunk. The ship's crews had escaped to a neighbouring island.

The squadrons had had their warning. Wings decided to

put the parallel search on standby. The comfortable life of the past fortnight was over. All day long the crews awaited the signal to go. That evening Wings briefed them for their search. Five aircraft of 999 Squadron, 'Abel', 'Baker', Charlie', 'Fox' and 'George', each armed with two bombs, would carry out the search. The third sub-flight, 'King', 'Love' and 'Mike', led by himself in 'Howe', would stand by as first strike-force, with 998 Squadron on second strike.

That evening all crews checked their aircraft: pilots ran their engines; observers plotted their navigation; air-gunners checked their wireless and their guns. Then the flying-crews, under the armourer's direction, loaded up their aircraft with two-hundred-and-fifty pound bombs, and topped up their aircraft with petrol.

The sky seemed very attractive to Bill that night. As he lay on his camp-bed he could see myriad stars overhead and clouds like islands floating across a black sea. These islands were dark and mountainous, but the foreshore was bright like a silvery beach as the moon rose in all its pale glory. There was a circle round the moon and Bill thought that had he been a soothsayer, he might have read the portent of battle. As it was, he forgot flying and slept a deep sleep.

At 0300 the next morning the five crews detailed for the search assembled sleepily in the lounge, where they drank hot coffee. Cars were waiting outside to take them to their aircraft. Bill hoped that the destroyers would come out and that he would be the one to sight them.

At last the news came through. A signal from the Blenheim informed them that the enemy destroyers had left harbour, and the hunt was on. Each one knew exactly what to do. At 0430, just as dawn was breaking, they taxied across the airstrip and took off, one by one, into the clouds. The weather had closed in during the night and visibility was little more than two miles. The cloud was down to a thousand feet, but they expected to be flying close together until the sun came up, when visibility would improve. Their tracks would diverge until they were ten miles apart, when they would follow parallel tracks to within sight of Arabia and return. The effectiveness of the search required very fine navigation so as not to leave any gaps.

The aircraft that sighted was to jettison its bombs and remain and shadow the destroyers, sending out frequent reports of the enemy's position and movements. The remaining aircraft would complete their search, in case another force were out, then close the enemy and attack with their two bombs.

B – Baker crossed the coast at five hundred feet, pilot and observer checking their instruments and the TAG tuning his wireless and trying out his Lewis gun. B – Baker was the extreme left of the search and its course was therefore straight out to sea. Bill took a backbearing of Port Sudan to check the plane's drift and made a small correction for the wind. As it grew lighter, his pilot climbed until he reached the best-visibility height of six thousand feet. After fifteen minutes' flying, Bill dropped a smoke-float to get an accurate measurement and direction of the wind, gave his pilot another small course correction and settled down to search the sea with his binoculars. Visibility had improved to more than ten miles and he felt happier that the search area would be completely covered.

At six o'clock, a hundred and thirty miles out, the engine suddenly coughed and spluttered, stopped, then picked up again, still behaving badly. The air speed had dropped off to below seventy knots and the aircraft was unable to maintain its height.

'I can't hold her,' Holy Temple shouted desperately. 'I'll have to ditch.'

Bill immediately gave his TAG a hastily scribbled message: *B – Baker ditching. Position 070 degrees Port Sudan 130 miles.*

'Get that off quickly, Black.'

He turned back to his pilot. The altimeter was swinging back at an alarming pace.

'Jettison the bombs,' he called.

Holy was already doing that and Bill felt the plane shudder as the bombs were released. The plane was now only six hundred feet above the sea. The bombs exploded on impact and the force of the explosion blew it up to two thousand feet. The needle had crept up to seventy knots again, just sufficient to maintain height.

'We can either go on to Saudi Arabia and be interned,' said Bill, 'or we can try to get back to Port Sudan. Arabia is thirty miles off, Port Sudan a hundred and thirty.'

'I vote we try for home,' said Holy. 'What do you think, Black?'

'I agree, sir. I don't want to spend the rest of the war in an internment camp.'

'What about you, Bill?'

'I'm all for going back.'

Gently, Holy eased his rudder, so as not to lose height. Quickly, Bill worked out a new course, allowing for the wind. The long, long journey home began. He gave Black a message to send, reporting their situation.

'I can't hold my altitude,' exclaimed Holy after ten minutes.

It was true. No matter what he attempted with pitch and throttle, the altimeter pursued its slow but relentless way downwards.

Another ten minutes passed.

'Message from L – Love, sir,' said PO Black. *Two destroyers in position 150 degrees Port Sudan 65 miles, course 330 degrees, speed 25 knots.*'

'That's the Italians,' cried Bill.

Quickly he plotted the position on his chart.

'We'll be passing only fifteen miles from them, and we have no bombs.'

'We'll be lucky if we get back, let alone bomb the enemy,' was the grim reply.

After an hour, they were halfway back and the altimeter was down to one thousand feet.

Bill could not help visions of sharks and barracudas coming before his eyes. They had been talking of forced landings in the hotel and the general consensus was that barracudas were a bigger menace than sharks.

Another half-hour passed.

'We might make it,' said Holy. 'The more fuel we use, the lighter the aircraft.'

The altimeter was at five hundred feet. They had thirty miles to go. Bill gripped the sides of his cockpit, urging it to remain airborne.

Five miles out and they were down to a hundred feet. And then they were over the coast, twenty feet below them, and Holy was bringing his aircraft down for a landing on the beach. No finesse. No turning into wind. Just stick back and close the throttle. And they were down. They learned later that four scraper rings had gone and they were very lucky to reach land.

A car approached them, bumping over the sand. A voice called out.

'You are wanted on the airstrip, Mr Hewitt. There's an aircraft waiting for an observer before it takes off.'

L – Love was the extreme right-hand aircraft of the search. Snowball Kennedy had directed his pilot, Killer Compton, down their first leg of fifty miles along the coast and then on to the eastward leg across the Red Sea. They were flying at six thousand feet. He had taken his first wind, corrected his course and plotted his track on his chart, then settled down to sweep the horizon with his binoculars. The sea was dotted with small islands. Ten miles ahead and to port was Barra

Musa Saphir Island and to starboard Tammarscia Island. But what was the dot in between them? He stared through his binoculars, and then spoke into his intercom.

'I think we've got them, Killer, two ships that look like destroyers, ten miles ahead, in between the two islands. Keep going on this course and you'll see them.'

Minutes later – 'I see them,' called Killer.

'Keep going until I've identified them for sure.'

Snowball consulted photographs of the Italian ships.

'Yes, They are the Italians. I'll send off a sighting report. Jettison your bombs. We'll stay and shadow them.'

'Can I have a crack at them?' said the ever-eager Killer.

'No, Killer. It's important to shadow and report the enemy's position, course and speed. If you attacked them you might get shot down and we'd lose them. See if you can cross their tracks about five miles astern so that I can check their course.'

Whilst Killer did this, Snowball plotted the position, and wrote out a wireless message in simple code, to which he added the course and estimated speed as they crossed the tracks of the destroyers.

'Get this off, Gibbons,' he said to his TAG.

At Port Sudan, Wings was waiting outside the wireless hut on the airstrip with the crews of the three 999 Squadron aircraft.

'Message coming in from L – Love,' called the wireless operator.

Wings hurried into the hut to watch the operator record his message and decode it.

Two destroyers in position 125 degrees Port Sudan 65 miles. Course 305 degrees. Speed 25 knots. Time of origin 0545.

'Right. This is it, lads. Take off immediately.'

The men hurried out to their machines, where mechanics were already starting and running up engines. Wings was to lead the flight and he had borrowed Sub Lieutenant Lloyd from M – Mike to navigate for him.

For the fifth time, Killer crossed the stern of the two destroyers. Snowball had sent off a confirmation of his first sighting report and was searching all round the horizon with his glasses. Where were the other destroyers? Then he caught sight of two of them, coming up fast from behind an island to the south. The two he was shadowing turned to meet them and, at a combined speed of sixty knots, it was only a matter of minutes before they had joined forces.

Snowball carefully reported these movements, giving the new position and speed: *Four destroyers in position 130 degrees Port Sudan 60 miles. Course 310 degrees. Speed 25 knots. Time of origin 0600.*

He knew that the strike-force would have left or just be leaving and up-to-date information was essential if they were to find their target. He was not very worried about the occasional shell-bursts. They were never very close and seemed to be a token anti-aircraft fire rather than a real defence, and Killer appeared not to take any notice of them.

At his suggestion Killer made a wide circle round the destroyers until he was five miles ahead. From here, Snowball would have an earlier view of the approaching strike-force.

At 0620 he saw them through his binoculars, four dots in the sky at about five thousand feet. As they drew nearer, the four aeroplanes went into line astern. Snowball could see them all clearly and through his glasses he could identify the pilots and observers. Wings was leading in H – Howe, followed by Bing Crosby in M – Mike, Biddy Bidwell in F – Fox and Hank Phipps in G – George.

Snowball watched the flak start, shell-bursts following the aircraft accurately, but ahead and five hundred feet below.

Wings flew straight on until he was almost over the leading destroyer. Then he put his nose down and as he pulled away, Snowball saw that the destroyer had turned to port. The bombs missed to starboard by about fifty feet. The remaining aircraft were going in, selecting their own targets. The destroyers had increased speed and were twisting and turning in all directions to confuse the pilots. Bing Crosby missed ahead and Biddy Bidwell missed to starboard. Hank Phipps was the last to attack and he was going for the fourth destroyer, diving across its bows. The destroyer's captain turned towards his attacker, but in doing so lined up his ship with the falling bombs, five of which burst along its deck, and Snowball watched in horror as it split apart in an explosion of smoke and flame. Within minutes it had disappeared completely, leaving only debris of splintered wood, floats and floating bodies.

After his attack Biddy Bidwell flew alongside Killer and indicated with hand gestures that he was taking over the shadowing. Killer acknowledged the message and turned away to follow the three aircraft led by Wings, heading in a northwest direction.

F – Fox was now the shadower and Wes Weston the observer responsible for reporting the enemy's movements. The first thing he noticed was that the three ships had regained formation and resumed their course for Port Sudan. He duly reported this. Then came the search aircraft, returning from their search to drop their two bombs on the destroyers.

First came Bolo Hawkins in K – King with Hatters Dunn in C – Charlie astern of him. They were flying at six thousand feet and Bolo went straight into the attack, diving through shell-bursts and close-range fire to drop his bombs from eight hundred feet. He aimed for the leading destroyer, but the Italian captain was good. He was moving fast, and as soon as Bolo released his bombs, the helm of the destroyer was put over and then brought back again. This had the effect of jinking the destroyer away from the bombs, which fell to starboard.

Hatters Dunn followed Bolo down. When he was into his dive, the destroyer captain brought his ship hard into the line of attack. Seeing that he was going to overrun, Hatters dropped his bombs early, at three thousand feet, and the destroyer had no difficulty in avoiding them.

Ten minutes later the CO arrived and made a solo attack on the last destroyer of the line. The flak was intense, and Lieutenant Commander Simpson had to twist and turn to avoid it. He dropped his bombs from a thousand feet and narrowly missed the stern of the destroyer.

The ships had been attacked by eight aircraft. One had been sunk and one had suffered damage from near misses. The Italian Admiral, in the leading destroyer, was determined to press on and complete his mission. At maximum speed the three destroyers steered for Port Sudan. All of this was reported by Wes Weston.

At a distance of only twenty miles from Port Sudan he watched the second strike develop. All nine aircraft of 998 Squadron were approaching in formation, three vics of three aircraft. The air was filled with bursting shells put up as a barrage by the destroyers. The formation split up as it approached the enemy, one vic going to starboard, one to port and one attacking from ahead. Wes was impressed as much with the efficiency of the Italians as with the courage of the pilots. Manoeuvring at high speed, the destroyers cut furrows in the sea, criss-crossing each other's tracks, and all the time sending up a steady barrage of shells and tracer fire and no doubt, Wes thought, close-range artillery which he could not see.

The aircraft formed lines astern behind their leaders. The battle was grim and ferocious. Wes saw one aircraft hit by shell splinters from a near miss and one turn away with a

247

damaged wing. The others pressed their attack home, weaving and dodging until the final dive. Huge fountains of spray enclosed one or other of the destroyers, which sometimes disappeared completely in the spray. Miraculously, no plane was shot down and no destroyer received a direct hit. There were several near misses and the damage and casualties on the ships must have been high.

As one of 998 Squadron took over the shadowing, Wes made his last report. The Italians had had enough. They had been stopped twenty miles from their target; one of them was sunk and one scuttled; the other three were turning away to the northeast.

Enemy altered course to 060 degrees. Speed twenty knots. Position 130 degrees Port Sudan 20 miles. Time of origin 0736.

They were heading towards Saudi Arabia. As soon as H – Howe, G – George and M – Mike landed at the airstrip at Port Sudan, they were refuelled and aircrew began arming with bombs.

'I'm too old for this game,' Wings said regretfully.

He had been impressed with the determination of his young colleagues and felt that it was now time for him to perform his real task, coordinating the efforts of the two squadrons. He wanted to keep up the pressure on the Italian destroyers. They were damaged but by no means finished and still posed a threat in the Red Sea. There were still no English ships to match them. With all of this in mind he ordered M – Mike and G – George to leave as soon as they were ready, Bing Crosby in M – Mike leading.

Both Bing and Harold Lloyd, his observer, had matured since their first operation at Tobruk. Harold was confident in his navigation and in his TAG, L/A Davey, who would receive and pass the W/T messages from the shadowing aircraft. Hank Phipps in G – George was looking forward to having another go.

As they were taking off, Killer Compton in L – Love

landed, followed shortly afterwards by Bolo in K – King and Hatters Dunn in C – Charlie. The time was 0800.

'Message from B – Baker, sir,' called the wireless operator. 'He has just landed on the beach.'

'Good. Get his observer up here at once. Send a car for him.'

Leaving Dicky Burd to supervise the refuelling and rearming with bombs, Bolo, as soon as he landed, hurried to the W/T hut, which had become the centre of operations. He gave his report to Wings.

'What I need here, now, is an experienced observer to act as ASO and keep a plot of the action. Do you think Lieutenant Burd can do it?'

I'm certain he can, sir.'

'Good! We shall have three aircraft ready to take off in half an hour, K – King, L – Love and C – Charlie. Could you manage with Midshipman Hewitt as your observer?'

'Yes. He's young, but he's a very competent navigator.'

'Right. I've sent for him. Perhaps you'll brief him when he arrives. And have Lieutenant Burd join me here in the W/T room.'

'Aye, aye, sir.'

Bolo hurried away to organise his new sub-flight.

At 0900, they took off, Killer, in 'Love', in his usual position on Bolo's starboard quarter, and Hatters in 'Charlie' on his port quarter. Bill Hewitt was navigating the flight, though both Knocker White and Snowball Kennedy were keeping a careful check. A report had come in just after take-off that the enemy was in position 085 degrees Port Sudan 48 miles, steering 060 degrees at a speed of 25 knots.

Bill carefully plotted the position. The enemy was only forty-eight miles away, but Bill wanted to make no mistake. Carefully he took a backbearing of the cranes at Port Sudan to check their course. At seventy-five knots, their climbing speed, allowing for the movement of the enemy, it would take them fifty-five minutes to reach their target. He informed Bolo accordingly.

Twenty minutes later, PO Mercer passed a message to him. 'Mike' and 'George' had attacked and scored near misses but no hits. The enemy was continuing on its course. At 0945 Bill was becoming worried. The enemy must be little more than ten miles away. Anxiously he trained his glasses on the sea ahead of them, and then he saw the three faint streaks in the water, the wakes of the destroyers.

'Enemy red one-oh,' he called, 'distance about eight miles.' He only just managed to keep the quiver out of his voice. This was a tremendous moment for him, his first sighting of an enemy at sea. All his training and the experience in the desert seemed to have led up to this moment.

'Right, Bill. I've got them.'

Bill was amazed how steady Bolo's voice was. It was like an ordinary conversation.

'See that cloud to starboard of the destroyers? I'm going to make for it.'

Already puffs of shell-bursts could be seen in the distance, but not many.

'I expect they're getting short of ammunition,' Bolo said.

The cloud was about three miles away from the destroyers and two thousand feet lower than the Swordfish. Bolo used it to screen their approach from the enemy. He waved his wingmen out to line abreast. His plan was for the three aircraft to make a simultaneous attack on the destroyers, thus weakening the Italians' fire-power on any one of them. They came from behind the cloud and there were the three destroyers below them. Already they had increased speed to thirty knots. Bolo had circled round the destroyers, approaching them from ahead, but as they came from behind the cloud, the destroyers made a hundred and eighty degree turn.

Bolo had already chosen his target, the foremost, and largest, destroyer. Now its stern was to him.

'Going down now,' he said.

By standing up and leaning over his forward bulkhead, Bill could see the destroyer over Bolo's head. The figures on the bridge stood out clearly gazing up at them. The big guns had ceased firing, but men were manning the pompoms and machine-guns. Bill could see their guns following them as Bolo turned his aircraft to follow the ship's movements.

The altimeter had passed one thousand feet and Bolo was still going down. We must be hit by the close-range weapons, Bill thought, they can't miss us at this range and we are flying straight into them.

Then an amazing thing happened. First one, then another, then a bunch of the Italians left their guns for shelter behind bulkheads. Just when the Swordfish was most vulnerable, the Italian defence faltered. Not so the Italian captain. As the bombs left, the Italian destroyer turned to port and back to starboard, the familiar defence manoeuvre used by the Italians in previous attacks. Bolo's bombs missed to starboard, but Killer was waiting for this. He had seen it when his was the shadowing aircraft. He began his dive seconds after Bolo, watched the Italian commit himself, and then aimed his Swordfish at the spot where he knew the Italian would be. It was a brilliant piece of flying and his bombs fell squarely across the bows of the destroyer.

Snowball watched the huge hole open up and, as the bows began to settle, the Italians taking to the boats.

Simultaneously with Killer, Hatters Dunn in C – Charlie was attacking the third destroyer. This had already suffered damage from a near miss, but again the Italian captain successfully manoeuvred his ship to avoid a direct hit. The bombs, however, dropped close alongside, and the ship slowed noticeably.

All firing had stopped now. The three aircraft circled the

stricken destroyer, the stern of which had risen high in the air as it made its last plunge. They were joined by the shadowing aircraft and Bolo signalled him to return to Port Sudan with the other Swordfish. He would stay to take over the shadowing.

Bill watched as the two destroyers resumed their course to the north-east at a reduced speed of fifteen knots. He sent out an enemy report, and continued to watch. Half an hour later the CO arrived in A – Abel with Biddy Bidwell in F – Fox, and H – Howe. Bill trained his glasses carefully and saw that his own pilot, Holy Temple, had replaced Wings in H – Howe.

Once more, the grim pattern of attack and defence ensued. The Swordfish pressed home their attack through the now weakened flak. The destroyers, which had speeded up, twisted and turned to avoid the bombs. Bill could see clearly now how difficult it was for attacking aircraft to hit destroyers moving and turning at speed. He could also see the damage done by the near misses. This time it was the undamaged one that suffered and Bill saw it heel as the bombs splashed close by, making a hole in its side just above the waterline.

The battle was nearing its end. The enemy was nearly out of range of the Swordfish from Port Sudan. The CO signalled to Bolo that he was taking over the shadowing and Bolo left to follow the other aircraft.

When he arrived back in Port Sudan at 1230, he learned that a last strike of five aircraft of 998 Squadron had left and that the CO was being diverted to Taklai, where an RAF Wellesley was awaiting a Fleet Air Arm observer.

They heard the end of the story later that evening when Sandy returned to Port Sudan. The last strike had failed to sink either of the destroyers, which had both suffered considerable damage. Sandy had joined the Wellesley, which was waiting with another at Taklai, and navigated the two aircraft along the track of the two destroyers. They had finally caught up with them near an island off the Arabian coast. The destroyers, in a sinking condition, had been abandoned by their crews, who were rowing towards the island. The Wellesleys had used the destroyers as targets for bombing practice, and had finally sent them beneath the waves.

Where was the sixth destroyer? An unconfirmed report had come in that it had scuttled itself in Nocra, a harbour in the island of Dehlac Chebir, north-east of Massawa.

The next day, 998 squadron was sent to search the islands, especially Dehlac Chebir, but no sighting was made, Wings concluded that the report was accurate and that all six destroyers were now sunk.

Epilogue

A week after the battle in the Red Sea, all the officers of 998 and 999 Squadrons were seated at dinner in the Red Sea Hotel. They had recovered from their weariness. Their aircraft had been serviced, repaired, or patched up and they were awaiting the arrival of *HMS Peregrine*.

Their guest of honour was the Admiral of the Italian flotilla, who had been picked up, together with the remainder of his ship's company, by a patrol vessel from Port Sudan. He was replying to a toast offered by Wings.

'I would like to pay tribute to you for your courage and skill,' he concluded. 'As a token of this I have the honour to present to you my ensign.'

Wings accepted the ensign on behalf of the two squadrons and *Peregrine*.

Glossary

ack-ack	anti-aircraft fire
air-artificer	highly qualified technician
Aldis lamp	a powerful portable lamp for signalling
angels	altitude of aircraft in thousands of feet
armourer	technician who looks after weapons and ammunition
A/S	anti-submarine
ASO	Air Staff Officer. The ship's senior observer
ASV	an early form of radar, showing a single vertical line with blips across it denoting ships
bandits	enemy aircraft
Barracuda	a high-winged monoplane that replaced the Swordfish as a TBR aircraft
battleship	the heaviest unit of the Fleet with fourteen-inch to sixteen-inch guns
Bigsworth board	a portable chartboard with a parallel ruler on a flexible arm
Blighty	Great Britain

bumph	official documents
buzz	rumour
chinwag	discussion
chow	food, a meal
C-in-C	Commander in Chief
comb torpedo tracks	turn towards a salvo of approaching torpedoes and pass between them
Commander Flying	the ship's senior Fleet Air Arm officer, normally a pilot – usually known as 'Wings'
confab	a discussion
cruiser	fast, large, lightly-armoured ship, usually with six-inch to eight-inch guns
cutter	large open boat
destroyer	fast ship of one to two thousand tons, with four-inch to five-inch guns. They carried torpedo tubes and depth charges
dhow	large commercial sailing-vessel with a single lateen sail
dish up	wash up
DCO	Deck Control Officer, who controls movement of aircraft on deck
DLO or DLCO,	Deck-Landing Control Officer, sometimes called 'Bats', who controls landings and take-offs
ETA	estimated time of arrival
FAA	Fleet Air Arm
felucca	small sailing vessel with a single lateen sail
Fiat CR 42	Italian biplane fighter aircraft
fitter	engine mechanic

FDO	Fighter Direction Officer
Firefly	fast monoplane that became the Navy's bomber-reconnaissance plane towards the end of the war
fish	torpedo
flak	anti-aircraft gunfire
flame-float	a float, dropped by aircraft, that emitted a flame for several minutes. Used as a marker
flaming onions	tracer shells of various colours
flap	emergency
flat	an area of deck space surrounded by cabins or offices
Fulmar	a naval two-seater fighter aircraft
formate	take up station in an agreed pattern
gen	information
gharry	horse-drawn carriage
gimlet	gin and lime
Gladiator	naval biplane fighter aircraft
G-string	a safety line for observers and air-gunners that prevented them from being thrown out of the open cockpit
goofers' platform	a space on the island of an aircraft carrier reserved for flying-crews where they could watch landings and take-offs
horse's neck	brandy and dry ginger
hostilities only	for the duration of the war
IFF	Identify friend or foe – an electronic aircraft identification device
island	the superstructure on the starboard side of an aircraft carrier that

	housed the bridge, chartroom, operations room, etc.
jellabah	Middle East cloak, worn by Arabs, that looks like a nightshirt
mae west	inflatable life-jacket
make and mend	a period free of duties
NAVEX	navigation exercise
parallel search	organised search by a number of aircraft following parallel tracks ten to twenty miles apart
Pilot	ship's Navigating Officer
PMO	Principal Medical Officer
rigger	an airframe mechanic
roger	message received and understood
R/T	radio telephony
SBA	Sick Berth Attendant
Schooley	the ship's schoolmaster who had many duties, including teaching, meteorology, navigation etc.
SM 72	Savoia Marchetti. Italian high-level bomber or torpedo bomber
smoke-float	a float dropped by an aircraft that emitted smoke for several minutes. Used as a marker
square search	a search in which each leg is at right angles to, and longer than, the previous one
TAG	telegraphist-air-gunner
tally-ho	target in sight
TBR	torpedo-bomber-reconnaissance
TSR	torpedo-spotter-reconnaissance
tell off	each aircraft in turn is to report the strength of my signal

VAD	Voluntary Aid Detachment – a women's service with a nursing branch
Verey pistol	a pistol that fires a signal cartridge in various colours
vic formation	formation in the form of a flat 'v'
wardroom	officers' mess in the Navy
Wavy Navy	Royal Naval Volunteer Reserve
wilco	will comply with your instruction
Wings	Commander Flying
WRNS or Wrens	Women's Royal Naval Service
W/T	wireless telegraphy – requiring Morse
yashmak	face veil worn by Moslem women
zog	method of signalling with the forearm, using the Morse code